First in; Last out

Greg C. Tanner CD

Cover picture credits to Stuart Moors. He is the owner and
photographer of
Anchor's Aweigh Photography

Copyright © 2024

Greg C. Tanner CD

Case ID #: 1-13859309341

eBook ISBN: 978-1-964451-56-5
Paperback ISBN: 978-1-964451-57-2
Hardback ISBN : 978-1-964451-58-9

Advanced Praise for First in; Last out.

"I first met Greg when he started coming to our local church. Everyone was drawn to him because he had his support dog 'Barrett' with him. This was our first encounter with a dog being part of our congregation and everyone wanted to meet them and make them feel welcome. His wife, Margret, was with them and we were pleased to have them join us for fellowship after the service so we could get to know them. What is impressive about Greg is an awareness that, in spite of his experiences during his overseas deployments and his struggles with drinking and prescription medications, he has somehow managed to survive and live in this present day world. He did this with the support of his wife, the help of a therapist, a strong will to survive, and with his support dog, Barrett, who is Greg's constant companion and best friend, giving him unconditional love and keeping him grounded.

Greg asked me questions about the book I had written and published and how I went about doing that. He went on to say that he had written a cookbook that he wanted to publish and then added that he had made notes about his career and personal problems and wanted to write a book about that. I told him the best thing to do is to just start writing and the words will come, and before you know it your manuscript will be ready to publish. The rest is history.

Greg's book, "First in; Last Out" is now a reality. This book will be a good inspiration for anyone who has been through the trials and tribulations of overseas deployment like Greg. If Greg can come through it and regain control of his life, then they can follow in his footsteps and also achieve success. "

Linda Mosher, author of
Surrounded by Death and Bureaucrats
Stories from the Nova Scotia Medical Examiner's Office

"In this breathtakingly courageous memoir, Greg Tanner shares his journey through life with unflinching honesty. With vulnerability and strength, he recounts events that led to his diagnosis of PTSD and provides insight into the long and difficult process of healing. Through his story, Greg shows us that trauma can happen to anyone, at any time, and that recovery is possible, no matter how daunting the task may seem.

Greg's story is a testament to the human spirit's capacity for resilience and growth. Despite facing unimaginable challenges, he emerges stronger, wiser, and more compassionate. His courage in sharing his story will inspire countless others to confront their own traumas and seek the help they need. At the heart of this memoir is the extraordinary bond between Greg and his loyal dog, Barrett. With unwavering devotion, Barrett stands by Greg's side, offering comfort, support, and a sense of purpose. Through their relationship, we see the transformative power of love, loyalty, and companionship.

First In; Last Out is a beacon of hope, reminding us that no one is alone in their struggles. Greg's willingness to share his intimate journey will resonate deeply with readers, and his triumph over adversity will leave a lasting impact. With Barrett and his family by his side, Greg shows us that healing is possible, and that love and support can overcome even the darkest of traumas."

Brendon Abram Maj Ret'd.

Former OC A3 RTF CFB Trenton

In "First In; Last Out", the author, a retired army engineer and instructor, takes the reader on an intimate and powerful journey through the trials of life and military service.

The narrative focuses primarily on the author's military experiences, capturing the intensity and camaraderie of his time in service. However, the true heart of the story lies in the aftermath of his service, as he grapples with invisible ghosts. The portrayal of PTSD is raw and unflinching, shedding light on the daily struggles faced by many veterans. The author's openness about his physical and mental health challenges, and stigma, is both courageous and enlightening, fostering a deeper understanding and empathy in readers.

Scuba diving emerges as an unexpected but profound element in the author's life and recovery journey. The underwater world, described in vivid and serene detail, becomes a sanctuary where the author can find peace and clarity. The therapeutic benefits of diving are explored with nuance, highlighting how reflection on this activity helps him manage his challenges and regain a sense of control and calm.

Barrett, his support dog, is a heartwarming presence throughout the book. The bond between the author and Barrett is beautifully depicted, showcasing the impact that support animals can have on mental health and recovery. Barrett's intuitive support and unconditional love provide comfort and stability, helping the author navigate the toughest moments.

The author's use of journaling as a recovery tool adds another layer of depth to the memoir. The entries are honest and reflective, offering insights into his thoughts and emotions as he progresses on his healing journey. This practice of journaling not only aids his recovery but also allows readers to connect more deeply with his experiences.

"First In, Last Out" is more than a memoir; it is a testament to resilience, the healing power of unconventional therapies. This book is a must-read for anyone interested in mental health, veteran experiences, and the transformative power of healing practices and animal companionship. It offers hope and inspiration, demonstrating that even in the darkest of times, there is a path to recovery and a way to find peace.

Dr. Robert Gilbert
School of Health Sciences,
Faculty of Health Professions,
Dalhousie University

Foreword

Canada is a democratic society that abides by the rule of law. Unfortunately many of our elected officials and the general public seem not to fully grasp the understanding that it is the brave women and men such as Greg Tanner that have given us our freedoms that we have taken for granted.

From the Boer War to Afghanistan peacekeeping and domestic security and assistance in Natural Disasters. These dedicated Canadians give it their all to ensure that you and I and our families are safe and can carry on with our regular lives. All they ask for in return is that if they pay the ultimate sacrifice ensure that their families are cared for. Also if they are injured either physically or mentally. Ensure that timely and appropriate benefits are in place so that they can carry on with their lives.

I'm grateful for the services that Greg has provided to Canada (and to other countries as well). The following pages is a testament from a humble Canadian that gave his all for the benefit of others. A remarkable insight to the fascinating world of a Canadian soldier. I wish to thank Greg's family for sharing him with all of us and especially his canine companion Barrett.

BRAVO ZULU GREG

Peter Stoffer
Chairperson
Veterans Legal Assistance Foundation
June 10 2024
Fall River Nova Scotia

About the Author.

Greg Tanner was born in Brockville ON, and shortly after his family moved to Montreal PQ. In the mid 1960's, Greg along with his two younger sisters made the move to Halifax NS, where he completed his high school education, and then joined the Canadian Army Engineering Branch. During his 23 year career in the Army he had postings all over Canada, a four year stint in Germany and completed four UN / NATO missions overseas. Upon taking his release from the regular forces, he enlisted in the Canadian Air Force Reserves and stayed an additional 11 years to complete 34 years in uniform. The Crowning achievement was the being awarded the Queens Diamond Jubilee Medal for his dedicated service.

His main hobbies included teaching scuba diving and camping, but after over 20 years of diving he was bitten by the boating bug in the late 90's. Switching from breathing underwater to cruising on top of it gave an opportunity to make new friendships and a experience different adventures. Active in the Canadian Power Squadron teaching Boating courses and served on both the Executive and Flag committees of the CFB Trenton Yacht Club including two terms as the Commodore.

Since retiring, Greg and his wife Margret have taken up traveling to such places as down Under to OZ, down East to the Maritimes, and down South to Florida visiting their family and friends. They have two daughters, Jenn and Jackie, In the summer months they reside on their Mainship trawler," Tapped Out" cruising Lake Ontario and the Surrounding waters with their faithful companion, Zoey, a nine year old female Shih Tzu, AKA the Bubbs...

This was the introduction to the cookbook I wrote while in Florida a few years back. A different time, for sure. I still cannot put my finger on it, but somewhere along the way, something broke, and I started to become depressed, then the slow, uncontrolled dive;

Dear Family and Friends,

Regarding my PTSD...
I was diagnosed in 2015
and up to a few months
ago, I did not acknowledge
this which was been
holding me back in the
healing process.

"IT is not easy to explain
myself or even remember
what it is I need to say. I am
hoping this letter can make
some sense of everything.
Because of my PTSD,
I can have real difficulty
explaining myself to others.
Apart from the memory problems,
PTSD is a complex disorder

To try and explain.

I have PTSD because of
extreme tramas - events
that I wouldn't wish upon my
worst enemies. This means
that various things, people, and
situations in the present 'trigger'
me.
They can trigger painful
emotional reactions beyond my
instant control. These reactions
may not make much sense to
those around me. They can
be sudden and feel uncontrollable

When I trigger, I may
become dysfunctional for
awhile. Emotions arise. I
have cried uncontrollably,
be frightened, or angry.

I may have troubles speaking
and thinking. I may be cash
extroverted & introverted.
It may take same time for me
to get back to my emotional
balance.
I cannot always predict when
I may be triggered, my
excessive emotions will happen.
These reactions have worried
and disturbed those around me.
It can be frightening. I do
feel bad, but it's beyond my
control.
PTSD is a physical injury —
It affects the brain.
IT is treatable, but not
cureable. It can manifest
itself in many other ways,
not just emotion.

I believe it appropriate to
explain to you the emotional
side of things. I may need
space and seem distant.
I may seem like a
different person.

Please know that I need
your understanding, and
deeply appreciate it and
efforts that you make to
understand my situation.

I am trying to
manage my symptoms
and sharing this instead
of deflecting or
ignoring what PTSD is
and look towards many
many good days. Greg/dad

Preface

Lay of the land:

When I started writing about my adventures, whether boating vacations of some type or about my passion for cooking a few years back, it was just for fun. Throughout my working adult life, I have had opportunities to write and speak to select audiences, both military and civilian, for work and volunteering, teaching continuing education courses for various clubs I was a member of. Along the way, there was an encouragement to write a "bio type" or my life story someday, but what would be the hook, as they say…what or why would you pay, if I'm lucky, but even as a free publication, what would make you pick it up or give it a second look. Hence, as a good friend said, "That is the rub."

I thought, "What are you going to write? Why are you writing, and Who do you want to get it?"

I think that, with all honesty, this is more for me, my journal, thought collecting and writing in a format that will, if it makes sense to me, it might for others who have or experienced something for reasons that are still not fully known, the mind reacts. A life changes in ways that one could not anticipate.

Getting right to the point, I'm now different. Not in *that way.* Shut up, you know who you are smiling at that.

But seriously, how do you rebuild and reclaim some presence after this? By the way, WTF [1] is this? I don't know, and I am not going to speculate or come to any conclusions other than, for me, it is an actual physical and emotionally crippling unseen and unpredictable weight that is sometimes easier to let roll over you than to drop the armor.

It has been a few weeks since I have felt like writing. It's not

---

[1] What the fuck.

really a block as such, but wondering in what direction I would be choosing to go rather than the rambling of no particular order. I got an email a few weeks ago from the Wounded Warriors Canada (WWC), a charity I donate to monthly. Not a whole lot, but a lot of not a whole lot is a lot. Anyway, the email was an invite to a big public media briefing at the Halifax library on Spring Garden Rd, downtown. Well, it was a Tuesday afternoon, and Margret was away. I had just got my UN NATO Veterans Patch and vest that weekend, and also a message from Rollie (more on him later) about the WWC and a foundation he is involved in also dealing with PTSD dog training and placement for veterans. Why not? What do I have to lose...

I did a quick Google Maps search, and yes, the library was still at 5525 Spring Garden Rd. Check for parking spots, not bad; have the Blue pass. Forty-five minutes to town, ten to centre, five to park, 1 hour. 1400 eta, 1430 start, 1300 depart...latest, 1245 to be sure. Fine time appreciation calculations.

Tic, Tac, Toe. Bing, Bang, Boom. Everything lined up. Got a spot up to the door 1355, locked. What??? I take a few steps back, yup, the Library, wait a note in the window, dated 2017, closed...

For a few minutes, it's like, WTF (what the fuck again) really, and because I am still a firm believer of hard copies, i.e. paper... I printed the email and read it again. Everything lines up, but it's closed. I'm about to ...I don't really know what, but it's ringing and getting dark and crushing on me. Breathe...breathe look. Across the street is the New library, all lit up, next to the hospital. Now I'm soaked and really uncomfortable, but that is the place. Good, got a few minutes to watch. Now, this is funny, and this might be taken out or moved later, but I was lying in bed with Margret between drops (an inside joke) and was thinking about the session with Darren that day and how it had moved through many topics. I was going to talk to her about it, but then the idea to write it down seemed better. I could cover more than a five-minute chat, plus I had more to add. It's one of these things that come to you days or weeks later, like a punch line, a name, a face, or a feeling. I want to address the thing that is uneasy or difficult for me, well one of the things. This is where you give a silent chuckle to yourself. That was my literary whit. Nuff said.

Several times over the past few weeks, people, total strangers have come up to me and thanked me for my service and asked me about the undress ribbons. Now, here is where I started to make a link. Now, this is nothing major and probably has been mentioned before, but as I had mentioned to Darren, I thought I was well-read in most areas, but mental health, even though my daughter has had her struggles with it, and I have lost several friends to "we regret to inform you of the sudden death of…"This started out as a way to capture specific events over a period of time collectively instead of small note pads and voice memos, which do, in some mysterious way, get misplaced or deleted and lose the full details. A few pages should cover me between appointments, right? Five turned to nine, then a break. I think because I put an end date to get my act together and get it done, that stalled the whole process. Regroup. A few days, good weather, back in the saddle, well, a soft chair anyway.

The following pages contain MY views, beliefs as I understand them, stuff that has not been written down before, and some need to know info to link it all up. I am a professional and will try my best not to drop too many F-bombs, but when there are, the computer almost goes like a frizz bee. There are some poor attempts to infuse humour in the not-so-nice bits, and there are several branch-offs or unintentional ramblings, but during the editing and rewording, looking at pictures to confirm the dreams, they say that they're worth a thousand words, so here are a few 1,000 or so.

Warning. The following program contains course language, violence, and adult content not suited for some audiences. Viewer discretion is highly advised.

How did I get here today?

Thoughts become Things. Three simple words with a simple straight forward message, Your thoughts become things. So simple, yet so hard to understand with any true confidence for some. I for one was at first. Let me roll it back a little bit in time.

I had just been discharged from the Trenton Memorial Hospital after 7 days getting my pain medication to a safe level that I could function at least for a few hours in some sort of normal fashion. That

Friday night after a round trip in the patient transfer service van to the Kingston hospital to see the surgeon who was going to do the operation on my back. I had fractured my L5 and the bone fragments were pressing into my S1 nerve with herniated discs. The disk at L5 was ready to rupture.

Excruciating constant electrified pain down my right leg and the pressure on my lower spine made walking beyond a slow calculated movement of only a few steps exhausting. I would have to wait at home for the next six weeks before the operation. OR days are already booked up and extra theatre time was hard to get. If I had been in a car accident and brought in with no prior assessment, you would be next in line he said. Real emergencies are trump cards. I do understand. It is the system.

39 days and a walkie. My daily consumption of hydromorphone was 2 x 18 mg slow release. 0800-2000 Break through quick dissolving 2 and 4 mg tabs used as required. 8-12 mg. Plus a shitload of other stuff to counter the other stuff you are taking. I went from 195 lbs and exempt on my last express test to 178 lbs surgery day with thin chicken legs and a cane using the hallway wall for support trying but not really succeeding in walking.

During those 39 days and the days after surgery the opioids had discovered stuff that had been pushed deep down into the "ya that was really fucked up hurt locker "and thrust up to what I have come to know as "the night terrors." That was the fall of 2012. A lot of things have happened between now and then.

I can now walk on a good day 3 km, on a bad day my cane and around the property is about it, but I am walking. How?

01 November 2021, I was paired with Barrett, my 13 month old 85 pound Labrador Retriever at the CARES training facility Concordia Kansas. Sponsored by Paws Fur Thought, he has changed my life in such a way that I am here today writing this, instead of being a memory to my family.

Acknowledgement and Gratitude page

Acknowledgements and my words of Gratitude to these great people who have in their own way, kept me between the double yellow lines and the shoulder rumble strip:

Gus Cameron III President UN/ NATO HRM, Fabian Henry CEO Veterans 4 healing, Kim and Mike Gingell, intake coordinators for PFT, Brendon Abram Maj Ret'd, Steinar Engeset, Chairman Convoy Cup Foundation NS, Linda Mosher author, Rollie Lawless who introduced me to the UN/ NATO breakfast club, Medric and Jocelyn Cousineau Co-founders PFT, Peter Stoffer, Chairperson Veterans Legal Assistance Foundation, Dr Susie McAfee Resurface North, Doug Allan VTN, Dr Finley Spicer MD, Dr Kate MacAdam & Associates, Hilary Stevenson TNPS, and Dr Maria del Rosario Hernandez for Pain Management.

To my team at LT-Writing for taking my notes and producing a book that enabled me to bring some focus on service dogs that I am proud to share with everyone else that helped out, a big thanks.

Communication within the family unit has its challenges. As a child you do want not to tell your parents about something bad in fear of them not understanding or maybe a punishment may follow. The same I think goes for parents not wanting to tell their children about something in fear of them not understanding or some possible avoidance issues.

To my daughters Jennifer and Jaclyn. Your love and support comes in different forms and I know that it is always there. Hopefully this book will help answer or at least fill in some of those missing years in your childhood and to understand a bit of who I am today.

Finally, to Margret, My wife of 42 years.

I am *Trying*. I do recognize that somedays or weeks it doesn't seem like it, but I am trying. Knowing that sometimes your support goes unnoticed by me and my efforts to communicate are challenged hurts you, I am truly sorry and hope that this book may fill in some of the gaps. Your strength has enabled me to get over the rough parts and at times, it has kept our family together.

Your husband,

Love Greg

Book description

A military veterans autobiography documenting his 34 year career in the Canadian Engineers, and the post release struggles with injury pain, depression and PTSD. After he was paired with his Paws Fur Thought Labrador retriever service dog, Barrett in November 2022, their two years of steady positive reintegration into Life was almost destroyed by a vicious and unprovoked attack by a dog at large on them both and what mental trauma's they endured to navigating back to where they once were.

Table of Contents

Introduction

I have been doing some sort of journaling over the years to keep my thoughts, both dark and cheerful, in some chronological order. This past 2021 was a challenge for everyone, with COVID-19 taking a commanding hold upon so many. But yet I could relate to the many restrictions/rules from my tours overseas. Ours were, in essence, as these ones were, to save and protect lives from imminent and certain death if disobeyed or not used as directed. We were issued with helmets, flak jackets, LBVs, gas masks, a full load (150 rounds 5.56), a C7 assault rifle and ROEs. These told us what we were aloud to do and not to do. i.e. the unauthorized use of deadly force. You cannot just shoot a person until they have shot at you BS. During this pandemic, we were issued with masks, gloves, testing kits, vaccines, and hand sanitizer and told of the current health measures that were in place, what we could and could not do to save and protect lives from imminent and certain death if disobeyed, or not used as directed. Interesting parallel, right? Now, let that sink in a bit. This is an insight into how I am hard-wired.

Now, before I go on, already off script a bit, my intended audience is Hilary from True North (TNPS), Doug Allen from the Veterans Transition Network (VTN), and Dr. Susie McAfee (Dr.S) from ResurfaceNorth (RN). I have identified with each one mentioned either through a retreat or regular sessions as a Safe person with a varied knowledge of my background. I will try to endeavor not to bring up too much of the past, doing so as a reference only. (see the above example)

After many note pads and voice memos, it is time to try to compose a discussion with the reader(s) as if it was a one-on-one, with occasion to address a single reader.

Chapter 1

What is going on?

Over The past several months, well 10 anyway, my life has slowly, although sometimes painful, had an upward drift, with gaining some peace and understanding of who and why I am who I am now. I am no longer a religious person (another paper in itself) and have experienced my fair share of near-death experiences that, on occasion, I relive when my back pain is amped to 11. (a back injury on 16 Sep 2012 that eventually resulted in a medical release).

In the summer of 2018, I had an invite to the HRM library to view a presentation from Wounded Warriors Canada (WWC) about service dogs. I was amazed at what they could do and how calming their effect was on people. Interesting, but I did not pursue the seed that was dropped. Moving to the spring of 2019, I was once again invited to a WWC service dog presentation, which also was a recertification weekend for the NS-based dogs and handlers, letting you have more interaction with the dogs. So, after meeting some dogs and their handlers, I entered into the application process to get a service dog. Then the pandemic hit. Fast forward to summer 2021. My walking was challenging, to say the least, and with the aid of a cane, I could manage a few 100 meters at best. This added to the frustration of dealing with the aftereffects of a serious concussion. This subject (my concussion) has been discussed in some detail with all of the audience. My biggest problem is my word association and a sudden total mid-sentence block. Also, my short-term memory is toast. My biggest problem is my word association and a sudden total mid-sentence block. Also, my short-term memory is toast.

After seeing the flyer for the Resurface North surf retreat at Hilary's True North office, I contacted Dr. S. On hold for now, but if there's more interest it is a go. The next day got an email saying that the retreat was a go. Sweet. Stuff is looking up.

The retreat at White Point Beach was, I think when I look back on it, they were the first dents in my armor. (recall my first day, Doug, When I talked about my vest? It is my Armor. Now, I'm not a huge guy, 6 foot 1 inch with my boots on, a buck 90 or so, black hat, sunglasses, beard, leather coat and vest. Not that I try to be intimidating, but as a civilian, what is your first image that most would project? I don't have to do a thing. The stereotyped biker picture popped into your head, right? Look like a patched-in member of SAM CRO. Well, that is my armor.)

I didn't forcefully pound them back out. I don't know why, but I left them there. One of Dr. S's team members asked me why I was there and what I felt about the last few days. I had told her that I was going to get my service dog in November, and I had not been away from my house except for doctor appointments or grocery shopping done concurrently in the last five years, so in true army fashion, I applied the retreat as a RECCE for the trip into the world. Successful again. Meeting some great people and getting wet in the process is a bonus. Now, before I go further, a clarification is needed. The reference to "getting wet" refers to going into the ocean. I was a PADI MSDT with over 25 years of diving all around the world. The last time I was in the water was in August 2012, removing a line from a prop at the CFB Trenton Yacht Club. I broke my back that September. I had not been in the water since then. Nine years of the fear was being literally washed away. With each wave breaking over me, I felt the warmth of the water, the taste of salt, memories of the Red Sea rushing back and the joy that I had from diving. Trying the basic moves and getting onto the board didn't really work out, but that did not take away from this great awakening experience. I am truly looking forward to the next retreat.

Although this discussion paper is addressed to several people, I will refrain from getting off script with personal feedback and save that for a real face-to-face conversation or even by phone after I have read this. I do not possess at this time the word -smith-manship required (?)

With some experience away from home, I was looking forward to the trip next month, and I needed something to keep my mind occupied. The AYC was running a Coastal Navigation course in

October, great. I used to teach the Advanced Pilot course, the next course above this one. Plotting tracks around Halifax harbour. Not too hard. I had been boating here since the 1970s when Dad joined the AYC and did four summers at the RNSYS sailing school before joining the Army. When I retired, I sold my power boat and bought a sailboat. We left Frenchman's Bay YC and piloted a Mirage 30 sailboat 2655 KM (as per the ship's log) to Halifax in 40 days. Down the St. Lawrence River to the Atlantic Ocean. The point is that I was plotting the trip in real-time, with the weather and the added responsibility of the safety of my crew, yet now I could not do nautical math for a simple tabletop exercise. 100s math is not bad, but not the '60s math, and I don't mean the TV show, but hours, minutes and seconds for tide travel calculations. I have this vast knowledge but cannot access it to do a simple course around McNabs Island. A little speed wobble, but everything is still under control. The course is not that important, but some things are not quite right.

The trip to Kansas was spooling up, and a few sessions with Hilary, before I left gave me some more reassurance and remembering about staying within my window of tolerance.

Add a binder of paperwork and the whole COVID-19 travel fun. Also, I might add that no THC or CBD is allowed across the border. Well, extra-strength Tylenol and scotch has its calming effects as well. A long and tiring week, but it will be worth it, right? I must mention that at Pearson International Airport in Toronto, after two countries, two flights and 18 hrs, the terminal was overwhelming, and I had a Chernobyl meltdown. Fortunately, Dan, who also got a dog, alerted the airport staff, and I remember this as if it were yesterday, " my friend doesn't do well in crowds ". The staff brought us to an elevator, just us and the two dogs up to the gate level, down a passageway and out beside our waiting area. Bypassed everyone.

A few clonazepam and a 3-hour wait until our flight. At boarding time, with no announcement, a flight crew member came over and escorted us onboard to our seats and made sure both dogs were good to go. Even though I had regained some composure, I could feel the eyes looking at me; some felt sorry, some embarrassed, but some had compassion.

Barrett, my then 14-month-old, 85-pound Labrador retriever Service dog was a steep learning curve. The winter was coming along, and walking Barrett in all kinds of weather, at all hours, it seemed, had its toll on both physical and mental health, being tested more than once with at one point, 31 January was circled on the calendar as his end date to get his act together. Loading up into the car was, at best, a struggle, usually with me lifting his hind end into our Equinox. We had difficulties while in KS, but when he went into a van that he was trained on, it was no problem. Well, I'm not buying a new van. Right? This was another problem to deal with as well. The speed wobble is starting to slide just a bit, but I got this. Not really.

I am now basically in a constant state of pain, with several 0 dark 30 falls in the snow with Barrett. Funny, I don't remember any additional pain except a now almost constant hangover. Two fingers of single malt twice graduated to three fingers, then three and three. A reference to a verse in a G&R song, "Mr. Brownstone," comes to mind: "A little was little until the little wasn't a little anymore," plus my Rx's and still it was there. The deep nerve pain was just running on autopilot. The wobble had, without realizing it, turned into a full uncontrolled 360 deg spin. Now, when I am trying to describe something or get a point across to someone I reference a common item that can be substituted in place. Imagine that you are on a spinning wheel ride at the park. I can picture it in my mind, not a Ferris wheel, but the..I'm at a block. When you are spinning around, the centrifugal force is slowly pulling you away from the ride, and the faster you spin, you'll feel the force lift you up, and you timed your release to miss anything i.e. trees or rocks. As kids there was always a contest of who could hang on the longest. Although I can't remember the correct word, you can visualize the scene. Now, this is me with the same feeling, but when I let go, it will not be in a park. My slow drift upwards was now a breaker on the shoals.

Margret Tanner ▶ Veterans UN   ...
NATO - Nova Scotia
October 5 at 9:43 PM · 🖼

Pictured with Greg is Dr. Susie McAfee at
the end of a two day Resurface North
Retreat at Whitepoint ,not knowing what to
expect I had a great time with 3 Engineers
on the retreat. Going out of my comfort
zone,(away from home)to engaging with
10strangers 168 km away was hard enough,
but the genuine understanding and
providing a safe outlet for us that suffer with
PTSD,Susie made my frist solo trip away in 5
years worth it. Cheers Greg
For more info check out www.
resurfacenorth.com

FB posting after the 2 day retreat with Resurface North

5

Chapter 2

Slap in the face-to-face!

03 January, I had an appointment with Hilary, but in my blur, I didn't read the full text, and it was a phone call session instead of in the office. The struggle to get Barrett into the car, the 40-minute trip in town just after New Year... just lovely, tell your mother. I plan to arrive, as usual, 15 min prior. Bathroom break for us both, then upstairs. Slick roads and slow drivers take up some time, but they are still on track. Google Maps says nine minutes out. Not that bad. When I turned the corner, it seemed odd that the parking lot only had three vehicles, and I'm sure Hilary didn't drive a blue cargo van or the delivery trucks. Well, maybe Hilary got dropped off. The stores in the park were open, so why not TN?

Unload Barrett, his break then to the front door. Locked, but there is someone inside, so I get their attention. He told me that there was no one working today. It is construction on the first-floor washrooms. Dam. Now I'm pissed off even more. Load Barrett back up and find a place to take a leak. I have had issues with (a sudden need to urinate) since my injury, which then becomes the immediate and only thing on my mind. I have spots tagged all over Halifax for specific reasons. Growing up here and then being posted here for nine years prior to moving back here gave me a home-ice advantage for hiding spots. So, off to Home-depot. By the blue space at the contractor's door, past the desk off to your right. In our load-up, on the road home. When I am driving, the phone is in driving mode. That's why they made it, am I not correct? Hilary was just calling as the phone switched over. Not calling back right now. Got to get on the road. Didn't even stop for a smoke. Can't stop now because then Barrett has to do his thing. Not in the mood. Not even close.

Back home again. It was nine days since I went back to town to drop Margret off at my daughter's. They had tickets to a show, and well, she had just about enough of the whole thing. It is just pain, don't let it run your life, I had been told countless times before. It was a cold trip in and a sad one on the way home.

A local friend, Heath, with whom I have had many conversations, dropped by. He spent a few months with the Army reserves during the Oka crisis, and when the current sitting Liberal government disbanded the Airborne Regiment, he wanted 2 Commando, so he got out. Did a few years with the New Glasgow Army Reserve. Suffice it to say we have shared enough to be able to talk about any subject, regardless of content. No judgement, just listening. Hilary and I have discussed the nature of Heath's relationship previously. So, Heath likes to drink and smoke weed. Interestingly enough, so do I.

A suitcase of Keith's and a 26'er of Famous Grouse blended scotch. Consumption rates are up; quality is reduced. A good single malt is savored and enjoyed over time, not chasing a green grenade. Barrett is fed and has his after-supper walk, so the smoking lamp is lit. The math works out well, too. 12 Keith's, and. 26'er. A beer, a double, repeat as required and a shot for coffee in the morning. Planning, planning, planning.

0630, and Barrett gives me a nudge. Morning break time. Just lovely. I felt like a semi-trailer ran over me. Everything hurt, and to boot, a sinus headache. Back in, off to bed. Barrett's back on the couch for some more rack time. 0730, alarm, more pills. I cannot even swallow without it hurting. Rolling out of bed, I was still loaded. The Metallica song Enter the Sandman is playing on the radio: "Sleep with one eye open, Gripping your pillow tight, exit light, enter night, Take my hand, We're off to never-never land" was playing on the radio. Why was the radio on anyway? Must have left it on last night. Yup, your lights are going out all right.

Going to be a rough one, buddy. Splashing some cold water on a facecloth, I gave my face a quick wipe so I would be able to pry open my eyes. They were literally bleeding. My eyes have the unique ability to go from hazel to green. Found out later that this is quite common. Now have two different coloured eyes like a husky; now that's unique. Anyway, they were green and with bloodshot eyes, and a distinct mark of a chain on my right cheek. It was the imprint from my medical alert bracelet. I looked like a cheap horror flick extra. "And the sign said, long-haired freaky people need not apply" My Grizzly Adams beard was, as my mother put it, "Gregory, you are looking very rustic". I weighed 212 lbs. WTF. I don't eat much, so why am I such a fat bastard anyway? There is an old expression, been around way longer than me, and I happened to be the recipient of this rant from my old, old TP WO, "Son, you look like you were ridden hard, rolled up and put away wet" that was after a 4 CER Engineer Reunion pig roast, drink your face off dance in Germany. Yagy, Yagy, Yagy.

The situation is not looking too bright at this time. Those flashing lights you are seeing are not floaters; they're your low-battery warning. I'm messed up big time. Bing 0830, more pills, and I still didn't take the 0730 ones yet. One hand full or two, sir? The choice is yours. Step right up and take your pick. Now, here's where things get a little weird of sorts, if there not already. Now previously mentioned was the fact that I was no longer a religious person, but through the years of counseling, personal research retreats, etc, I have developed my own methodology taking certain techniques, practices, or lessons learned. It's great when applied but comes into question, like when bad shit happens, and you're doing everything correctly. But I can now, I mean today as I am writing this, see that it was working like it is supposed to. I just didn't see it. Big picture stuff, not cruises or the winning lottery ticket, but a treehouse for my grandson Carter, and putting a dock off the front of the house to swim and dive from. Real-world things that I can create that would bring joy to others. At my DWD ceremony, a retired four-ringer engineering officer gave me a small five-by-ten maroon leather-bound notebook. Something you can even get at the Dollar Store. It read," Stay calm and carry on." That saying has been around forever, but what made this special is that he had a white crown embossed above the quote. He was a boating friend as well and had observed my struggles after my injury.

The white crown represented my rank of Warrant Officer. The pages are all blank, with no lines, so you can even sketch if you feel the urge. I currently have 149 pages completed thus far. It is not something I read or add to every day, but it is there as a reminder to remember. This morning, page 99 reads, "Every single human being is meant to be in joy. It is our natural state, and we know it because when we feel negative emotions, we feel terrible. We want to be happy, and the biggest thing to realize is that happiness is a choice because it is a feeling generated from the inside of us. We have to make a decision to be happy on the inside now, to magnetize a life of happiness on the outside. I do have a choice, and when I really felt joy was when I was weightless just below the thermocline a few feet above the bottom, just observing the kelp ebb and flow with the swells, the occasional bug, no outside noise, just the sea. If you close your eyes and slow down your breathing, you can actually hear the shrimp snapping their tails. Bubbles from the regulator expand and rise up, leaving the telltale sign that a diver is below. The small feeder fish chasing the silver shimmering ever-growing air pockets. Yes, I do remember.

Now, what can you do within your sphere to get things rolling along? I'm sorry, but I must digress at this time. This event happened 36 years ago, which literary defined my life and diving career, the reason why I rose to MSDT with over 1100 dives logged before my injury. We were in Spain on leave, staying at the Eden Rock full pension resort nestled on a rock face overlooking the Costa Brava coast. Three pools, a private beach, and no kids. Our daughter Jennifer was three at the time. She was staying with friends back at the PMQs. They also had a daughter born in Lahr about a week after Jennifer, so they grew up together. A few of us would take turns baby/house-sitting during the summer period. July was the month off. Fall Ex part one, six weeks in Hohenfels doing training, back for a few weeks in September, then back out for another five weeks for the live fire Ex. Sorry, I'm way off-topic now. Regroup.

We had been doing the tourist thing and I had pre-arranged for some diving through a German club from the Lake Constance region, our sister Club. I think it was the third or fourth doing afternoon day boat diving trips that the dive master brought us to a beautiful secluded area only accessible by boat due to the sharp rock ledges. The thing about this special dive was that there was a tunnel open at each end, about 20 meters in length. A sandy bottom enabled you to squeeze through just before the end. Air check. Good 100 bar.

Now I had my own fins, mask suit and BC, but I hadn't decided to get DIN or SAE connections. Hence, the rental regs. No problems swimming or crawling through. A few scrapes here and there, but that's diving. Breaking out into the sunlight, I rolled on my back, watching the other divers above me, and I followed the anchor line up to the tender, watching the boat gently roll with the swells overhead. Rolling back over, the dive master was about three or four lengths away. Everything's looking good. Gas check, 50 bar. Time to drift over to the assent line. I did a big scissor kick and exhaled. Breathe in, I said, breathe in. Nada. A vacuum. Not good. Now, I have relived this event at least 1000 times, and sometimes the clarity is shocking.

This is where the choices come in.

1.) Free assent 105 ft to the surface, dangerous but doable

2.) Get to the DM and get some air. Very doable. He is 20 ft away.

With the effects of CO_2 building up, the blackout slowly starts. Shake it off and swim, Swim. My O2 level was dropping, and the burning in my lungs was almost all-consuming. I got to him and gave the world-recognized sign for an out-of-air emergency. Well, the first thing he did was grab my pressure gauge and tap the dial. An air bubble came out from behind the red needle and went to the top of the dial. Now, with the needle pinned on the stop, approximately 15-20 seconds have passed. Not a lot of time, you would think. Not to go all Big Bang Theory on you, but At 105 feet, you are at 3.17 atmospheres plus pressure, 46.59 lbs per sq inch, crushing your chest. So now, time is of the essence. He gives me his reg, and we do a few minutes of buddy breathing. Calming down, we exchange the OK sign. A German diver saw what had transpired and came over to us. He had an octopus regulator (one of the few), and we did a controlled ascent with a safety stop of 5 meters. 5 at 5 was the rule.

Hang and do a bit of deco. Back on the boat the DM felt bad because it was their gear I had rented. A bottle of water to cleanse the rubber and salt out. On the way back in, the older German diver, in his broken English, said, "Kandanish good? Militar? He asked. "

We exchanged some mix mash of my bad German and his English. Once we were back and unloading, he came over to me and said in a very rehearsed manner, "You are good in the water; no panic. Auf Wiedersehen." When I got back to the resort, Margret wondered what happened. I had basically lost my tan and was still wired from the whole experience. Going over the dive trip and the decision that is now before me. Grabbed a bottle of Sangria, and by the pool, we talked, and ultimately it was my decision. Dust yourself off and Get back on the provable horse that bucked you off, or take up jogging. I hate running. Do it five days a week now.

The next day, I went to the dive shop, and we decided on a nice 20 m dive and a new reg set. I was ready to crawl out of my suit when he dropped the anchor. You could feel it when it took a bite in the sand as the boat slowly pointed into the wind. A DM briefing on the dive site, gas check, timer on, and roll off the side. Just like falling off a log. One hand on my mask, the other on my weight belt, splash. I kept my eyes open and watched the water embrace around me and I took a deep breath in. Cold, sweet air. A gentle descent by the anchor rode to the coral and sandy bottom. This was an area known for moray eels, and I even got some pictures. God, it felt great. Forty-five minutes bottom time, relaxed, in my happy spot. Remembering on the beach last fall and the hidden nugget that was almost never found, I wanted that again. When we were doing wrap-up for the retreat, I never let on to the newly acquired dents that were still there.

A few times, I drifted off for a bit on the deck when the yoga bend you like a pretzel class started, wondering how to get a handle on this rekindled sensation from another lifetime ago. But how to get there now? A full stop, reboot, circuit breaker if you wish. Cold turkey, big time. No booze, Rx mind-numbing drugs, smokes, and sleeping aid pain pills. I might be half-batshit crazy, but I'm not stupid. I stayed on the CBD 20 mg gel pills because they work, and I know that a full-blown case of the DT's about to set in. The Army way, as they say: balls to the wall. No use in doing four withdrawals. Let the Concurrent activities begin.

The next month or so was marked on the kitchen calendar, but I wasn't really in the note-taking mood. I might elaborate on it in a future paper, hallucinations and all, if I told you that after those six weeks, all was sunshine and lollypops, well...... a little bit of sunshine.

Now, I have to jump into the present day to this down. On Wednesday, 15 June, Margret was working at Shaws restaurant located in West Dover, the 1-6 shift. It is her away from my time, and the tips are pretty good, too. I was walking Barrett up behind the garage and heard sirens in the distance. Following the sound, it went around the cove and stopped. From my vantage point, I can see over to West Dover. I can actually see the yellow house of a mutual acquaintance of ours back on track. I could hear but no visual, so off we went doing our afternoon walk up the hill along some deer trails. Back to the house for some relaxing time on the deck. Barrett has found the remains of a discarded stick and as I stir my coffee, I am thinking things are starting to look good around here.

Chapter 3

Update: AED

Now a quick update from the February timeframe. I have now been sober for five months and a few days. No liquor of any type or any anxiety meds for five months. I have been temped on a few instances, but to start over again is not in the cards. A few smokes a day, and my bud 0.0. And honestly, a bit of King Kush every now and then does take the edge off. No hangovers, and when Barrett comes into get me up, I'm usually just lying down waiting for him. A quick walk for his break, and sometimes, if were lucky, you can catch the sun cresting the rocks at Prospect, leaving a golden sheen on the rising tides swells. Coffee on the deck, watching the lobster boats do their runs, and I can now, with reasonable certainty, name the boats by the engine sounds. No two are alike. Example: The Casey V is a 40 ft cape with a 10-cylinder cat and four-inch exhaust. When a south west wind is blowing, you can hear the Casey a few miles away. Miss Leary Cove had been around since I can remember. Smaller in size and has been repowered to a six-cylinder diesel. We all had little turtle backs (a type of fiberglass dinghy) to explore and fish around the local coves. Damn, where was I?

Barrett taking a break during our walk.

Oh ya, so I went to pick Margret up at the end of her shift, and she told me that a friend of ours had a heart attack around 2 pm. Chris came over from the UK years ago. He sits on the director's board, as do I for the East Dover Comfort Centre (EDCC). Chris also runs Yoga twice a week at the EDCC. Now, here are some times to remember. His wife works with Margret, and she got a call early into the shift to get home now, but no reason why. After she left it was about 20 minutes for the Fire Department to show up, and another five for the ambulance.

She said it was there for a good 15 minutes anyway, and when it left, it blew by the Firetruck in full mode. We heard nothing until Thursday morning. He is doing good and needs a stint and be back home fingers crossed Sunday or Monday. So 20 minutes for the FD, and another five for the ambo, plus turnaround back to the Emergency Dept another 25. You are really pushing the golden hour.

Now, remember when I said that was getting a bit weird? Well, here is the set up. For the last six years in the military I was in the Emergency Management Cell for the largest Airbase in Canada. To tie this up quickly, my educational journey in EM was a continuous learning curve. And if I wanted to go to school, the Military had the money for training if you could substantialize the courses, and also, the ability to pump out a few good memos never hurt either. Four years of night school and DL courses plus many exchange training exercises with our American counterparts. We got to see a lot of they're really neat secret squirrel shit that was unseen to others, but because we were in uniform, the doors were wide open.

And you know the Americans love to show off their Gucci kit to us poor Canadians. HLS and FEMA packed quite a punch after 911, and Katrina's lessons learned were applied. When we moved back here, the person who was sitting on the Western Region Joint Emergency Management (WRJEM) was stepping down, and I would like to slide in. New, fresh eyes and all that stuff.

A meeting once a month, some interesting presentations so what the hell. Got to spend the government's money wisely.

My dad passed away on 16 October 2019 at the age of 83 from congestive heart failure. He had had a heart attack Aug 2000. I just came back from Kosovo that July after seven months away. Mom also remarked that it was a long time for the ambulance to get here. When I really hurt my back in 2020, even though I wasn't deemed life-threatening, it still was 30 minutes, give or take, until they arrived. The decision to call wasn't mine, I can reassure you, but after around three hours of attempting to crawl from the bedroom to the ensuite, I finally collapsed, exhausted and broken again. The trip is another discussion altogether. It wasn't nice.

So the following day, Thursday, I got a call from our neighbour who lived across from the EDCC. She said that the door was open and wondered if I was in there earlier that day. Nope. Now, just a bit of a rewind. After Dad passed, I wanted to do something, but what to honour my dad. We just happened to be asked by HRM EMO to produce an emergency plan for our community. Just what the doctor ordered. Right in my wheelhouse and all that jazz. Some of the examples given were just lat and long positions and location names, Zone 1, etc, and several pages that no one would read anyway. At one meeting, the HRM fire Lt and I did not see eyes on a few things and received the standard blurb about him doing this for 30-odd f'n yrs. What does an army guy know anyway, right? Apparently, SFA, according to him. My EM plan was a six-page PPT. Our one road in communities was a pain to him. So, my plan was based on the greatest hazard that we would face, realistically, the estimated arrival time from the call-to-door response.

This is a copy from the Phillips Heart start manual, which really emphases my point.

"IMPORTANT NOTE: For every minute of delay, the chance of survival declines by 7% to 10%."

I mentioned that some google maps currently show that my house is a wooded lot. Nope, I'm wrong. The internet doesn't lie. Thats what they use. I guess we are on our own. What an A-hole. The boss at HRM loved it and posted it on the EMO site. After my dad passed, I bought a Phillips AED, an alarmed box, and signage for the community centre. A good tax deduction for donations. Now, for access to the AED, I installed a weather proof box and the spare building key in it. There is also a sign on the window and door.

Getting back to the phone call, She had said she knew nothing about Chris. A while later, we got a call from another neighbour who said she got a call from a friend who works at the So'Wester restaurant at Peggy's Cove. See the pattern developing. EMS had dropped off an AED to them from a call they had responded to nearby yesterday, and neither the FD nor their bus was missing one. They said it was on the scene when they arrived. Thanks for the return, and have a good day. When the SW staff conducted a check on all the registered units, all were in place. Someone from the village remembered that there was a unit at the EDCC, hence the phone call. Today Margret got a call from one of the directors and told her that it was indeed our AED . I am elated and exhausted all at once.

I am letting the last few months stay at rest right now, concentrating on tomorrow. We, Barrett and I are currently on good days doing a two km round trip to the EDCC and back. We stop at the look-off and just sit, watching the ever-changing landscapes laid out before me. There is a divot at the top of the cliff where rainwater collects and serves as a mid-walk drinking spot. People drive by and look up. I wonder what they think.

It was just one regular day, and I received an email from Dr. S that they are planning to run a few more retreats, with an extra day tacked on this round. Are you serious?The booze weight has been coming off, and I can deal with 186 lbs. Clothes fit again. I've got some extra energy, but pacing myself. I had the recent opportunity to attend a five-day workshop/retreat laid on by the VTN in March of this year, and even though there were other facilitators participating, I will keep my direction on Doug. This was something that, yet again, was delayed due to COVID. As always, no names, no pack drill. I will say it really shook something up. My safety was that I only lived 12 km away, so if I had to bug out, no worries, home before you knew it. After the second day, hearing and sharing stuff long packed away in their own compartments was taking its toll, and I had become physically sick thinking about the next day.

The wife said bail if you want. You don't know them from Adam. But here is the rub: I did know two of the guys from years back. Never actually met each other, but we remembered the crusty old base RSM in Gagetown in the early '80s. Been to the same

16

postings or tours: Beer gardens in Lahr, the clubs in Opeagia Croatia on a 72 hour, the tomb of the unknown solider at the Hero's Square in Budapest, or on Roto 1, the UNHCR refugee camp on the way to Zagreb. We went past, well, it was usually a 40-minute drive to reach the ramp for the checkered route onto the main cleared highway, then another few hours to the airfield. The UN QM was located here as well as the main airhead for the troops on the ground. There was a building, more like a cellblock and our logistical and senior staff stayed here. So the deal was it was a six to seven-hour road trip, wearing your full kit, crammed in, and was it hot.

I'm, well, I was 6 ft one, now just six 0. Lost that bit during the operation to decompress the sciatic nerve and remove the bone fragments from the fractured vertebrae and the disc; as the surgical report said, " as I started the incision at the L5 level, the disc material oozed out... well, you can visualize that image because we have all seen doctor and emergency shows showing operations, blood and guts... beach scene from Saving Private Ryan. That on surround sound half-lit, your hair is tingling, and when the bombers come in to do their run from seaward, the sound starts from behind, and I have actually ducked after the fly over. Glad we have established how my mind uses examples to set the hook, an instructor trick, so I really have your attention. Now, back to the UNHCR refugee camp. There were reported to be approximately 40 thousand people there living in old tents, burnt out cars, tanks, old fuel tanks and every other imaginable shape of shelter to gain some protection from the elements. We all used to joke about this next bit, and D you know that this is no BS.

Our trips were usually every five or six weeks, taking a different helper, usually someone who needed a break. Remember that I had mentioned, or maybe I didn't, that as Engineers we had in the Middle East Orange cards which enabled you to cross into Syria on short notice. Say that day. No problems. We went everywhere. Some trades were strictly static, and a few months were on the camps. The Orderly Room, Supply techs, base support pers. On these trips, it was two were two vehicles on these trips so we had a signup sheet so if they were off shift and wanted to get away from it all, they were a welcome change. The same goes for all my other tours. Solider first, trade as required. Moving along, these and sometimes young 19-year-olds, eyes wide open, and I imagine I did the same thing on my first trip, a long six months before. It was just routine for us by now, but to see some of the facial expressions, and now, 25 plus years later, remembering our snickers or remarks that just rolled off, Holy F. Did you see that MCPL? Yup, you going to have a beer at supper? Just everyday stuff.

So as the tour was winding down for us, the Dayton Accords had been signed the December before. The polling station equipment, official ballots and around 30 personnel who would over see the election process took place on the far side of the camp, and the triple cat wire concertina fencing was erected by the Combat Engineers.

So we had to do our last trip before the election was to be held, so one last time the Zagreb for an ISO pick up. The regular trip up and back, but we noticed that a lot of the old cars had been dragged out from the fields, and a mobile car crusher was being set up. Hardly looked like it could crush a beer keg. But they are industrious out of a necessary need to survive. The roto till pulled carts, .50 cal in the trunk. Remember that I had said the estimated population of the camp was around 45 thousand. Even at the PSTC Peace Support Training Centre located at CFB Kingston, there are pictures of that camp and a famous one of the five or six-tier high guard hut at one of the major intersections posted in the halls.

The 10-day course did it four times. Why? Because of some badly worded Training orders, stating the expiry date of your knowledge retention is only 12 months, everyone was doing a tour, home for 14 months, three months of workups, and a ten day reunion party. Even funnier, since even after all the training and tours, my job then was the standards WO. The training directive orders (TDO) state that a train the trainer (TTT) course is required as a requirement. Since we were the Readiness Training Flight (RTF), we taught the Camp Mirage roto's the same course but in-house. So, to do the TTT, you have to be current with the Kingston course. No worries. Done it four times. Don't check me, check records. But it is time expired and my tours meant squat. Hey, a staff car, quarters at the Holiday Inn downtown. Did I mention Kingston? Maybe the Hip is playing somewhere. So the ten days on course, and a five day train the trainer. It's not much smarter, but a great two weeks. Thank Steven Harper. This one is on you.

BlackBear Casern C.C Jul 1996- Jan 1997.

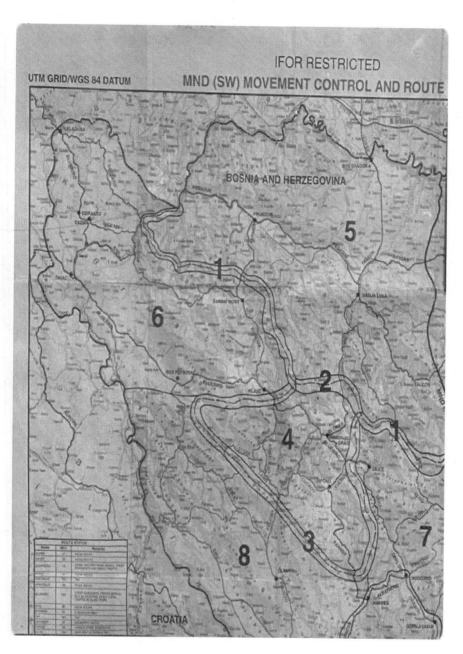

The map of our AOR

Rolling into BlackBear Casern.

Clearing pit at Coralici.

Chapter 4

To qualify or quantify

See what I mean, way off topic; well you need to know some of this so get the full picture. There was, like I said, about 45 K housed at the camp. When we rotated out in January 1997, the trip to Zagreb was a fleet of buses and ten-ton trucks with all our kit winding up the mountain roads. We were really doing good on time when it dawned on everyone: the UNHCR camp was gone totally. Piles of metal blocks from the car crusher and lots of dirt mounds ten feet or higher. But no people. All gone. Off to another Refugee camp, I guess. Lots of rumours circulated, but with the tarmac in sight, that was just the way it was. Now picture the area that size that took 40 minutes to drive through and tents for miles, gone. It was like it wasn't there. I heard that they were good at doing that.

I AM back from the future, sort of, well from page 34 or so, the rabbit holes I've been down to confirm or deny some thoughts. It is clear that these lateral tangents are meaningful, but then the conversation point has been lost, and sometimes, no matter how hard concentration efforts are, nothing, nada, zip. Maybe that's a good thing. J.H.C. on a cracker, see what I mean?

I have decided to capture these off shoots as appendices that then can be referenced if and when required. It's not the approved Purdue Owl format, but it keeps all of us on the same page.... I know, don't quit my day job.

See Appendix A for a more detailed description of the UNHCR camp.

Since this paper will not be printed by me anyway, save a tree and all that stuff. Shit, where was I? Oh ya, since I am adding appendices, why not figures as well? I will stop after figure 11. It will be a figure 11. An army reference. I will clarify this off line. Doing that, Tokyo drifts again. Back to page 34.

Christ, all that from a mention of a five-minute conversation at coffee. Hey Doug, I guess this automatic writing thing you were talking about is real. Had to go back for about three hours to find my main discussion point, which was the VTN five-day program. Now, before I drift off once again, a tremendous experience covering stuff to be maybe only said once, with a group of, hey remember Doug, I'm not the touchy-feely type, and an open, non-judgmental, safe environment. And by the way, the picture of the bell curve came in handy.

To quantify or qualify? I want to mention my current healthcare providers, both mental and physical. I don't know why, but it feels like something that needs to at least be laid out in some form of structure. For my physical care, I have and am lucky to have an MD, yearly check ups, scripts, etc. The standard fare. My Chiropractor, Dr. Kate, for several years, has been doing acupuncture with an electric current flowing up and down my spine. Sometimes, it is like nine-inch nails in place of the needles and jumper cables up to a battery charger. And sometimes, she cannot even put a needle in.

Now for the mental health side. I think that deep down, my fear is how when I'm finished reading this, things will change professionally no, but in the eyes, yes. Hell, I've changed, but I'm the one that's damaged goods.

I had started and nearly completed a nifty engineer-type style flow chart to try and project the multi layers in my somewhat fading grey matter called the brain. How many Billions of brain cells did you incinerate during the Scorched Earth advancement? Don't have enough fingers and toes to add it up. Back to work on Appendix A.

Using my best Superintendent chart skills, the boxes and flow arrows, wyes, and subordinate boxes emerged on the computer screen. Follow the left arrow for a yes and to the right for a no. Now, to visualize the response boxes, both good and bad so I can get the creative juices flowing.

A few soft balls for a warm-up for the big game. An imaginary yes response, good, carry on to the next. It was really feeling good to see the 3 D image rise up, but now I could see a few No responses hanging down. Out of curiosity, what is, of course, expected, we all grab the low-hanging fruit to sort of say, well, because it is easy, and the survivalist instinct kicks in. Lets try another one of the orchards offerings. A little bitter but palatable. Another Yes response to perk up and now to look and observe the fruit. Which one is the ripest to pick? The logic says so. It's got to taste better.

Transfixed on the colour that has multiple shades as the sun shines off the moisture. How will it feel in your hand, the bumps on the bottom, the slight prickly sensation from the leaf as it slips thru your fingers, the slight sweet smell of apple in the light breeze, and with a quick snap, bam, you're ripping into it, core and all.

It's Whacked, right? How did that taste, sunshine? Hard going down and worse on the exit route. Once again, with the cinematic description. Clive Barker is a well-known Director of horror movies. I do not know what your fair is but suffice to say there are some graphic scenes throughout the flick. In the move Hell-raiser, upon opening Pandora's Box, Pin Head introduces the main character to unimaginable horrors. Now, that doesn't really make sense to me; if they are showing the images, someone had to. A Catch-22 situation. Pin Head asked the main if he wanted to open the box, and after a minute, the answer was yes. Of course, it is. Otherwise it would be a short seven-minute Cannes Film Festival Foreign entry. Say that five times quickly.

With the slightest of touches, the embossed insignia within the centre circle on the top slowly sinks within itself, and without any distinct pattern, small doors open on the now glowing box. Instantly as the last door opened, chains with meat hooks burst from across the room and embedded themselves into his back, immediately pulling the flesh from his muscles, letting out a shrilling scream, and with a wink of his pin-laced eyelid, another set came from the opposite side and grappled into his chest, essentially slowly skinning him alive. WTF. To triggered to carry on right now. Break time.

Chapter 5

My 1-866 number call

Looking at the imaginary monstrosity staring back at me from my MacBook Air, well, it's choice time, once again.

Now if I retained anything from the five-day VTN experience, it was, why did you react that way, know that it is OK, and try to understand, not with a magnifying glass picking the fly shit from the pepper but Breathe Leo, Breathe. An inside joke and another Appendix, anyway. The Main point is that you respond to, instead of reacting to and losing, your now not so tightly wired shit. The experiences and tales told out of school were, well, once again, I lack the mental fortitude to express the whole thing. But that's good, right?

The question pops up on the screen, "Are you sure you want to delete this file?" Damn straight. Burn that bitch. We now return to our regularly scheduled program.

A very rocky start. The first 1-866 number I called was the hardest thing to do up to that point in my life. I had become just consumed with the whole release paperwork mess, a two-year F'n nightmare that ultimately crushed any belief in the care after release bull shit. The whole event can be wrapped up in a tight bow.

As a part of the information gathering process I had to write a second person account of my military career up to now.

Second person account essay for the clinic after third visit Spring 2015

"…Greg grew up in Halifax NS, where he completed his high school education, and then joined the Canadian Army Engineering Branch. During his 23 year career in the army he had postings all over Canada, a four year stint in Germany and completed four UN / NATO missions overseas. Upon taking his release from the regular

26

forces, he enlisted in the Canadian Air Force reserves and stayed an additional 11 years to complete 34 years in uniform.

In his service with the Army as mentioned above included four missions overseas. His first six month tour was to the Golan Heights in the fall of 1992 to the spring of 1993. This experience filled him with honour and pride doing his first UN peacekeeping mission and also some unsettling emotions of shock and disbelief in the way different cultures dealt with their civilian population. We (Canadians) in comparison were wealthy beyond imagination. Their value for the human life was extremely different from the western world, and as UNDOF Peacekeepers we were the buffers between the Syrians and the Israelis. Listening to the Logistical Officers (LO's) on each side of the border gave him a raw and brutally clear impression of what each nation's feelings were towards each other. What was taught in their schools, and what their ethos were based on. When crossing into Syria, aka the dark side, (reference to the living style of rock huts and their lack of technology) if there was anything with Hebrew markings found in the vehicle, it was immediately burned and you were refused entry across the border and were marked as a Palestine sympathizer and would be treated harshly if you tried to cross again. Because it was our job to be impartial / neutral we always checked carefully before each crossing. Breaking this rule also could bring disciplinary actions against you from the Commanding Officer. When Greg returned back to Canada, he found it difficult to fit back into the family unit. We were all told that this was the "norm" and in time things would be back to normal. He was a bit short with his two daughters when they wanted the newest doll or toy. The images that he had seen on the "dark side" of children playing in the dirt with a piece of scrap metal or a few broken toys still were fresh in his memory. "Be glad you have what you have" he said more than once to them. Within a few months things were back to the way it was before and life was in a routine again.

Greg's second tour was of a different nature. It was going to be a NATO mission OP Alliance (IFOR) involving several other countries and were there had been recently war fighting vice a relatively static (the UN had been in the Golan Heights for over 20 years) mission. With eight weeks work up training in Valcartier, then another two in Gagetown prior to deployment, then it was off to Bosnia and Herzegovina (the former Yugoslavia) that July of 1996. One of the first and most lasting sensory reminders that Greg noticed was the incredible stench of garbage, dust, food, tobacco and body odours that enveloped the country. It seemed that everybody smoked in country. Dead animals were ever present in the minefields, and also in the local rivers. They had told that the insurgents poisoned the wells with dead bodies, and destroyed the electric pumps that supplied the local reservoir for the town the Canadian Contingent (Can Con) was in. The main camp housed 500 personal and his primary tasking with his section was to keep the water, sewage, and gas utilities running, and supporting the other two camps when required. Because of the localized fighting all soldiers carried their personal weapon at all times when not inside a hardened structure. He carried a C 7 assault rifle and whenever he went off camp, flack jackets and load bearing vests were added. Greg found this at times challenging due to the lack of resources, and working with the local civilians. He noticed that some workers were genuine in their gratitude towards the Can Con, but many others were in it for the quick bucks to be made in supply's and working on the camp. His labours assigned to him were glad for the work, since the local industry and farms were destroyed over the last few years during the conflict but some of the locals employed by the Can Con were caught stealing, and on many occasions asked Greg for favours, could he buy alcohol, smokes, chocolate etc, and would get upset or even shout when he refused, knowing very well that it would be used on the very lucrative black market for their own profit, not presents for their family. He tried to explain that it was forbidden for him to do so, and received the cold shoulder. His attitude was shifting from being there to make a difference, to doing his job, and a resentment towards the Serbs stayed with him for the rest of the tour. To this day things like the smell of boiled cabbage, and burning garbage sometimes trigger a chill down his spine. There were Rules of Engagement (ROE's) that were strictly followed, example: you could not engage the enemy unless you were directly under fire, or if you were in fear of yours or of another soldiers life. The insurgents knew this and after a day of drinking slipovich ,commonly referred to as *slip in the ditch*, they would drive by the camp and discharge the weapons over the camp. Greg often wondered where the tracer rounds landed, in the hills, or maybe in a family's roof or yard, and how many innocent were wounded or killed by this act. One day just a few weeks before he was rotating home, Greg was walking to the water plant and he saw a flash, then a puff in the dirt in front of him and a faint Zing sound. Looking up where the flash came from he could just make out a person with a rifle. "The fucker just shot at me" he thought. He was either a bad shot for missing him, or a very good one, just giving Greg a warning. From then to the end of the tour, his senses were in a heightened state and and several times he got drunk thinking if it had been a few feet closer….

Because Greg was not from Valcartier, when he returned to his home unit there was no real debriefing when he got back to Halifax. He remembers one day soon after he was home yelling at his daughter for walking on the grass. For the last seven months, grass to Greg meant minefields and injury or death. Get a grip on your self, he often told himself. You are back home. It was hard to decompress and sometimes process it all.

Several months later, in June of 1997 he was posted to CFB Trenton to the 81 Airfield Engineering Flight. The change of scenery was good. He had been in Halifax for nine years, and with the freeze on promotions it was a chance for a fresh start. Meeting with old friends from previous courses and tours felt good to him, and there were many discussions at Friday's happy hour about their experiences. We were all Army Engineers, first in, last out, was our motto and there was no place for the faint at heart. You saw shit, did shit and carried on. Because his Military Occupation Classification 613 (MOC) was relatively small in numbers, approximately only 70-80 members that could be deployed, rotations were coming on every other year. Greg's next tour was back to the Golan Heights and he was slated to deploy March of 1998. Being a "veteran" now of two missions, going to pre-deployment training was like old home week, meeting up with old friends. At least on the summer tour you will be home for Christmas he consoled himself.

This time Greg got more involved in the camp sports, playing

29

floor hockey and organizing and going on many scuba diving trips whenever he could. His first tour there had been right after the first Gulf war, we still had bunker drills for SCUD's but now there was a more relaxed atmosphere. Club Med was the nickname and Greg found that he could cope and really enjoyed his tour. Getting to know a bit about the customs and culture made it a little easier to understand, but he still did not have to like it. The Israelis, he felt, considered themselves as the privileged and the chosen ones, and that everything they did was justified. Their air of arrogance gave him a bad taste, and knowing that he was not a raciest, he still had a growing dislike for the Jewish people. The difference he found between the Arabs he had met in the local shop in Syria and the Israelis was that they had a ritual of building a friendship, which included having sweet tea or Turkish coffee, then offered their goods, and then wanted to bargain with you over the price. It was a fun game, but you could never just go in and do a five minute visit. They considered that it was an insult. On the other hand the Jewish shopkeepers were crying poor if you offered a lower price, and they were more interested in turn around and profit. They would steal your watch, then sell it back to you if they could.

Back in Canada, Greg got promoted and assumed the position of crew chief. There were more responsibilities and with a few newly trained corporals in his section, he also took on a mentoring / coaching role. His home life was ok, and he went on a few one month deployments to the USA to some Air National Guard units on exchange training. It was interesting to train with different pieces of equipment and Greg was enjoying his job. Once again the call came for a deployment, this time to Kosovo. It was a short notice tasking, the primary person's checklist had been red for some reason, and you needed either all green, or they allowed a few yellow if they deemed it not critical to the mission. Since he had only been back 11 months Greg's checklist was still all green, and in November he was off to CFB Petawawa for field training. This was for five weeks, then home for a few days, then the flight overseas. It was 14 December 1999, and he was off to the Balkans again. The main thing that Greg liked was that he was going with 2 Combat Engineering Regiment, from which he still had many friends from his Combat Engineering days and that since it was an area of high danger, the extra pay was about $2500.00 a month.

His main responsibilities were to finish the construction and set up of the camp's ablutions (these were contained in a sea container, and the sides dropped down to make an area about 24 ft x 20 ft.) They were a new acquisition for the CDN Forces, and this meant trial by fire. None of his crew including himself had ever seen the units. Greg and the rest of the section were living in modular tents, with 10-12 men per tent. With the wind and snow blowing about, this made for some sombre nights. It would be after Christmas before they were housed in the new shelters with beds and lockers instead of cots and barrack boxes. Because there was lots to do working seven days a week was the norm. When he got a chance to do service calls to the company camps that housed the infantry, even after a long day, Greg looked at this as a way off the camp and to see other parts of the country. It reminded him of his time in the Black Forest many years ago. Back in the land of beer and bratwurst. Sometimes his trips brought him into an area that had recent conflicts and he witnessed lots of destruction, and the poverty that is the direct result of a war. When he had to go on a supply run, usually an interrupter came along. It was your responsibility to ensure his safety at all times. We always traveled with a full load, weapons, five mags, flack vest, and helmets. On one trip he was going into a town, and because of the damage to the buildings and roads, some detours occurred. At one point the "Muslim interrupter" got extremely uncomfortable because we were in an area that he knew to occupy insurgents and he feared for his safety. Greg thought it was part of an act, based on his encounters in Bosnia, but then became conscious of the fact that there were really "bad guys" and they would not hesitate to engage you, NATO forces or not. That is the true look of fear.

On the trip back to camp, Greg listened to some stories of what his interrupter had seen done to family and friends. Although he did not give all the details, he felt uncomfortable and had a sick feeling in the pit of his stomach. We had to drive past a field that was dug up, and nothing around it. It was weird, no snow, fences, building, or markers, just black earth. He said that it was a mass grave from a year ago. The Serbs killed many from a town near by. He didn't pry for specifics, but he could tell it effected his interrupter.

Greg's first R&R wasn't until the end of February. He had been working 12 hr days seven days a week for almost two months, and was looking forward to a break, if not just for a few days. The designated area was in Slovakia, a small town by the mountains. After a day on the bus, and several border check points he arrived at the hotel. Once he was checked in, a few bottles of Heineken and a long hot bath. Greg and a few others hung out together, safety in numbers. After a few beers, a trip to see the sights was in order and enviably he and his buddies got convinced into seeing a show in run down club. 100 or 200 korunas to get in and you can see dancers all night. Another 100 korunas to check your coat and a frisking before going past the curtains. These bouncers looked like the stereotype Russian, KGB thug you see on tv. Black leather square cut coats, closed crop haircuts, pockmarked features, smoking and bad teeth. Everyone in this part of the world smoked and had bad teeth. In we went and a round of Piccolo champagne showed up. He had seen this before as a newbie in Germany many years back. It was how the new troops got broke in. It was more of a lesson to learn early and relatively cheaply into your tour. You got hit with a tab for 50 to 100 depending on the club and amount of drinks. If you paid that then you could talk to the girls or whatever else you could afford. The "old married guys" wanted to leave with a few others, but some of the younger ones wanted to see the show. Even though he didn't touch his drink, another round showed up for the table. "Let's drink up and go" on of the other guys piped up, and we started to make our way out. One of the larger bouncers, stepped in front of the curtain. He was directed forcefully back and handed a piece of paper. On of the guys grabbed it. It was a bill for 10 drinks, and five girls. The amount was equal to $250 marks each. $1250 marks, that was over a grand Canadian. One of the bigger guys in his group challenged the bouncer, and was pinned up against the wall. They demanded our wallets and basically robbed us of what we had. As we went out and tried to get our coats, there was a bit of a shoving match, and we were pushed out. Greg remembers one of the bouncers yelling, "Fuck you NATO, not so tuff now" or words to

32

that effect. Back at the hotel everyone relived the past few hours, and got drunk. From then on he had a growing dislike for the people there, and trusted no one.

Once Greg was back in camp, he concentrated mostly on work. He once felt sorry for the civilian workers, but now looked at them with cold eyes and viewed them as a commodity not really people. There was a term assigned to them now. YAKS. This was a reference to the pack mule. Young Albanian KosovarS. As a rule you could not give rations or other supplies to the workers, and they knew this. "Chief give me this, give me that. You are rich" they hounded his crew daily. They knew that the tour was coming to an end, and we were leaving. Part of Greg wanted to help, but the other part said to himself, not my problem. He was going home soon which was far far away from this shit. On his second R&R, Greg and a close pal Gerry Olsen a WO in the RCD's, is friend from their CLC course, went to Greece. He did some scuba diving, ate out at the local street restaurants, and tuned out as much as we could. Gerry and Greg didn't draw a sober breath for a few days. Before long it was back to the grind to close up camp and return to Canada. Greg returned to Trenton in July 2000.

Within a month he got word that his father had a major heart attack and was in intensive care at Camp Hill Hospital located in Halifax, NS. With special emergency leave, he went home, and stayed there for six weeks. His dad was out of the woods, but had a long way to go. He had a quadruple bypass and there was extensive damage to the heart muscle. His hero had fallen. There was nothing that he could do. Watch and pray. Greg had to go back to Trenton, but kept in contact daily. Finally his dad was released and started his long road to recovery. Later that fall, Greg got promoted to Sergeant and then a posting message to Moncton for the following year. Since his daughters were in grade nine and 12, they were not leaving school, so he went by himself from August until February the next year when he put in his release. Due to the pettiness and a clear abuse of authority, the career manager at that time had been the course MWO on his QL 5 course and He had 23 years in the Army, and when he and his wife did the math, of the 20 years of marriage he had been gone for over seven of them. Greg had a trade as a

33

Plumber and could make it on his own. He got out in May 2002, and returned to Trenton.

The reason why he got out actually stemmed back to August 1992 at CFB Chilliwack BC. While on his 6 month QL 5 Plumber Gas fitter course, prior arrangements for Greg and his wife Margret had been made to attend a Childhood Cancer conference in Winnipeg August that year before the course message was released. Once the course dates were finalized the conference was then addressed. With the memos written and staffed up approval was given to attend pending the grades warranted it.

With the week approaching the leave pass with the CO's memo and minutes for reference was sent in to the orderly room with a copy of the tickets as proof of return. That Wednesday after PT a call was sent out for Greg to see the MWO ASAP. It seemed that the MWO took exception that CPL Tanner somehow pulled a fast one on him, and he was not going anywhere because he was going to miss a code test end of story. Greg explained that arrangements were made to write the test Monday 0800 instead of PT.

Well that made the MWO even more engaged, cursing Tanner and made some threats like " if you think a CPL can bypass the CoC behind their backs….. " Rant for a few minutes, then dismissed him to the canteen area to sweat it out. He was off to the CO to get to the bottom of this.

Around 30 minutes later the MWO returned, throwing Tanners paperwork on the table and he told him to enjoy the weekend, because the RTU paperwork has been started. The course was buzzing with the recent developments and what was the story? Greg has been known to be a bit of a stubborn individual when he felt that a wrong doing had been done, thus adding to the slightly heated exchange.

That Monday morning 0730 the MWO was waiting and escorted Tanner into the oil burner boiler class area to a single desk. Placed in a line was a brand new Fire Sprinkler code book, a cleared CFSME scientific calculator, a pad and pencil. " take your seat. You have 90 minutes for the EO. I will be staying right here. Any questions? Start"

Greg was pissed and just focused on the test. At the 90 minute mark, the MWO walked over and with a bit a satisfaction in a smile as he shuffled the papers. Dismissed to the canteen to wait it out, the rest of the course was filling in after PT.

The test score was posted and a 92%, and Standards was to review because the MWO was convinced that Tanner somehow had cheated, and had made the MWO look bad.

Fast forward to 2001, and that MWO was now the Engineer Career Manager ready to exact his revenge on the unsuspecting Sgt.

Consequently Greg got out of the Army May 2002. Later that August he got a call to fill an instructor position on base so he joined the 8 Wing Air reserves in August 2002, and for the next 11 years enjoyed a interesting, challenging and rewarding career. After the surgery he couldn't meet the physical requirements for the universal service and was medically released after a two year battle with VAC and NDHQ...."

The release MO got posted, and NDMC or whoever runs the DMED cell had a question reference my medical category. Unfortunately, he got posted, and his mail was binned, I guess. My DWD was 06 July 2013. Because of the mess, I released 06 Feb 2016. Great, but I haven't been paid in two years. The VAC monthly pension and a savings account for the new house got chewed up but safeties were in place as always. A Huge paper war ensued, and after answering everything in about three memos, basically, if you read thru the lines, they Screwed up royally and all my back pay, with the incentives, was dumped into my bank account with no advanced warning, less taxes of course. My former OC Maj Don Paul just shook his head; idiots was all he said. One day the Maj and I were coming back from a meeting on the North side and as we were driving by the RCAF museum he pointed out that the CH- 113 Labrador that had been recently added was in fact his old airframe tail # 11315 that he flew out of CFB Comox as a SAR bird driver and also an instructor. Nice. He had shared some of the more funny missions rescuing lost hikers or ski bunnies that took the wrong trail. On thing Don was very proud of was his rotary wing flying skills and the ability to be very quick to adapt to the unfolding situation.

This is where the " Don Paul Plant" was generated from. Doing SAR sortie's in mountainous terrain locating a flat spot to land may not be a possibility, and time constraints for multiple hoists could be hazardous to both his crew and the people being rescued, so the DPP was created. Not to get into the massive aerodynamic and physical stressors aka gravity that comes into effect, so once the hover has been established and the decent has began a count by the foot from the Nav goes on until the one foot. Now the hard part. Once on the ground, usually the power is reduced so loading / unloading can happen. Kind of hard rolling backwards down a slope doing that so Don decides to plant the Labrador then doing that pilot shit slowly applies forward motion to counter act the falling off the mountain thing. I cannot remember the slope % but it was pushing the limits. But that's what they do, right. I'll leave the rest of that for Don.

Apparently, No one told Ottawa I was in the hospital, and wondered why I went from a G2 02 cat to a G4 04 cat after an exempt express test six months prior at 51 years old. A few calls to the bank to correct their mistake. Nope, direct deposit from the Federal Government. Cha Ching. After all, it wasn't like the pay officer had to cough up the cash for his Fuck Up, didn't he? But would't make a great story at the fire pit.

Back to the phone call. Did the eight sessions and then was recommended to see Dr. C, who was a psychologist in Trenton, where the questions, tests and a few appointments were penciled in before we were scheduled to move back home.Sold the house and boat, bought another house and another boat. Weren't we down sizing? Got a referral from Trenton to see a person here in Halifax once on the ground. Again, tests, questionnaires, the standard required stuff, but forcefully having to remember specific details… aren't you supposed to forget this…

"Have you ever attempted suicide before, and if so, why didn't you succeed?" Or words to that effect. That's one of the reasons why I'M here. You think if I had completed the attempt, I wouldn't be here, right? All I can say is that because of the paperwork and the fact that I am a professional, there is no slagging of establishments. Eighteen months later, now on Hydromorphone curtesy of the ER Doc from my ambo trip earlier that year, my home life self destroyed, and I became a full-blown junkie. Yup, I SAID IT. I had done the dance with the devil after my operation, and at 176 lbs, 16 weeks on 50 mg a day, the day had come to a stop. So, I went cold turkey. Way different than alcohol withdrawals.

After three days, Margret called the doctor because I was sweating profusely, trembling, could not stay still, sleeping, and had weird eyes. She didn't know I had done a self-imposed boycott on drugs.

The doctor freaked out, but since I had gone through most of it, it was no use to take a 1 mg pill to feed the fire.

Now, I find myself in the place where I told myself I would never go back to. As I mentioned it was 18 months of sessions once a month. One word: Non-Compatible. Ok then, one and a half. So messed up on the Hydro, and just really pissed that no one understands. Shit, I don't even know.

One day, I was the FSM for the A3 Readiness Training Flight CFB Trenton, to I can't even run a lawnmower. This position will be the subject of Appendix B. Carry on. So, using my infinite wisdom I was going to explain what is what and get them onto my program. The 40-minute drive to town was just pouring more gas on a smoldering dumpster fire. If you haven't picked up on the theme of early arrival, parking spots, quite spots. This was one right here. They have a plexiglass smoking area with a bench even. Sweet. No one around, but if they were, hey, I got a scrip, what's your problem anyway? Out of control is all I can say after looking back on the whole think. Out of control. Anyway, I sparked up a blunt that even Snoop Dogg would be proud to smoke and choked that back in about seven minutes. Timings to meet. Ten minutes out. Smoke, leak, then attitude adjustment time. Needless to say, things got ugly, and when I posed an engineering question to my psychologist, I left before I would have to be escorted out. Now, here is the burning question that I asked after I said that I was fed up, " What do you think the bearing pressure is required to be applied to the corner of your fourth-story picture window before it flexes and loses its integrity? A computer, a chair, or a person? Fuck you, and some other words describing what I thought of their PTSD help. Shit.

After calming down a day or two later, I called to offer my

apologies and explain that it was the morphine and a bad day. You understand, right? You deal with this type of thing.

It is what your headshot noz said on your bio page. This was the September timeframe, and the next available appointment is...... November. Got you loud and clear. You don't know anything. Probably smoked cheap dope all through university anyway. Draw a line under it and back into my world.

Getting back to the camp. Say, on a good day at a Blue Jays Game there would be approximately 40-45 K in attendance. That established the density is too great, so I was thinking about the geographic lay of the ground, and if you went from Trenton to Belleville, it is around 20 km. Same distance, but not doing a buck twenty on the 401. The population for the Quinte West was at the time I was posted there 41 K. So now, having that total landscape wiped in six weeks, where did they go? From the little bit that I saw, the stories from our interrupters or witnessed on the Balkans tours images can still be seen sometimes. Crap, what was the original point? Anyone remember? I'll scroll back. Wait out.

Had to reread and chill a bit. For some reason, and I am admittedly a slow learn, it is all right to not be busy all day and slow down to actually see what I have and the encompassing support system that is around me. I finally remembered what was the overarching link to all this. The ride in the park. Still cannot remember what the spinning wheel's proper name is, but it was the sensation of release and floating backwards in the air with the meat hook body piercings. I don't know, but I shook it off before the chains reached their stops and tore the flesh from my broken, defeated body. Was this a week later or two? Not really sure about that. It was enough to leave some sort of imprint and make the hamster wheel jump off its A-frame. Something that I either daydreamed or, more to the point, had a conversation with my dad, Barrett, and I walking and stopped every-time a certain section of the property was reached. A discussion about the sale of their home, where we had been living for five years while building our home a few lots over on the family land, and that my job was done. Everyone was looking a head, so should I. I remember that Margret was a little concerned. Where had I been, and am I ok? We were gone for about two hours. Felt like 30 minutes.

38

Chapter 6

A little rant

It's been a few days. The automatic writing thing is great but also sucks. Sometimes, the flow is continuous, and sometimes, well, mostly small memories or quick flashes. Make any sense? Trying mindfulness and grounding techniques more often than not, sometimes an hour can pass just watching the cove or the random cloud formations moving slowly opposite to the breeze, leaving cat's paws on the lee of Round Island, a mere 100 Ft from the shore. Looking down at my list of tasks to complete in order to go diving, it had amazingly been pared down to just a few go/no go items from a seemingly endless, almost impossible milestone to reach. Pick up regs from the dive shop next week, and get dressed. Minor fine-tuning will be ongoing, as normal around here. Work smarter, not harder, and with maximum comfort and minimum effort. Not just some words. We all want these things; it's just that the approach and definitions may differ. The last time the sun was out for more than two hours, We were sitting on the deck Q 104 playing just sitting. Still had things on my list to do, but I now had the luxury of a little time break due to the weather coming up in the next 48 hours. Anyway, the Readers Digest version is I still have the steps poured into the rocks, but instead of 10 more bags of cement, I will just do a small leveling pad and use some of my acquired 872 trapezoid paving stones for $40.00 (yet another, well chapter) to build the steps. This can be expected as you expand your cognitive skills. Some rise to the challenges, knowing up front that at some point in time, you will be put into harm's way and how to expand your survival skill set. And some have just as important roles that have called them to serve in their own capacity. As I mentioned in the preface, these are my expressions, thoughts, and experiences that I am choosing to share with you, not because I have to.

Time to work on Annex B. I also started doing a version count. 1.6 at present. Depending on what I am using, the most up-to-date one might not be that one.

Moving along, Sore and had a bad day yesterday. Tried to reel it in, with limited success. Didn't have supper until 2230, Barrett's last walk, and rack.

Sunday and feeling somewhat intact and Barrett is still sleeping at 0830. He knew. Daddy needs some downtime, just like a new day for him. Coffee on the couch morning walk can wait for a bit. Margret's off to Terence Bay to get a lamp, and I just might break out the skill saw and cut some 2 x 6 for the boarding ladder. But hey, the pain is still there but manageable, right? Barrett plops his cow-sized head into my lap, getting my attention in more than one way. He was making sure that I wasn't going anywhere. The sound of an email arriving woke me up from a gentle sleep. Good news, so things are looking up. What is on this Sunday anyway? Rotating through the three channels was no effort. I was going to flick on YouTube and watch stupid rich people at Miami's Haulover inlet. Million-dollar go-fast boats with quad 350 HP outboards, plowing into the 15-foot rollers. Now because these Boaters see that they are on a professional camera, sometimes they would give an exotic dance and even fall overboard sometimes. One channel is called the "Chit Show," Back on track. The Hip's Farewell Tour documentary was on CBC; go figure. Need something to relax. Another email. And good news again. Gord starts "Blow at High Dough," and, well, my allergies started acting up, you know, watery eyes, runny nose. Pollen season here. Been a fan for years, and at Belleville's Harbour Fest, there was a really good cover band doing mostly Hip, and it sounded not half bad. Music and memories. Good and bad. Hootie and the Blowfish. One of the few workout CDs I had in Bosnia. Time, their big hit was a warm-down set. I, like everyone else, pick the rhythm of the song to match your workout. Once back home, I never purposely put that CD into play again. The theme that I am picking up on is Bosnia gets pulled into a conversation so quickly, and that opens up another map to look at.... See what I mean; this is why appendices are included. This will be continued in Appendix C.

Around halfway through the concert, Heath texted me if I wanted some fresh cod. They just came back in. Sure fresh fish and chips English style with french fries. Bonus. Turned out to be a great day in the end, with leftovers for lunch tomorrow.

Well, no beating around the bush. Appendix A seems to be rearing its ugly head around every corner, so without another excuse to think of, we shall proceed with the show.

I had started to do some intense editing and decided it needed Chapters instead of a long story with no breaks. Hell I took lots of breaks to come back to the Now. Appendix A is now the next Chapter 7. Formerly known as <u>Appendix A</u>

Camp Black-bear. We were deployed to Velika Kladusa, Sector North Bosnia and Herzegovina June 1996. After three months of work-up training at CFB Valcartier (Valcratraz, affectionately to others) with 5 Regiment Genie Du Combo. 5 CER in Anglaise, and a month of leave before the deployment date, you can see how a year just vanishes before you know it. Anyway we would travel to Zagreb, Croatia every six weeks or so for supplies, with different co-drivers along for security. Figure 1. The point where you felt a little safer was getting onto the main highway at Turan, then to Karlovac and a large truck stop that was a cleared halt area. The other fun six hour trip was to Kljuc, our most southern camp. That halfway point was Bihac. Camp Black-bear was on the edge of the Joint Krajina Serb/Muslim separatist Control area. (This is info directly taken from a map of Territorial Changes in Bosnia and Herzegovina since Jan 1993.) Now, back to the UNHCR camp.

The Kupljensko refugee camp was located in the Krajina region, where the Croatian government permitted about 25,000 Bosnian refugees displaced from the Banja Luka area to settle in this area. Some sources place the population to be 55 K. "According to International, the Croatian government troops condoned and committed widespread abuses in the Krajina, including looting, arson, and killing. Extremists opposed to the return of the Croatian Serbs continued to commit murder and other acts of persecution and terror in Krajina throughout 1996 without impunity, according to the human rights groups in the area" I will paraphrase the next part, but the local population of 3-4 thousand by the end of 1996 that returned to Cazin and Velika Kladusa, even though assurances from the local government promised safety, many still were abused and terrorized in other ways. I told Margret this story a few years ago during a dark time. Just only one example of the shit that no one back here ever heard of or saw on the news.

** Note** This was inserted several months after this chapter was written. How the memory does its thing. Remembering something just from a sensation, smell, or song. See what I mean? A curve ball from nowhere**

When we arrived as Roto One, Roto Zero did the basic construction and infrastructural groundwork because the UN council agreement was only supposed to be a one-year commitment. It ended up that PM Jean Chrétien decided to extend our dates to some years down the road. This meant the camp was now changing from a temporary camp to a long-term camp, and the headquarters was now going to be here instead of Coralici Another Canadian camp and the NATO HQ are an hour south of us. Its main area was a cement factory, and the administration buildings were now being used by different countries, or a carpet factory. Either here or Kluge. Can't remember right now, and I do not feel like breaking the flow. The other incident could have been when a Polish armored vehicle's weapons loader didn't do a full safety check on the anti-tank rockets strapped on its side and, well, during a Multi Nation sporting event, the rocket launched all by itself into the side of the HQ. You want to see everyone fuck off to the high port to their designated bunkers. Tanks, APC, BMPs, and Cougars were all fired up, and crash routes opened up. The blood was pumping that day tell your mother. Canada, now signing up for the duration, wanted its own HQ, and looking back at it, that was not my impression, well, back in November 1996 anyway.

Now, after years of military school, history, and current tours, your optics move from tactical to operational. I was a part of A3 WG Ops for six years, and some of that shit was pretty cool, so it would really open up some eyes. Not in any bad way, but in some of the JTF guys have and do. Some of my lifelong friends were deployed with them. We did tours together... great respect for them. As the FSM, we all (the other SSMs and FSMs) went to the Chief's coffee break, the last Thursday of the month, and did the usual catching up and then went back to work just in time for lunch. That was a gimme. Once a month to get together when you could, and I think that in the course of a year, I might have attended three or four. Thursday was range day, and if it was a course of 30 or more, I went as the RSO, adding to the range staff. Just had a quiet chuckle, range days...fucken box lunches. We always had to order the rations a week in advance, but because sometimes the influx of orders when the cadet camps showed up, that was pushed back to three weeks. It was becoming an administrative nightmare. Rob T, one of our RCR Cpl's weapons instructors, also did rations, vehicle work tickets, the classroom instruction for the C7, 9mm, foreign weapons (AK 47, RPG, etc), and the base team goalie. Anyway we just went with expected from our past records, just a click away. Sometimes you hit, and others it was a miss, but in a good way. Hence, fucken box lunches. Sometimes, they ordered 30 and 6 staff, plus coffee urns, snacks, juices, and water. Add in that each student shoots 65 rounds during the test, plus ten sightings. Most used 15. Then there are the misfires, lost rounds in the snow, x students. That's a lot of ammo. The quick math is 2550 rounds of 5.56 mm. Sgt Dave Chalmers was the IC, and we had been friends before I came to work here. He ran me through the ranges before I went on tour, so when I did get posted to the RTF, I had the home-field advantage coming as their new boss, so tagging along was a good break from the office.

It usually started out with a box lunch Recce on the one-hour road trip to Kingston. The Joe Louis or Carmel cakes were great with Timmie's. Hey, when it is -20, you burn a lot of calories. After the targets were set up, the range clear with the green flag, the students came in. Briefing, relays, then coffee break. More snack cakes, Peekfreans cookies. Clean up, range live again, and so on till lunch. Processed meat, sometimes mystery meat, chicken legs, deep fried, a bag of chips, and a Vachon cake. For the healthy part, an apple.

When we were finished at the end of the week, there might be 15 to 20 leftovers in the fridge. So what we did was break them all down into their common groups. Sandwiches, cakes, cheese sticks, you know where I am coming from so no need to drone on, sectioned in the canteen fridge. Friday afternoon, you could come and, if you wish, grab a few things to take home before the best-before date on Sunday. Yeah, I know that in the eyes of the Military law, that is illegal, but many families, including mine, got to share in the after-exercise clean-up. As young privates and Cpl's, you almost relied on it to help you along. To support our Engineer Reunion Dinner and dance cost, the Regiment would be on exercise the month before, and for the last three days or so, we were on hard rations. The Chief Cook ordered the meal for Dinner, kept it in the freezers, and shelved the can goods. Different times back then. You mention a subsidy for a dinner now, forget it.

I remember when we came back from Germany, I was posted to CFB Chilliwack, the Home of the Engineers. Every trade, course, for every rank engineer related, was there. Combat Engineers to Civil Engineers. It was the first family day of the summer. Margret, my oldest daughter, and I, with some other recently posted-in friends, all showed up at the cook's tent at the same time to get out burgers and hotdogs for the kids. We get our stuff, do the fixings, and go to grab a Coke when I hear, "$3.50 for the food and pop, please." What? This is Family Day. Since I had gotten in eight years earlier, we had never paid for the family day BBQ. We sometimes fed the wives rations and they got to shoot blanks from a .50 cal turret mounted crew serve weapon on an APC. Mine did. Anyway, that was a bit of a wake-up call. Welcome back to Canada, the land of the poor. You got paid some extra for going to Lahr and even having a good time; we saved up a bit. More than we ever could back here in the 80's. Lots of people bitched about the Beer and Brat medal (SSM) when it came out. Since then, other NATO missions or tours not of six months, but accumulated time now count towards the decoration.

Holy snapping. Just scrolled back to find out what was the original thought train I was on. We were building the new CCHQ VK. As my thought is this, yes we needed our own HQ. This is for a few reasons. Coming from me now is the need for transparency if we are becoming a bigger stakeholder in the NATO mission. We were nicknamed the Kool-aid Brigade. Canada was dry, but other countries were not, so at the Officer's mess parties with mixed attendance, the Bar was open for all. This was a diplomatically protected area, so anything goes. Red passports with the white crest. Lots of weight. Sometimes good, and sometimes not so much. If a 4-star General and the local officials are in attendance, when in Rome. That mission went on for years. I did roto 1. Think that it was in the twenties when it closed down. Lost a few friends there over the years or later when they came back home.

Back to the camp construction bring up the next level in support. This included more locals as trade helpers cleaners etc. There was this particular young girl, about 20-21, and was at that time six months pregnant, working in the bakery section. The other female military were planning a baby shower, with small gifts from Canada. Her husband was Muslim and was killed at a checkpoint coming here one day. End of the story. When her expected date was due, the MIR staff checked her out, and she was off. Nothing else was ever mentioned, and frankly, I hadn't really noticed. The staff has changed so much around here.

Around November she just shows up, working back in the bakery. She looked a little different. Tired, pale. But hey, she had a kid, and they lived in a house with a corrugated steel roof and old tires on top because of the wind. We come to find out later that when her husband was killed, she was passed around the guard shack a few times. Since it was a Serb soldier(s) as the father, I guess that the old WWII stories of the women that gotten beaten, shaved heads, and forced miscarriages that slept with the enemy, well, the apple doesn't fall from the dictator's tree, does it? The same happened to her. My helpers Hibbo and Rambo gave me some graphic details about the back alley shit going on. I take it with the source considered. Maybe they just want to see how much I can take? Scare me? Even if one afternoon of quiet chatting was true, Holy F-bomb. I think that I was so involved with working 12-14 hrs per day. Went from 14 Dec 1999 until 24 February 2000 for my first R&R. 60 plus days straight, but it was better driving from camp to Platoon houses than base maintenance. My QL5 CPLs can and need the experience. I was told that the course had changed and the oil burner package wasn't ready to be delivered so ...... so what do you say. Another one of those Stratospheric decisions that the political whips snap when the general public gets a teary eye and demands across-the-

45

board decisions. Short-term gain, but the long game is ….By the time it trickles down to the rank and file, they will be onto another portfolio, and it will be someone else's problem. I know that I am throwing a lateral, but I have to qualify my last sentence. CFB Chilliwack was closed in 1995, so the school quit teaching in '94. My 6A (SGT's course) was September 2001, which was the first in almost eight years. We were all friends from our other courses, just a bit heavier and wiser than the last time we met. Everyone had, on average least three -four tours. Some five or six. Throw in the occasional flood or two, some ice storm, and rebuilding damages of the aftermath, no one had time to go to school, let a lone create a new Complete package. Needless to say, in the first few weeks, the boys had a steep learning curve to climb. No fucken way I am looking after and servicing 28 Oil burners and hot water tanks. That is good apprenticeship material. Nothing too hard, but the basics. End January the boys were good to go. There is also a red liquid chemical, non-toxic used in measuring the CO in the appliance exhaust so adjustments can be made for optimum performance. Well, some loadie decided that the 15 pages of paperwork substantiating the importance of the 4 oz of fluid. Nope, not manifested so in the bin. You're shitting me, right? Nope. Well, I as might as well go home. If I cannot test the equipment, it will not run. That's BS. NOPE. It was poured down the drain. I almost lost my shit. What's the problem? Just buy some when we get there. Well, if you haven't noticed from your hotel room, there is no downtown where we are going. If it was a vile of mercury or another heavy metal ok, but. Thousands of dollars of damage was done due to eyeballing the burner flame at negative 19 centigrade. You opened up the back of the MEC abolition to work on it but were totally exposed to the elements. We were using an Overhead Protection Shelter for wind protection. But you can't see it from your room. Enough of this for a while.

I am going to go directly to Appendix C. Something got stirred up the other day. Barrett has a bit of a tummy ache, so he is resting in the coolness of the house. This gives me an hour or so to write.

The "Hi Mom" picture. Found the water leak….

The ISO graveyard in Zagreb, Croatia.

Me and Rambo, on of my Bosnian helpers I had during construction of the camp.

Chapter 7

FSM A3 RTF

I have been working for a while on collecting and trying to organize what I thought would best explain my job. What was important, relevant and brevity being the main focal point. I took over as Acting Flight Sergeant Major from the retiring MWO in December 2009 until August 2010. The previous summer, when Maj Stewart was the OC, I did a 4-month stretch as AFSM between postings, so this should be just another day at A3 RTF. Nope, Spoke too soon.

On 12 January 2010, a 7.0 magnitude earthquake struck Haiti, leaving its capital Port-au-Prince devastated. Spool all hands on deck. We had just finished 10 days of surge training for the mission to Haiti, 16-hour days, and compressing the training to Just in Time (*Just waste* of your time, you mean) and need-to-know stuff. Once again, the anal Wing Admin DAG (Departure Assistance Group) staff come running around waving pieces of paper and chanting, Waver. They need Wavers. *No tickie, no shirtie.* Sorry about that. Luckily I held the rank and position to offer my interpretation and give alternate solutions.

Example: When I was on my 6B CE Superintendent course in March 2006, we had a mess dinner where you get to meet all the graduating phase four officers that we had shared some class time together with. Captain Bill Clarke, Infantry Officer (PPCLI), was changing majors to Engineering and was seated at our round table of eight. If we are supposed to work together and collaborate instead of taking corners might as well start with the breaking of bread and drinking of the wine. Consequentially, we must play nice with others. Example: Will you Pass the Port, Sir...... please?

Fast forward to 8 Wing Trenton January 2010, and Captain Clarke was going as the RECCE ENG O departing in 48 hours. But guess what, his qualification was, you guessed it, expired by two months. Nope, the rules say.......

What the REMFs ignored to do was read his UER (Unit Employment Record) past page one. The Captain did two tours in Afghanistan, thus his change in career. We quickly chatted to catch up a bit, then into my office with Sgt Dave Chalmers the Unit weapons Chief instructor and RSO. After some more reminiscing, I passed the 9 MM Browning to the Captain. Prove safe, unload, check, load, check, unload, and prepare for inspection. Clear. Safety check. Sweet, all done, Sir. Have a good trip. Drills were performed in front of two instructors and Base RSOs. The big green P. That's how we sift through the Bull shit now if you are wondering about the above acronym REMFs.

Rear Echelon MotherFuckers.

200 km safely behind the main force FOBs and Camp lines. I used to get this comment a lot when we had to drop in for supplies or do maintenance every six weeks or so.

"How come you are getting $2500.00 a month tax-free for danger pay, anyway?"

Why you cheese whiz eating, KD slurping, paper pushing, crying if I get wet, and coming out of your concrete four-story building located downtown in a city, going for after-work restaurant dinners with a few beers dickhead? We are not even in the same Country, that's why. We are under canvas, eating ration packs before they expire (Easter weekend in Kosovo with 41 AEF, the Camp's easter meal was boiled in the bag).

Well, they blew up the downtown and, on occasion, continue to do their civil engineering on the roads, which are sketchy at best, oh ya, and they are still shooting people here. F'n A hole. So, $2500.00 per month, divided by 30 days = $83.33 a day, divided by 24 hours = $3.42 an hour. Would you do our job for that generous gratuity? What does a Starbucks *crapachino* cost today anyway? That is my value comparison of risk and reward. I don't need a reward for doing

MY job. Doesn't even cover that. And don't choke on your two beers a day at your sit-down dinner downtown. I bet you don't even know what a ration pack is, do you? Ever seen one besides Cornwallis? No, sorry, the old boot camp closed by then, so the new recruits could be inside all day in the MEGA plex St Jean. Can't get wet. You might melt snowflake. Camping in a parking lot. Don't get road rash leopard crawling under the low wire entanglement. I probably never even heard of Heartbreak Hill. Humped my sorry ass up there a few times with full kit, and the heavy old, but indestructible FNC1A1 Rifle. "This is one of Canada's main Cold War battle rifles. Chambered in 7.62x51 standard NATO ammunition. The FNC1 saw service in the Canadian Army till it was replaced by the C7, (M16A1E1) design. 5.56x45 Standard NATO caliber in 1984."[2] The Local Chapter of the Hells Angles MC has better small arms than us, or as a matter of fact, they are better equipped than our Regional Police and RCMP forces, which, unfortunately, as it has been displayed by the media time and time again. Armed Peace Officers enter a situation when the assailant has high-powered rifles and high-capacity magazines with the knowledge that the initial responding units will be drawing on side arms only. Not right, that's for sure.

One of the weapon sections Cpl's had been looking for other employment as his 20 years was approaching. Bruce Energy (Nuclear Plant) was using the police and army networks to look for instructors with lots of "selected experience etc, etc."

He did several interviews and made it through to the next round of skill tests. He had to take a few days of annual leave to attend the training. It had been several months since we had heard anything and he finally got an offer/probationary, of course, but he was good to go. I happened to see him at the annual CFB Trenton Charity Fun Run the following year. All decked out in the black Gucci kit, Oakley's, and Predator custom Tactical boots—lots of training and lots of good weapons. Guarding nuclear shit, you need it. And he

---

[2] https://www.canadiansoldiers.com/weapons/rifles.htm

was loving it.

Sorry, where did that come from? Break time.

07 February 2010. Mr "Call me Russell" Williams, the 8 Wing / CFB Trenton Wing Commander, was charged with two counts of first-degree murder as well as two counts of sexual assault. Court records showed Russell was involved in 82 fetish-related home invasions and attempted break-ins between September 2007 and November 2009. I remember Captain Paul Peloquin, the unit's training officer and Excel spreadsheet guru, coming into my office and closing the door behind him. This can't be good. The last time he did that, he broke the news that Major Glen Steward, our just retired OC, had died of a heart attack the fall before at the age of 65. It was my first time as the FSM and Major Steward, having been an active pilot for over 25 years, then going to flight safety wasn't really the talking to the Men type. He was flight crew all the way. His favourite expression was, "We all make hamburgers for someone." Everyone has a boss. It might be the CDS, but we all answer to someone. His death unexpectedly hit me. He was the person who presented me with my Warrant Officer rank at the promotion parade. Even though he was my boss, we had a great working and after-hours relationship, which made that news a huge shock. I had visited his home on more than one occasion and we held his retirement party at the CFB Trenton Yacht Club. There were not too many places on the base where all ranks could get together and have a drink since they tore down Carneys in the early 2000s. I have lost friends either through accidents, cancer, or by their own hand, and we process each a bit differently. Sorry, back to the present.

He told me to get the unit assembled in the main classroom for a briefing immediately. Ok, I thought, what gives now? Another disaster somewhere else where are deploying to was where my train of thought was going so I asked him what is so urgent anyway?

"The Wing Commander was arrested last night in Ottawa on murder charges. The whole Wing Admin staff have been up all night with the RCMP going through the Col's files and are taking everything with them." I did a bit of a double take and asked him,

"What did you just say, Sir?"

He confessed to killing Jessica Lloyd and Cpl Marie-France Comeau. "Holy Fuck, that's really messed up. I saw him last week at the barber's last Wednesday afternoon. He had just finished up, so the customary pleasantries were exchanged, and I sat down as he left. Spooky, man, fucking spooky.

Well, you can imagine the shit storm that just hit 8 Wing. When everyone was seated Captain Peloquin gave the same info as he relayed to me a few minutes before and let the shock sink in. The 1 CAD (Canadian Air Division) three star Lt General, and his staff are going to be here this afternoon to brief the Wing Squadron Commanders, and tomorrow in the gym, there will be briefings in the morning for these units, and the afternoon this group. Wing Operations Commanding Officer LCol Murphy was the A/WComd until 1 CAD did the who's who on the promotion list to slide in once this shit got under control. LCol Murphy was already posted outside Canada this APS (Annual posting season) more commonly referred to as the silly season. We know people who were all packed up and clearing out, and a message arrived stating, for whatever reason, the posting was cancelled.

Because the investigators literally cleaned out his office of anything electronic or paper, this also, unfortunately, included the years, funding, and budget requests that were due before the mid-March PWGSC spending frenzy could begin and what was expected in the following fiscal year. Our civilian staff hires, and renewals of contracts and MoU's Wing wide were now void. This had essentially, number one, gave the Wing a kick in the nuts, followed by the number two, uppercut to the chin. The huge problem is not that the documents could not be reprinted, but all the signatures required to process over the 2000 personnel files. Some of the signing authorities have been posted or are now retired.

1 CAD staff had issued orders that all pictures of the Wing Commander posted in every building be removed and destroyed. Souvenir hunters were starting to appear, so when his uniforms and decorations were seized, they were burnt in the base waste incinerator. That was step one.

The next was to have an Assumption of Command parade. Some of the staff were bitching about going to a Change of Command Parade as some were calling it that I was quick to interject. A Change of Command refers to a passage of command between the outgoing and incoming Commanding Officers. This was not the situation. The whole Wing was in shock, and with so much heat and light being focused at Trenton, the new WComd shortlist had to be pulled up and put into action ASAP. Morale was dropping with all kinds of rumours and speculation on what they were finding in William's stashes of "trophies" and pictures which were later broadcast on national and international news outlets.

Eleven days later, on 19 February, Col. Dave Cochrane was selected, and the parade took place in the CC 177 hanger with local political and Captains of Industry in attendance further enforcing the community support for the Wing. On a side note, the CFB Trenton YC was celebrating its 50th anniversary that summer, and Col. Cochrane was in attendance, seated at the head table with some of our elder statesmen and founding members. During the weekends, events both on and off the water, he attended on the docks and touring the occasional vessel. His reward for stepping up and taking the job was a posting to Australia at the Staff College and the rank of BGen when he returned to Canada. Our eldest daughter and her partner were living in Canberra and working at the U of Australia as Marine biologists. Margret and the Col's wife were chatting about their posting and places our daughter had visited. Small world sometimes.

Since the signing authority for big-ticket items was getting sorted out, training was still pushed on with special circumstances attached to purchase orders. The city of Quinte West also felt the betrayal from one of the highest commands and employers in the area. An institution that had been previously looked at for safety and a secure presence with many strong working partners now was viewed by a cautious and less trusting population that we in uniform felt. All the good work 8 Wing/ CFB Trenton has done was forgotten that day in an instant.

The Ramp Ceremony

"Arrival Ceremony in Canada"

"Upon arrival of the deceased on Canadian territory, a ceremony may be held to commemorate and remember. Members of the family(s) of the deceased may be present, as well as dignitaries from all levels of government and all military representatives. If available, the unit of the deceased(s) may be represented and should constitute the pallbearers detachment. A quarter guard, bagpiper, and trumpeter may be present for the ceremony. The ceremony begins when the preparations for the arrival of the aircraft are completed. The military chaplain leads the way, followed by the detachment of pallbearers as the coffins are moved to the hearses. The family of the deceased may be positioned directly beside the hearse to pay their respects. The ceremony is concluded when the convoy leaves the gathering place."

https://www.canada.ca/en/services/defence/caf/military-identity-system/drill-manual/chapter-11/chapter-11-annexes.html#annex-a-7

When a member of the Canadian Forces is killed overseas, they are repatriated to 8 Wing for the Arrival Ceremony in Canada ramp ceremony. As described in the above text from the CF Manual of Drill and Ceremonial Annex A to Chapter 11, it can be quite overwhelming for all involved. Security for the family and VIPs (the PM, CDS, and Governor General, for example) space is at a premium, so not all CFB Trenton / 8 Wing personnel that wanted to attend are able to.

The other spectators, news media outlets, and civilians attending were gathered on one side of Highway 2 that divided the base, and the military personnel wishing to attend lined up on the centre median and on the other side so when the Hearst and family drove out the gate" the ceremony is concluded when the convoy leaves the gathering space" the first thing that came into sight was uniforms lining the first leg of the trip before going on RCAF road then to the 401 and the trip to the Toronto coroners office.

The first time that I attended a service with some other fellow engineers was when I got a call from Captain Terry Muldoon, the past Wing Fire Chief, just before lunch that day. If we were available, a quick call and we would meet up by the guard shack. Captain Jim Bolan, the former 8 Wing CWO, had gone to the dark side by taking his commission and now worked at the RTF. Also attending was CWO Levesque, the CWO for CCC, our Chief back at 81 AEF years before, and WO Mike Breskie a firefighter as well. We had all worked together on the MSS (Mission Support Squadron) for rapid deployments up to six months in duration anywhere in the world. The fallen sapper was originally from Cape Brenton Island and accordantly, Terry had his own CBI membership flag with him. We were standing right next to the intersection on the centre median beside the signal light pole. Between us, we both held his flag, and an Engineer's flag was between the other two.

As the first black stretch limousine's shiny chrome grill could be seen, CWO Levesque barked out, "8 Wing personnel, Attention. To your fallen comrades, Salute."

It is a powerful moment when that big black vehicle with a casket rolls by. A welling up inside, that sudden short but deep inhalation and fighting back the tears. You didn't show expression on parade, unofficial or not. You are in uniform. Funeral parade practice was a week-long lesson on my ILQ with different positions being shared between company members. As a Sergeant, one of your possible responsibilities could be arranging a funeral parade at the fallen member's home hometown church if it was requested by the family. Not everybody loves a parade.

I was concentrating straight forward, burning a hole in the Restricted Area sign hanging on the airfield perimeter chainlink fence, trying to breathe deeper and stare ahead. Things were working to the plan as laid out when the second last limo slowed down and then stopped. WTF is going on. There is no traffic because the Military Police are holding turning vehicles so as not to interrupt the convoy. The window in the last door rolled down, and all I heard was a broken female voice saying, "Thank you so much," and I broke the golden rule: Avoid Eye Contact at all costs. Whenever a call for volunteers or in class and the instructor is looking for that answer, look away, look away. It was just a millisecond, and our eyes met. I saw her eyes, and mine welled up. Dam, shit. You had to look? It is 10 years later, and it was like last summer. Break time.

It was July, and summer leave was beginning on 01 August. Looking forward to some relaxing times on Tapped Out anchored at Sandy Cove, and after the year it has been so far, I really need a break. I was doing something on my computer, when there was a knock on my door. Captain Katherine Woodburn stuck her head in and gave a quick scan of the room, slipped into the chair and started crying.

"Oh my God, Katherine, what's happened? Is it Scott?" (her ex now, but he was OPP at the time).

"No, no, it's Pat."

"Pat... Pat who?" I asked, racking my brain of all the Pats I know, male and female. Katherine worked on the third floor with the regional Army Cadet program.

"It's Pat Audet from the Flying Frogmen Scuba Club." She choked.

"No, No, shit, shit." His big, jolly image popped into my head instantly. There had been a group of brand new, freshly minted Open Water divers that hung around after hours. What, how, why questions raced quickly from me, just absorbing that bombshell. BBQs at his home in Frankfort by the Trent Severn Canal after a pumpkin dive or a bonfire and Bailies after an ice flow race on the Otonabee River up by Trent University Peterborough. Still, how did this happen? "He was over there with 430 Tactical Helicopter Squadron and involved in a helo crash at an American FOB a few days ago. There were other casualties as well, but all I was thinking was about Pat."

Katherine got up, came over, and just gave me a sob and a hug on my shoulder as she made her way out. That was 06 July 2009—a bad month for Canada. From 08 June to 01 August, we held ramp services for 8 fallen soldiers.

It was like going to a funeral parade outside the church, but now eight this month, and two more engineers that's messed up. Sometimes, if the day was almost over, a toast at the mess to our fallen was in order, and if there were some antidotes to share or an embarrassing but funny event that occurred early in their career. Sgt

58

Dave Chalmers and I were at a Range Safety Officer conference held at CFB Kingston. On the second day, we found out a mutual friend, an RCR then remustered to the Engineers, had taken his life a few days before. We regret to inform you of the sudden death of Cpl, MCpl, CWO, Captain ..... NATO standard death message, bull. Lots of beers and shots went down range at the mess that night. Taxi chits were definitely required to get to our hotel after the last call.

Over those five years, I estimate that I attended around 20 repatriations and Major Glenn Stewart's service. Just lock that away with the other unpleasantness, right?

Since I was released, I haven't attended any funerals except two—Margret's and my dad's.

Time to bust up a gram of VetSelect Master Rockstar indica, roll a cone, and regroup.

"Just can't live that negative way .... make way for the positive day," Positive Vibration quote on the Bob Marley cigarette rolling papers.

National Defence — PERSONNEL EVALUATION REPORT (PER)

SECTION 1: IDENTIFICATION

K50 016 063 TANNER	GC	WO	PRes	CE SUPT	00307	04

SECTION 2: GENERAL

ANNUAL 01 04 10 31 03 11 81 13

2 13 A Member's Preferred Language of Completion English ● French ○ Either ○ CFB TRENTON 0125

SECTION 3: DETAILS OF EMPLOYMENT/NEW QUALIFICATIONS

Pri: RTF Emergency Management WO (12), RTF A/FSM (4), RTF A/Readiness Training Officer (4); Sec: Building 56 Security Officer, Commodore Trenton Yacht Club

Basic Emergency Management Instructors Course, Tabletop Exercise Design and Development, Advanced Leadership Qualification

SECTION 4: PERFORMANCE (Rated By Supervisor)

1. Supervising
2. Eval and develop sub
3. Team Building
4. Leading Change
5. Working with Others
6. Problem Solving
7. Decision Making
8. Effectiveness
9. Initiative
10. Verbal Communication
11. Written Communication
12. Applying Job Knowledge/Skills
13. Resource Management
14. Accountability
15. Reliability
16. Ethics and Values

17. Conduct On/Off Duty

WO Tanner's performance was outstanding. (1,12,13) As the A/FSM, he had a meticulous knowledge of training requirements and was a patient and supportive role model and mentor. He masterfully managed staff, resources and took rapid, effective action to resolve manning, training and morale issues. (2,3,5) As A/FSM and RTO, he clearly proved he was a highly capable and reliable supervisor. His expertise, guidance and strong, dynamic leadership moulded the unit into an extremely effective team during surge operations. (7,14) WO Tanner's comprehensive knowledge of areas of responsibility combined with his innate ability to transform budgetary decisions into responsible actions was noteworthy. (10,11) A master communicator, WO Tanner drafted several Op Orders and emergency management correspondence, provided insightful training reports and effortlessly completed unit administration. A first-rate orator, he was comfortable addressing all audiences and briefing senior staff. He was an articulate speaker who had a commanding knowledge of his subject and presented his thoughts in a cool, confident manner. (8,9,15) A highly reliable self-starter, he always looked to improve operations. Significant contributions include coordinating deployment training for the MSS, developing, designing, evaluating Ex Vendetta, and liaising with local authorities. (16) WO Tanner displayed his dedication through a balanced home life and commitment to the community as Commodore of the Trenton Yacht Club.

SN, RANK, NAME, MOS, APPT: F34 365 878, Maj. B.K. Abram, CELE Air, OC A3 RTF 8 Wg

SECTION 5: POTENTIAL (Rated By REVIEWING OFFICER, For Promotion To Next Rank)

1. Leadership
2. Professional Development
3. Communication Skills
4. Planning and Organizational Skills
5. Administration
6. Dedication

POTENTIAL RANKING

0 of 0

PROMOTION RECOMMENDATION

(1) WO Tanner has outstanding potential to perform at the next rank level. A top performing Sr NCO, his outstanding work ethic and solid leadership are indicative of an NCM with unmatched potential to succeed. As A/FSM and RTO he clearly demonstrates that he is ready to lead and mange subordinates to operate as a highly successful efficient team and to assume the responsibilities associated with higher rank. His remarkable management of subordinates comes from an innate ability to employ the appropriate leadership style for each situation in order to complete the task at hand. He effectively promotes teamwork and cooperation amongst his subordinates. (3) With communication skills that will serve him well as an MWO, he ensures vital and pertinent information is exchanged, contributing to a harmonious workplace. An articulate orator, he calmly delivers his thoughts confidently to any audience, ensuring full comprehension regardless of subject. (4) His development and designing of exercises clearly indicates he possesses the planning and organizational abilities of a MWO. (5) As A/FSM, WO Tanner consistently displays the administrative and organizational skills indicative of an MWO. (6) Extremely dedicated, he willingly accepts any task assigned to him. His inspirational outlook and work ethic are second to none and clearly indicate he has unlimited potential to operate at the next rank. He is a superior role model who displays absolute loyalty to superiors which instils dedication in his subordinates.

SN, RANK, NAME, MOS, APPT: H32 220 843, LCol. D.J Ziprick, ACSO, A3 8 Wg 16 May 11

SECTION 6: ADDITIONAL REVIEW

WO Tanner is ranked 1 out of 17 Reserve WOs at 8 Wg. He is a remarkable tradesman and exceptional NCM. He readily assumes greater responsibility and consistently attains the results expected of higher rank. His exacting standards and positive impact on team achievements assure optimal results and mission success. WO Tanner is highly recommended for immediate promotion.

SN, RANK, NAME, MOS, APPT: A82 416 516, Col, D.B. Cochrane, ACSO, WComd 8 Wing

SECTION 7: MEMBER

THIS REPORT HAS BEEN READ AND DISCUSSED 19 May 11 Reserved

Fuck, I *loved* my job.

FNC1

C7A1

Browning 9 mm pistol

CAPORAL
Blais, Karine Marie Nathasha   13 avril 2009
12ᵉ RÉGIMENT BLINDÉ DU CANADA

MAJOR
Mendes, Michelle Linda, CD   23 April 2009
INTELLIGENCE BRANCH

SOLDAT
Péloquin, Alexandre   8 juin 2009
ROYAL 22ᵉ RÉGIMENT

CORPORAL
Bulger, Nicholas Ashley   3 July 2009
PRINCESS PATRICIA'S CANADIAN LIGHT INFANTRY

CAPORAL-CHEF
Michaud, Charles-Philippe   4 juillet 2009
ROYAL 22ᵉ RÉGIMENT

CAPORAL-CHEF
Audet, Patrice Yvon   6 juillet 2009
430ᵉ ESCADRON TACTIQUE D'HÉLICOPTÈRES

CAPORAL
Joannette, Martin   6 juillet 2009
ROYAL 22ᵉ RÉGIMENT

CAPORAL
Dubé, Joseph Robert Martin   14 juin 2009
5ᵉ RÉGIMENT DU GÉNIE DE COMBAT

CAPORAL
Bobbitt, Christian   1 août 2009
5ᵉ RÉGIMENT DU GÉNIE DE COMBAT

SOLDAT
Courcy, Sébastien Joseph Gérard Omer   16 juillet 2009
ROYAL 22ᵉ RÉGIMENT

Canada's Book of Remembrance page 234 from the book: In Service of Canada (1947-2014)

Chapter 8

Kosovo

/ Appendix C

KOSOVO

When I was deployed to Kosovo, this was a town that was about 10 minutes away from our base. There was a Company housed beside the factory and a platoon house on the outer ridge of the town. We were located right on the Serbian border. It was an every-second-day trip to Glogovac for service work. We drove past the factory every time, twice a trip. We often shared stories with the Brits who were guarding the factory. Found this in one of my rabbit hole adventures. I could not write this, let alone read it again.

Description

KOSOVO: GLOGOVAC: ALLEGED DEATH FACTORY GUARDED

Jul 21

(18 Jun 1999) Natural Sound

British troops are guarding the site of a Serb "death factory," where up to 600 innocent civilians are reported to have been massacred in an orgy of revenge by Yugoslav forces.

The killings are said to have taken place at the Feronikl factory, a smelting works in Glogovac taken over by Serb special forces during their 15 months of terror in Kosovo.

Local Albanians claim that the plant's smelting ovens were used to dispose of hundreds of bodies of the Serbs' victims.

Some of the victims are believed to be buried in mass graves close to the factory.

The Feronikl Factory in Glogovac.

Witnessing the ruins of the smelting works, it is hard to imagine the horrors that are said to have taken place here.

The disused factory was taken over in the spring of last year by the Interior Ministry police and specialist anti-terrorist units.

The sprawling complex of foundries and outbuildings was reportedly used as a holding centre for Albanian men captured during the Serb campaign against the K-L-A rebellion, which broke out in the spring of 1998.

But local witnesses say that after the factory was bombed by NATO on April 29, the Serbs set out on a campaign of revenge against ethnic Albanians in the region.

In all, up to 600 people are believed to have been killed in the "death factory."

In a chilling echo of the Nazi Holocaust, the plant's smelting ovens were reportedly used to dispose of hundreds of the bodies.

SOUNDBITE: (Albanian)

"They (the Serbs) used this place as their main base. Here, they tortured people, brought civilians inside, and executed them here. We heard that possibly the furnaces were used to burn people. It was completely surrounded by police."

SUPER CAPTION: Rusde Karaxha, KLA Soldier

Eight hundred meters from the factory is a mass grave with 66 unmarked graves, said to contain the bodies of some of the factory victims.

However, local Albanians suggest Serb forces also used the site to bury victims of atrocities committed in surrounding villages.

They say that following the bombing of the factory, special police and anti-terrorist units teamed up with the Yugoslav army to take their revenge.

One of the first places to suffer was the neighbouring village of Cikatova Vjeter, where 64 men and women aged 12 and upwards were murdered.

SOUNDBITE: (Albanian)

"They brought bodies from surrounding villages and brought them here with trucks and buried them here. They used civilian Albanians to unload the trucks. There were all kinds of bodies. They came two weeks ago with a bulldozer and then buried them one by one."

SUPER CAPTION: Local Villager

British K-FOR troops - who are stationed in Glogovac - moved in to secure the site on Thursday.

War crimes investigators will soon begin to uncover the secrets of the "death factory."

One problem, though, is that the factory and the mass grave sites have not been cleared of mines as yet.

SOUNDBITE: (English)

"We've had reports of several (mass graves) - we've seen two. I don't have the full details. We've been given a list of 51 names for one of the grave sites, and we're looking into that. Part of the problem with these graves is that there are mines in the area. And what we're trying to do is trying to take them off. When we can get in an investigation team, that would be useful."

SUPER CAPTION: Major Nick Walsh - British K-FOR Forces

There are reports of other mass graves in the area.

Scores of victims from a massacre in the nearby village of Vrbovac are believed to lie in a mass grave at Shavarina, less than a mile from the Feronikl plant.

Kosovo Atrocities Recounted In Detail

Format

News and Press Release

SourceHRW

Posted

27 July 1999

Originally published

27 July 1999

On the way back from Skopje, Macedonia, we used to stop at Camp Bondsteel, an American Base Camp. It was about halfway back, just off the main highway. Americans... have a Burger King franchise there and a huge PX. It was in one of those inflated domes, like some of the indoor golf or sporting venues you would see here. Burger and a shakedown range, a few new CDs, and sometimes a tee shirt. Back on the road again. Past one, well, let's just say you're at a very high heightened state of awareness journey, and onto the next portion of the leg. It's not nice on the road at night here. Anyway, there was this huge cement plant right on the new border, with miles and miles of trucks and semis waiting for days, sometimes for a crossing. Depends on the border guards' attitude.

So the locals don't like your green Armored LSVW with the squeaky breaks blowing by them up to the border. We got guns, sunshine. Well, so do they, proudly displaying their AK-47s, officially known as the Avtomat Kalashnikovs, which is a gas-operated assault rifle that is chambered for the 7.62×39mm cartridge. Developed in the Soviet Union by Russian small-arms designer Mikhail Kalashnikov. Literally 100's of millions were produced. We even had a Chinese version in our foreign weapons vault. So after a wait at the border were off again. Beautiful countryside. Reminded me of the Black Forest area, except for the blown-up shit. There were several rivers and valleys to cross, with one area with several tunnels blasted through the mountainside. What was told at a briefing earlier about the Serbs placing anti-tank mines in the tunnels in the shadowed area? Occasionally, you would see a vehicle on the side with the front end twisted off. This day, we were driving the 10-ton cargo trucks. 8-speed tranny, or it had an automatic overdrive mode. Mash the accelerator and let the turbo diesel whine. This mode is so that anyone can drive the truck in an emergency. Two vehicles, two people loaded for bear. As you approach the tunnel, you are supposed to take off your sunnies before entry. Most trips ok, but when the sun is going down, the game is afoot. More shadow to play with, plus at sunset, the glare is blinding. It was getting late once we got through the border and got underway. The usual chitchat kept the mood light.

Only a few months left and 1 R&R to go; let's get back to camp. You always slow down at these approaches, and this was the second out of three. All I remember is Mark yelling, Left, go FUCKEN left. Hard turn straddling the double yellow lines; as I take a quick peek in the side mirror, black diesel fumes were billowing out like a tractor pull event, blocking out the tunnel lights. The glance was to see if the other HL was still there. Full pull mode. Freaked both of us totally. He said that he just got a glimpse of two square wooden boxes a few feet from the wall. Right in the passenger tire tracks. The majority of the Yugo/USSR Cold War era anti-tank mines. Low cost to manufacture, non-metallic so mine detectors can't pick them up. The Smoke time. DND has a rule that there is to be no smoking in a military vehicle. Well, in Canada, that applies here. It is a whole different ball of wax. Our HLVW has bulletproof protection, so there are layered windows and armor on the doors and a blast blanket on the floor. No A/C or windows to roll down, so you prop open the door to get the air in. Fun, fun, fun.

I was a Combat Engineer for eight years before re-mustering to Plumber Gas fitter. Among the skill sets as Combat Engineer's is basic to advanced controlled demolitions and mine fields. Laying and picking them up. I had the sub-trade specialty HA Basic EOD. A six-week course at CFB Chilliwack. Air, Land, and Underwater munitions. Around 150 different types. You created your own book to include all important info with your added notes, etc. I did EOD while I was at 4 CER, Germany, so all the Warsaw Pac mines were included. I used to give the MAT training (Mine Awareness training) for the Camp Mirage roto's. Scope creeping into Appendix C. I did a scroll back, and I am in Appendix C. Time to shut her down for the night.

Our camp in Kosovo. 4 down on the left and 2 in was our eight man Weather haven canvas shelters. Utility corridor was the road between the tents.

Chapter 9

Bell curve meds

It has been about a week or so since I have done any writing—a week of good reflection, comradeship, and just doing something a little different. As mentioned in the preface, this paper is addressed to several parties, so individual experiences and discussions will remain where they took place. I will talk about things in a general context to hopefully keep everyone in the loop as needed without crossing that imaginary moral line in my heart.

What I have been dealing with for approximately the last six months is my medical cannabis ordering. My reorder date is the eighth of each month, give or take a day. So, as it turns out, that day has been landing on Thursdays to Sundays most months. Sucks big time. Now, once again, using the engineer in me, and after almost seven months of no booze and sleeping aids, clarity, and sometimes the not-so-common common sense, I was doing the big bell curve thing that Doug had covered. It also matched up with what Hilary and I discussed about the window of tolerance. So here is how I explained it to my pain management doctor.

Example: You are a type two diabetic and require four injections a day to stay healthy and out of potential physical and internal damage.

Me: I take CBD oil 20 Mg 3 times a day and a 20 mg THC gel pill before bed. Same, same four and four, right? (plus a little bud as well)

Example: You know the date is in a few weeks. Call the pharmacy ahead and pick it up next week. All is good. It is a prescribed medicine that, after years of testing and doctor reports, does work to alleviate the ailment.

Me: I know that my date is coming up, but due to the delivery delays, I must now:

1. Start to go on half Rx at week three and through to after the expected delivery,

2. Look at my calendar to determine where and what I can now do for this period, then drop the nice-to-do work and pare it down to the must-do things, i.e., chiropractors and TN appointments.

3. Smile and wave, avoiding anything remotely triggering an event.

The result, unfortunately, is that these constant peaks and lows can rear its ugly head. Now, I must be very clear about this next part, and the readers, I hope, will take away from this that I am not making any excuses or apologies for any of my comments or actions over the past years. I have made amends with all concerned parties, hopefully anyway.

We were at a bar one night, listening to the band, having a Heineken 0.0. A familiar sing-along song kicked in at one point, and the atmosphere was really electric. (well, to me, anyway) I was rocking in my chair and getting into the groove. Just as the song was winding down, I heard an older lady behind me say, "Oh, isn't that nice? He looks like he is enjoying himself."

I stopped in the chair, and, for the lack of a better word, got up. LABLED was all that was racing through my now ringing head. Wearing my Veterans tee shirt, I had Barrett with me. It was not that the actual words disturbed me; it was the tone and the delivery. They were an older couple, 25 years older than me. It was the grandmother tone that we have all heard when they talk about someone who is "special" (I paused here for about five minutes searching for the politically correct term, without avail. I will just let you picture that image), and I genuinely mean no disrespect to them. My Grandmother spoke that way when I was little, so it is just that. My grandson knows more about the IPAD and video games than I will ever retain. But can they build a shelter, fire, or basic camping skill without an App? I guess that's the Generation X, or the millennium age thing.

Sometimes, it is just as simple as that. People are either scared of the vest/crest/tattoos or are overly sympathetic towards you. They are also afraid not to say or do anything that would somehow unhinge or send you into a tailspin in the COSTCO hotdog line. Watch your F'n fries A hole. Once again, you do the Toronto Globe and Mail headline test. "Will your intent or actions bring question or disgrace to the uniform that you wear?" Force-feeding a large soft drink into someone's face checks the YES box. Sorry. Another break.

Red Hot Chill Pepper's song "Black Summer" was released in February 2022. The station Q104 played it a lot for the next month, giving them their 14th number-one single. Thanks Anna Zee. I was involved with the final stages of withdrawal, but hearing the catchy rhythm and the Welsh accent (my Grandmother was English, and my son-in-law is Irish) caught my ear. If you ever get a chance to listen to Christy Moore, an Irish Artist, download or stream the song "Weekend in Amsterdam." It will give you a chuckle.

I didn't research the band or the song's meaning, just the radio and Entertainment-Tonight type show doing interviews—some dark stuff. Been there, but I am looking forward to the other side of this DT thing. Still, it gave me some little kick trying to remember if the two add-lib vocals between verses were.

"Hit me now, and Get it on."

Which one was the first? It gives me that little .... you know, the little tongue click to the beat, with the occasional head tilt waiting for that part that feels good. What was I upset about before? Hey, Weezer's "Hash-pipe" is up next... Where was I going with this?

The cover for the Song Black Summer is a guy standing on rocks in the water, looking up at a setting sun, light streaks piercing the cloud layers, and a red orangish ball. So today was the regular Tuesday trip; Chiro made some quick stops, saw Mom, and took her out shopping if needed. She usually has a friend go with her during the week, so a quick catch me up, fix a thing or two, coffee, and on the road by 1630. Highway, our exit, then the road home. We had a lot of rain and wind, so the boat had a few inches of water, which I had to bail out.

My next-door neighbour had just come back from a dive. A local kid's outboard fell off his tin boat yesterday off Scott's Point in 35 feet of water. He did a grid search, but the current was building up with the tide already on the flood. He had only a short bottom time. He wanted to know if I could go and do some research tomorrow. Are you freaking serious? Sorry, just got back my Zeagle Tech regs, but my tanks are still getting hydro'd. I was drooling at the thought of a bottom search in the shallows. It would have been a Great first dive. I apologized and offered the standard, maybe next time, buddy answer.

Breathe, Leo, Breathe. You want to do this your way, not with the added pressure of a search in a place where I have never been, with Big tides right now. Nope. Your own pace. There is the urge to call back over to him to say that I have changed my mind. The two-stroke outboard's distinctive high ringing sound brought me back to the now. Good luck I called back with the nod and wave. All is good.

Chapter 10

Nine months

Barrett and I have a pretty good routine now, after, wow, I have had him for NINE months. It seems like years since Kansas and the trip. Switch gears right now.

Our walk is usually around 1830-1900 hours up the driveway, to the garage, then up the trail cut through the scrub brush, leading to the top of the granite mountain behind the house. Yup, high ground. All arcs of fire are covered. The whole property is lit up with solar lights. That is what runs my garage and power tools. Wired it up like a boat, 2 x 90 amp solar panels, a 12-volt breaker panel, a battery switch and wire leftover from the trawler.

All my cables are 00 cables to the batteries. Then wired in a 3000-watt inverter and LED light strips for the work area and the Captain's Cabin (the 16 x 20 ft room) with all my sails, charts, scuba gear and any other nautical-related items. I have brass casings from WWII shipwrecks in the Halifax harbour area. Tiles from a hospital ship, Leticia, and a few cannon balls from Port... Cove. A safe zone for anything that has to be said. Came in handy in several situations. Dam, scope creep again.

Oh, The walk and the song bit. So we get to the top of the hill. I just happened to turn to my west, and there it was. Pow. Overlooking Whistlers Cove towards the sunset, the image was remarkably an almost perfect reflection of the song's background picture. When you really slow down and visualize the YouTube clip..... I can feel the hair on the back of my neck stand straight up and the chill that gives me the shakes. What a great end to an awesome turnaround and another mark in the save column. These bursts of, just stuff, with the slimmest of threads to draw any remote connection, just all seem to link up. Remember, It's not your job to figure it out. Your job is to start embracing the wealth that already surrounds you.

For the most part, our civilized world is divided into many races, and based on their geographical location on this planet, they have developed their rituals and traditions. These, in turn, get passed down through the generations so their ethos is maintained within their sphere. Yes, this is a very, very rudimentary lens that I am using, but I am trying to get a point across. As a military, we are steeped with traditions and some very old customs that, to the average Joe, ya, well, why are you scarlet coloured mess jacket and waistcoated mess dress or Mess dress uniform as it is known? Miniature medals and other accoutrements are also worn. Mess dinners were created so that we could blow off some steam but also, in a relaxed setting, receive some tutelage from the guest of honour, usually some Generals or even some Captains of industry. The toasts, the bagpiper, and the passing of the port are all deep in our customs, and then, after the guest of honour has made his intent to retire to the bar area, pee break. I sometimes wondered how the old Generals held their bladder. Christ, a 40-minute car ride to town has me bursting sometimes.

So, where am I going with this? We in the Engineering Corp have a book titled, "The Canadian Military Engineers Book of Customs and Traditions, affectionately known as The Red Book.[3] Well, because the cover is RED. Simple right? It is required reading on our 6A Sergeants course. Non-applicable things in it now, such as hosting an afternoon with the Troop Commander and how to lay out the Luncheon menus. (see references) But there are also lots of interesting tidbits of forgotten history.

Rudyard Kipling has several quotes in the book, and interestingly enough, if you look up the history of the Iron Ring, you will see that Rudyard is quoted in there as well. I will not get into the brass tacks of the story, but suffice it to say that he talks about professionalism, pride, and humility. We all have to respect the unknown factors. The biggest ship in their time was the Titanic. Big and strong, but little was known at that time about the heating and annealing of metal, and we all found out later that big can be misleading. Tough on the outside, weak and brittle on the inside.

---

[3] https://cmea-agmc.ca/customs-and-traditions-canadian-military-engineers

I had a few nights when a group of us Engineers and some others closed out the mess, singing,

"We are, we are, we are, we are, we are the Engineers.

We can, we can, we can, we can demolish 40 beers,

Drink rum, drink rum, drink rum, drink rum, and come along with us,

For we don't give a dam for any old man, who don't give a dam for us. Hey!

Chimo."

There are several more verses, even with a part "Lady Godiva showing off her Lilly white hide....." At the men's Christmas dinners, the song sheets circulated amongst us newbies to learn. Moving Along......

Amongst the readings in this book are things like duty, honour, respect, loyalty, courage, and ethical standards for all engineers. Now, as I said before, these are my interpretations and feelings that I am now dealing with, looking for something that even remotely contains any of the above six fundamental building blocks with which I lived for 34 years of my military career and am trying to in my still transitional phase to civilian life, almost ten years later.

I think one of the main reasons why I am not on Facebook, Twitter, Instagram, Snapchat, and on and on is just how now it is more important to get "likes" than lend a hand or heaven put yourself in harm's way to help or save another person, regardless of where, or who they are to step up. You see it all the time: 30 people with iPhones taking videos and texting. By the way, the person is bleeding out or is in distress while your ego rating goes up a few stars or whatever you fucks get. Now, this just took a hard left turn.

On my ALQ (MWO course), we had ten weeks of DL assignments to be sent to RMC for grading before going to St Jean. One of my assignments was to select two principles of war and apply them to the Allied and Resistance forces. Argue that both Generals had completed their mission. Look at both sides. Ok, so I will.

I can put into this context what I have personally experienced.

76

What images you see on a screen, either on a phone or a 60" curved flat screen, they are just that. Images. When we went to the ice storm relief in Montreal for 19 days, the shots you saw on television in no way compared to seeing in real life 200-foot hydro towers twisted in a mostly unrecognizable mass of grey steel for miles. The same goes for sailing around the Gaspé Bay and Percé Rock, cutting through the waves at seven knots plus from 100 feet away. Awesome sight.

The same goes, I think for the stuff going on today. After the phones are lowered, gasps are heard, and a hand quickly comes up to cover a drawn mouth. Now, here is one observation that I have made, and maybe I am not the only one, but here it goes. No matter what demographics the crowd is made up of, no one is arguing or picking fights with each other, just enjoying the scene unveiling itself right in front of them. Then, the yelling to call 911. Wait, one, my FB page is exploding. I'll fucking FB ya.

Sorry. The R.H.C.P. song cover image thing. Look what happens when you take that extra step towards the hilltop. I will take a crack at Appendix B, A3 RTF FSM.

I left off by talking about the events following the arrest of the 8 Wing Commander that February.

"About three pages to be finished in this chapter instead of the reader having to flip back to that chapter. I think it would disrupt the rhythm."

Chapter 11

Black summer

Back from finishing off Appendix B. I went to a place the other day. Triggered Monday night. No sleep, and Tuesday morning was starting to suck hard already, and not even a drop of coffee was in sight. I found a picture. It really shook me up.

Wait out. Slightly off-center right now. Hilary is going to earn her money this week.

It has been about a week since I last sat down to continue. The picture will remain where it is, and after a good session with Hilary, some pain and guilt have been understood, and I will work on my acceptance of the events and look at my life now. I needed some relaxation and mindfulness to acknowledge my feelings and thoughts. Water is the common denominator here. Either on top or underneath, she has her tranquil effects. My present watercraft is a 16-foot, southwest-deep, Vee fiberglass boat with a 20 HP outboard that is my "fishing" boat.

With the deep ocean several 100 yards away, a sturdy boat is necessary if caught in the wind and tide shifts, which can cause a confusing sea within a few moments. Off White Island, it is on average 110-130 feet deep, with the shoals only a foot away, the jagged granite peaks awash at high tide, waiting for the wary tourist / Credit Card Captain—lots of fun. Off the green spar buoy, set the line, and just let the tide drift the boat back to the cove entrance over a period of two Budweiser 0.0 and a smoke. It is like having the world's biggest wave sound machine with special effects of the occasional spindrift cresting the gunnel, adding that salt taste to the beer. One of the locals was out the other day, and he showed me all the little nooks and crannies throughout the adjacent coves.

He had lobster fished for a few years on a Cape and had a wealth of knowledge not listed in the Aid to Navigation publications.

Which side of the big rock in Back Harbour can you pass at low tide? Lobster Cove and the hurricane party hole. A quick explanation of a hurricane hole. It came from down south where there were, you guessed it, hurricanes. A cove or area that has shelter from almost all cardinal points.

Sometimes, it can be between two small islands where the same opening accesses the coves. Had a few in the Thousand Islands by the Bateau Channel. Man, could Lake Ontario whip up quickly when she wanted to. I have sailed from Trenton to Toronto several times on several different types of boats. The quiet and stillness of being in the middle of a Great Lake, with the gentle night breeze, is enough to keep up the sails but not enough to make it uncomfortable. As the moon is in the final phase, the pulsing glow of the GTA is a sight that can be seen 30 miles away. The cooling towers at the Darlington Power plant have red flashing lights so planes and boats can use these as reference points. The CN tower has an eerie orange haze that seems to be now ever present, leaving a residue on the decks after a rain storm. Hey, where was I? Oh ya...

The album cover picture. Back to the water again. I was going diving that week, looking for my mooring block. It is a one-ton Jersey Barrier (the highway dividers) with 30 feet of chain and my 36-inch white mooring ball. When I bring the boat down here in September, she will need a place for the nights. Once again, with the physics.

Now, to get something rigged to get my tanks and gear out of the water without bending over and doing a straight lift of around 75 pounds with the integral lead shot weight bags of my Zeagle Tech BCD. When I sold my 34 ft Mainship MK III Trawler, we kept the St. Croix seven-to-one mini stainless steel crane. I used to use it to lift the dinghy's 15 hp outboard. The crane was $600.00 back in the 90s.

Some modifications to the two-inch AL pipe that supported a 25 amp wind generator for the boat battery banks. There is no need for that right now, so now a quick drawing and a few measurements. Also, the nice thing about this setup is that you can remove the crane for easy storage. I mentioned that it was worth $600. Crows (

midnight madness-shoppers) like shiny things, so lock up your stuff, or the ownership will be passed to someone who needs it more than you. That was about as polite as I can be on this. You mess around with people here and piss them off, well, they burn your boat. He owed money to some less-than-stellar individuals.

A local contact was made, and he does aluminum welding. Materials were picked up, and a time to meet was set up. Picked up and returned on the same day, $100. cash. $250 in town, with a two-week wait. Half that would be my cost in fuel and bridge fares. Next, the weather.

I got the crane mounted, and we are all set up for my first dive in ten years—just a quick memory jolt. My last dive was in Trenton at the Yacht Club, working on a prop and line issue. That was the mid-end of August 2012. Well, this is mid-August 2022, and as I let the air from my BCD, the water slowly covered my mask, and a small breath slipped under the surface. Ears, check, mask, check, equipment, check. How are you <u>doing?</u>

Great.

Let's go exploring. I had a towing bridle done up, so Roy and Heath towed me out the 500 m to the area, and I just let go of the line and glided over the bottom, drinking everything that I could see. It was a bit murky for viz, but I was in the water and could feel the warmth of the body heated sea water go down the middle of my back just like it was last month when I was in diving. At no time did I feel uncomfortable or spooked by the bottom.

We found the float line from last fall that I had used as a winter marker, about six feet below the surface. The retrieval and attachment of the mooring ball took about three minutes. Shackle off, shackle on.

Done.

Once the ball was back in the water, I followed the anchor chain to the bottom, gave it a few pulls to unkink it, and a quick feel along the links to feel for any damage. Oh shit, I should check my gauges, shouldn't I? Having too much fun. 20 ft at the mooring block and 2550 psi of gas in the tank. That's over an hour's worth of bottom time or at least three 20-minute dives. What I have as a mooring block is a one-ton Jersey barrier for the weight. You know, the big blocks on the highway for highway medians and temporary construction.

The block had wedged itself into the side of the shoal from the tide, locking it in place. Secure for Wind Gypsy I and the dock. Popped up to the surface and hitched a tow back to my dock. Nice little swim around checking the anchors for the dock and the fishing boat. Ten feet of water at the end of the dock. Sweet enough room for the big girl to get in of offloading. Finished off the dive after around 20 minutes. I got the BCD off in the water and hooked up the St.Croix crane and with the seven-to-one ratio, it was like lifting around 8-10 pounds. Excellent. You have to like when a plan actually comes into effect with the expected results. There were a few little detours and side-off shoots, but the end result exceeded expectations, with more good prospects opening up each day. (the big secret is you have to look for them. Just waiting and pinning time away, sometimes pleading for something to show up, is just that. Waiting. Get up and Look at what is around you. More on my take on this later).

Chapter 12

The text

I got an interesting text a few weeks ago from Heath. He wanted to know if the spot by the wharf was free so some vacationers in a camper could stay for a night or two. Before COVID 19 there was always someone day parking, maybe drinking too, or just staying the night. They are usually gone by 9 or 10 o'clock—no one is there tonight. The weather was starting to fade and the mist was coming in. They had stayed at West Dover the night before and wanted to explore the area for a day or two. I had texted that the spot was open, and then, for some reason, I shot off another text saying that they could park up by the Captain's Cabin for the night since the weather was deteriorating.

A few minutes they arrived in a little Ford Transit panel van. It was all done up inside with a bed, shelves and drawers, an area for their cooler and stove. Nice little setup. The creature's comfort level is set for your own level, so if you are happy, great. We had been camping in the BC interior when I was posted to CFB Chilliwack after Germany, and Jackie was born there. We had a 1983 Dodge minivan and a tent. All that we needed was packed in the barrack box. Good to Go. We were on site when a 40-foot bus-style RV pulled into the lot next to us. Out came the awning, the sat dish was locking on its signal, and the genny was flashed up. It was a sweet ride, but then a cool $250K was the sticker price. Way out of our snack bracket, for sure.

But hey, we were happy campers. Anyway, getting back to the story within the story, A short while later, you could hear some clattering and rummaging sounds. Then, the RV door opened, and the wife approached our site. She was wondering if we had a can opener that she could borrow. Sure, I can lend you one. I have one of the ration pack openers on my key chain. Thanks, and off she went, but just to come back a few minutes later. "How does this work?" was the question. The Army, in their infinite wisdom, made these so they fold and sit flat so you cannot accidentally puncture yourself by sitting on them. Demo done, and again off she went to feed her hungry crew. Now, back to what I was originally talking about.

So, they ended up staying for eight days. I could write pages and pages, but some things need not be shared. Everyone had a fantastic time, fish fry-ups, exploring around the coves in the boat, just being on the sea. Suppers were at the house, out on the deck, taking in the view over the cove as a backdrop. Here are a few takeaways from the whole experience:

Hellen and her partner, Bernard, were French and had a limited English vocabulary. No worries, I can get by a bit. After about an hour of giving the lay of the land and where to and not to go on the property, we are up in the Captain's Cabin having a Bud 0.0, and they have their drinks. Then something funny happened. My friend Heath, who came up with, they said, "Hey, Dude, I didn't know that you spoke French."

Fuck, neither did I. Well, that's a bit of a stretch. I lived in Montreal until I was six, then we moved to Halifax for Dad's work. I had to do extra English classes in grade one to get "the proper pronouncement." Then, French in grade and High school, throw in a tour with 5 RGC, Fifth Regiment Genie du Combat to Bosnia Herzegovina.

Vallcatraz, as it was known that have been there. CFB Valcartier Quebec. Three months of work-up training, all in French. And add a six-month French course that I did in 2001. I just started to come back slowly, and I even found myself thinking out the translation for our conversations. So after a few days, we were having chats fully in French. Blew Margret and my kids away. Me too even. It's amazing what no booze and prescription drugs can do to the mind without really trying. The fog is slowly thinning.

So the other big, big takeaway was that Helen was involved in a car accident when she was 22, and her leg was severely injured. Then, when she was in hospital, she had a stroke and lost the use of her left hand. This happened in her first or second year of

Architectural Design at the University. Due to her limitations, the school said a different career choice should be sought after. Not liking that answer, Hellen's physiotherapist care person suggested some different avenues to persist for funding and school assistance grants for aids.

She got a special mouse and pad to fit her hand for easier control of the buttons. To wrap this up in a nice little bow, Hellen has her Masters in design and works in Montreal for a firm there. They have a triplex in the St Catherines St area. Living in the middle one, renting out the other two for their travel fund. Hellen and Bernard have been backpacking around the world, tenting in Peru, Cambodia, and Africa for a few years. About three months is the duration for the trips. They definitely look for the path less taken.

Now, they are in Newfoundland for three weeks before heading back before the weather gets too cold. They sent some great pictures of the cliffs and the rugged shoreline. As a parting gift, Hellen had painted some pieces of wood with a scene of the cove and an anchor on another piece. What I got from this encounter was someone who did not like the cards that were dealt for that hand, and instead of folding, played on to see the next card and then another. Speaking French was a bit of a shock, but after we started to talk more, the school French was long gone, and the working-class French came out, new swear words and everything. Bernard had been in the France forces for 25 years, then got divorced, etc, then met Hellen on one of her trips and agreed to meet again. He ended up coming over about four years ago. That's my translation anyway. Like I said before, I could go on for pages and pages, but maybe I'll return later.

Was having a bit of writer's block, mostly because I have been Wind Gypsy I (WGI), my Mirage 30 sailboat ready to splash in a few weeks. She was on the hard for two years, and I had lost interest in her, just due to the fact of the work required to see the boat in. This got the juices flowing as they said, by the way, who exactly are they? Eh?

Catching Pollack off Blind Bay. We had 10 people over for supper that night.

Chapter 13

The water

Over the years, the water has become my place to collect my thoughts and find peace and tranquility. The last two are things we all want, but finding them can be a daunting task. I briefly talked about diving in Spain, and my big decision at that time was to go back in and face the chance of the unlikely equipment failure or regain my freedom from the surface world, even if it was just for a few silent minutes.

My introduction to scuba diving began back in 1982. I was posted to 22 Field Squadron, CFB Gagetown NB, as a Combat Engineer. They were running a Combat diver pre-course entry to diving to see who could or wanted to try diving. The course was three weeks in September, for the full course was out at FDU (P) later in October. Thirty tryouts for 15 spots. Lots of PT, running, pushups, with twin 80's even. Wearing weight belts and harnesses, and of course, diving in the pool. That was the Fun part.

Since I wore glasses and was a V3 vision, seeing underwater was amazing. With the 25% refraction and clear water, it was almost too much to take in. Wow, how cool is this? Things like jumping off the 3 M diving board with all your gear on. Well, you will have to jump off a Destroyer deck or a chopper at 10-20 ft. Hold your tank strap, check the weight belt buckle, and regulator in, hand over mask, and give the OK to the DM. Then jump, oh yeah, cross your legs and point your Finns down just before you hit the water. You have to protect the groin region from sudden de-acceleration and the force of the water as you break the surface straight to the bottom, wearing approximately 100 pounds of gear where two divers were waiting to help if needed.

Man, the first time you hit the water from that height was a shock, but once all the bubbles left, and I got orientated, it was different. An excellent different, you know? Then you did your mask removal and recovery, tank off and back on, and a few other skills before getting the surface signal and the thumbs up. It was challenging but great three weeks. Because I was a V3 at the time, I failed the vision part of the medical. No biggie, there just happened to be a NAUI scuba diving course starting that October, so it's worth a try, and I had some experience. So I did the course, and the checkout dives were going to be in the spring. Too cold to do any diving in the St John River. Anyway, we were going on exercise for 5 weeks, as were most of the other guys on the course, so it made sense.

I got a posting message to Germany, 4 CER, Lahr that spring for four years. Sweet. Germany was an active first-line base. You had to have certain generic courses because we would spend seven to eight months in the field on exercise and training with different nationalities of Military Engineers. APC track course and dozer, 2 1/2 MLVW, 5/4 truck, Comms, and QL 5, a 6-month course done at CFB Chilliwack. Germany's field time consisted of different Exercises or foreign nation training.

Gun camp. Three weeks of machine guns, the General Purpose Machine gun, (GPMG), and the 50 cal. Thousands and thousands of rounds were fired from different vehicles and ground-mounted positions. Humping the Five-Oh was a two-man job. One had the gun body, and the other had the tripod, spare barrel, and spare ammo. We also interacted with they're diving teams as well. Even though I had done the NAUI course, I still dove and some of the guys in our troop, The Two Troop Tramps. (Andy Capp from the British comic strip was our mascot).

We had his picture stenciled on our dozer blades and on the M548 cargo carrier doors. My c/s was 28A). Some of the other guys were civilian divers, so we all hung around with each other. If I was working at the Lahr Sub Aqua Club and some of the guys needed air, I would fix them up instead of them flashing up the dive van and setting it all up for their compressor. The boys would be going out for fun, and if it was OK with the Dive O, sometimes I went.

I did much diving in Germany, France, Spain, and Austria. Each has its attraction: coves, underwater ledges, wrecks, caves, and currents. Whenever you felt like something different to shake it up, you had to select special spots that were kind of off the grid or the beaten path. It was always an adventure.

The running joke at home was that I would be back in a few hours; seven to eight o'clock at night soon was the regular, so when we went out with a group, Margret and Jennifer would come along. We ended up with a 1972 VW camper van, and that was the Dive van. It was all decked out with two beds, a fridge, a sink, table. When you wanted to go to bed, just a clip here and a strap there, the roof popped up, and the longer bed was up there. Racks for my tanks and spots for extras and spares made it easy to access something quickly. Then you weren't tossing the place inside out while wearing a wet suit. It is not a pretty site. I know. I've seen myself go there once or twice.

I base much of what I build and do on safety and with a certain sense of urgency in acquiring the said item. Working with high explosives, weapons, driving heavy track vehicles, motorcycle and Dispatch Rider Instructor, HA EOD basic, and a few side shows out of town. Then there's the whole breathing underwater thing.

You either get it, or you don't. I will use this next term very loosely, but sometimes it's just natural. Not to compare myself to any natural in sports, music, the arts, or flying we all know someone who is a natural. When you can assimilate with an environment like that, it's magical. I love to watch the Volvo around the world ocean racing, but that's where it stops. Long distance, no worries, leaving Table Bay, Cape Town, South Africa, with a 30-knot wind coming off Table Mountain, nope. There are eight crew on a 65-foot high tech 5 million Euro sailboat. With 25 knots, the average speed of forward advancement, and water constantly over the decks, awesome to watch, but not my cup of tea. Some of the skippers have done this six or seven times. Now, that's a different level of commitment.

So for shits and giggles, I am going to dig up my old log books, take a few minutes and get back to the early years, taking a drift dive through some ancient and forgotten times, good times.

My first dive in Germany was by the Austrian border in Lake

Konstance. There is a local club that we are friends with, and they have been diving with the Canadians for a few years. Usually, six to eight went in a group. Each either shared a ride or free-wheeled on their own. (families). It was a five-hour drive through southern Germany, mountains, vineyards, and sprawling forests. Much rebuilding was done after the wars, but there is still evidence from WW II in some smaller villages deep within the interior areas.

We usually got a campground spot, or if we were all just guys, we split on a hostile type room by the club. Just two rooms, with a bunkbed and a few twin beds. Hey a place to secure your kit, and it wasn't canvas. The neat thing about this area is that there once were train tracks around the lake. During WW II, the resistance blew up the rails to stop the Nazi supply system. There were some tracks and a boxcar along with masses of twisted metal. Since it was a lake, there were no tides to worry about, so it was an anytime dive spot. Fifty feet for forty five minutes, just taking it all in. Your mind is trying to process what you see, familiar but not quite right, you know?

Sometimes, you can make sense of it, and other times, WTF is all I could come up with. I think that that, for me, best describes my PTSD. I have seen much shit in my life, but there have been a few occasions where the WTF factor cannot even come close. I will skip this and get back to something on a lighter subject.

We went to Toulouse, France for the Easter long weekend to check out some shore dives. Once again, we contacted the local dive shop for air and dive locations. We had our VW van then, so I shared it with Ray Raymond. He was an MSE OP, a trucker in civilian talk, and had been diving for a few years also. Ray and I dived together for the next two years and developed a comfortable "buddy system."

If you were on the bottom grubbing and lost sight of each other, it wasn't the panic drill to pop up and search for your buddy. We were usually only a few meters away in the silt-screened water. Plastic arm slates are great for direct communications underwater. Great for directing students on their drills. There are PADI instructor slate kits with all the info on them, and the last slate has just lines to write what you want.

So, how do you write underwater anyway? Good question. The slates were made of SDR 30 sewer pipe. The white stuff. It already has a curve, so you cut the pipe in half, then about six-to eight inches long , depending on the length of your forearm. A few holes and secured with surgical tubing. That also allows for the expansion and contraction of your suit. We just used small golf or IKEA pencils to write with on the end of the tubing.

Later on, a white drafting eraser works to take off the marks in the post-dive clean-up. If I can see and understand it, I can usually build it. Within certain parameters, of course. Why spend $35.00 on something I can create and modify to meet my requirements? I even have some with my pre-written notes on for a particular dive. Another slate had your decompression table and stops, if needed, drawn out in the unlikely event that your dive computer will crap out on you.

After a few years of diving and courses, I was a Dive master, and got introduced to Tech Diving, and extreme depth diving, as well as Nitrox. Some of my first Tech dives were under the ice at Cold Lake, AB. During the annual Winterfest, there are even stock car, (NASCAR wannabe's) oval races on the ice. Yup, stock car races on the lake that you are about to dive under only a few hundred feet away. Just a bit left of centre.

With the ice being over three feet thick, several rounds on the chainsaw cutting a triangle-shaped hole takes over an hour. When you got close to the water, you climbed up from the hole in the lake; I'm just going to use this sentence as an example of what your mind translates from what you just read—climbing up from a <u>hole</u> in the lake.

Anyway, I just had to re-read it, so it made sense to me. Good to go. Why a triangle? There are only three sides to cut. The normal thinking for a hole is square or rectangle. Who digs a triangle hole in their yard unless it is for a plant or decorative touch? Tell anyone to dig a hole, and, well, the point is proven.

When pushing the sport up a few notches, so does the safety and site prep. As the DM, I had a 150-foot long line on my harness, which was tied to a pickup truck's hitch. I cannot drag that away, for

90

sure. The students had 100 feet, so they could never go past you. A two-section modular tent was set up with a Herman Nelson heater hose coming in for the much needed heat for thawing out when you surfaced. Here is another maybe unknown tidbit about lake ice. It looks primarily flat on top, with the pressure ridges along the shoreline, but on the underbelly of the ice, there are inverse valleys created from the ridges and small, well-two-foot dimples in the ice.

Now, remember, this would all be upside down. One of our cheats, or hacks as it is called now, was to take a cigarette and a few wooden matches in a ziplock baggie in your BCD. When you found a large enough dimple, we exhaled enough to drop the water level down so our mouth was above the water. Picture someone in a capsized boat, breathing in an air pocket—the same deal. Carefully get the smoke out without getting it wet. Remember, no bare hands: full gloves and a dry suit. Once you get that done, using the striker piece, you get flame, and smoking commences. It was just a few drags, but it was a quick buzz. And to freak out the students, you kept a lung full of smoke and when you dropped back into the water and exhaled, the bubbles were full of smoke. Another stunt was Moonwalking. With a dry suit, it is well dry inside. You wear a type of long underwear called Wooly Bears.

Air provides buoyancy and warmth. No water gets into your suit, so when working or teaching consecutive dives in a day, you're still dry and warm, not all pruned. So, back to the Moonwalking. Once under the ice, you inverted and put some air into the suit. Now, your feet are stuck to the ice by the force of the air in your suit. Puffy feet is the term and the most feared plight to find yourself in. It is not an urban myth, but the occurrence of this event is so rare. Well, that's how myths start.

The biggest fear is to have your inflator stick, causing a rapid and vast amount of air to enter your suit at an alarming rate of speed within seconds; you are looking like the Michelin Man at 75 feet. NOT GOOD. That is why we teach dry suit courses, to be able to 1. avoid accidents, and 2. how to quickly problem solve underwater, without caving to the natural urge to get to the surface. You have lots of gas on your back, so stay there and sort it out. That is the last option. Unfortunately, I have met all too many new divers who

91

bought all the Gucci kit and don't really understand how and why it does what it does.

Remember, it is underwater, so it works differently than on the surface. I had an old tee shirt from the Golan Heights that said, "I've done the Red, Dead, and the Med." This is a reference to the Red Sea, Dead Sea, and the Mediterranean Sea".

Mask removal demo at 30 feet.

The dive boat.

Israel - Touring Map and a few diving pictures

Chapter 14

The Red, The Dead and The Med.

I did two tours in the Middle East, September '92 to March '93 and May to November '98. On my first tour, I was a DM, but now I was an Instructor, and I was looking to dive into some old sites from '93 to see what has changed in five years. I had hooked up with a guy named Remo on my first tour, who was a retired Israeli Defence Force (IDF) SEAL and owned a dive shop in Akko, an hour north of Tel Aviv. We took a weekend trip to do a RECCE of the old haunts and see who was still around.

Remo had sold his shop and was now the PADI 5-star Rep for Israel. Nice to know. With the old stories coming out over a few Maccabee beers and some hummus. Always a staple of Middle Eastern bar snacks. Olives, pita bread, and assorted pickles made consuming the beverages much easier. The snacks represent the cultures; some different hummus versions were just at the next pub. The other beer was Gold Star. Maccabee beer is named after the followers of the Jewish leader Judas. And the Gold Star refers to the Star of Bethlehem. Shit, you learn at the bar. Three years of Sunday school condensed into a four-hour Pub crawl. Did I mention that I loved my job? The perks sometimes outweighed the hazards.

Eilat is located at the bottom of Israel, with Jordan on the right border and Egypt on the left border. It is about an eight to nine drive hour down past the West Bank, past the Dead sea, and the Dead Sea Salt Works. There is a place where you can go into the sea with benches, showers etc. It was located at the base of Masada, built by Herod the Great between 37 and 31 BCE. It was invaded by the Romans from 73 to 74 CE, where the war ended with the mass suicide of the remaining 960 Sicarii rebels. It is now a UNESCO World Heritage Sire. Good tour. If you ever thought of investing in salt stocks, in the tour, we were told that there is enough salt to feed the world twice over. That's why road salt is $5.99 for 25 Kg.

After the pit stop, we got back on the road to our next stop, Yolvata, the only city you leave the Dead Sea district before Eilat. The driving is all on steep roads around lava rock mountains. The Jordan border patrols drag a pipe with chains on it behind their vehicle. The road is sand, so if someone tried to scale the two razor wire fences at least 4 m, their footprints would leave the trail. There is also a second fence 5 m away making up the laneway, so even if you made the first fence, getting to the next one by the road and scaling it unscathed would be almost impossible. Several vehicles are doing the route with staggered times so no pre-set schedule could be followed. BTW, the valley that you would have to climb is at the extreme pro level, so the use of natural defences works here. Smoke and stretch break, then the last burst before the big city.

As UN members, there were apartments that you could rent out for a few days when in Eilat. $20.00 each per night. Six people per unit. That gave you a place to rack and wash your kit. The main part of the city was only a few minutes away. With the vehicle keys in the desk draw, (this prevented the urge to go sightseeing later when you had a few). Craig, the owner of Aqua Sport was a Canadian from BC and dove on the North Sea Riggs for 15 years before getting bent once too many times. His wife was the travel coordinator in the UK office, and when he retired from saturation diving, running a Dive resort was a good fit. Now since we were in Canadian Military, CANEX stocked favorite Canadian beer brands, because truthfully, the two national beers sucked. With this little tidbit in mind, before the trip, we pooled some cash, about $40.00, which got us four flats. (24 beer x 4). After our first day of diving at his bar, we started into the draft on his tab. His office was on top of his bunker. Every large building or business had a bunker in case of enemy shelling. Craig and I chatted about some dive areas to visit later and then he breaks out a few Montecristo number 4's brought in from Egypt by a friend. Cubans are hard to get over here.

I opened up my kit bag and brought out a 12 pack of Molsen Canadian and gave it to him as a welcoming gift. Into the special bar fridge, it went. The party and stories went late into the night with everyone having a smashing time. The demographics of the tourists ranged from, young blond Swedish and Danish beach bunnies to the retired 65-plus group with cash to burn. The latter group consisted of mainly UK types. Even witnessed the black knee socks and sandals on the beach, with the long shorts coming down, leaving just about an inch of white skin to bake in the 38 C plus weather.

Now here is an other nice to know fact about this area of the world. Everyone carries here, from teenagers to bank tellers, especially the male adult population over 18. They have to serve for three years, then three months every year until 55, or they cannot longer do their duties for a variety of reasons. The state transportation is free to use, and if more soldiers than civilians wait for the bus, they (the citizens) just get the next one. The reasoning behind this thinking is that if the Army is called to duty, you have no excuse to get to work. Interesting, no? Maybe we could learn something from them. But then, on second thought, our population would be up in arms because we are getting something free on their dime. Fucken. A-holes. We also get free housing and don't pay taxes, I was told by an anti-military person one day.

News to me. I guess that I'm getting a huge refund this year. Ya right. The sad part is that the general masses really know very little about what their troops actually do besides the once-in-a-decade scandal. Someone recently asked me how I could do another man's bidding on world affairs. First, it is not a man but a small organization called the United Nations, with around 50 countries as members. Have you heard of them? And to boot, a Canadian PM, Lester Pearson was the President of the United Nations National General Assembly, dubbed the Father of Peacekeeping. They even have a Training Centre named after him, and an Airport too. We may as well throw a Nobel Peace Prize to top it off. So there. Sorry about that. Where was I?

Their sidearms consisted of the 9 mm Jericho, Glock 17 &19, and the H&K P11. The assault rifle of choice was the M4A1 Carbine. Plus, throw in a few AK 47s just for the poor folks. And all on the beach. No kicking sand in my face, thank you. You would get blown away today with the values of this generation.

We were planning a night dive to Moses Rock to see Clown fish. The big danger was that they have poison spikes on the top of their dorsal fin.Thats why you always wore some type of glove. Look but don't touch. Heard that before... Calm night, six of us made our way to the beach in front of Aqua Sport. Last minute checks, lights, glow sticks, shore light. Splash time. It was a smooth sand bottom with few references, so the compass route was the choice. Moses Rock was about 300 m offshore, only in 25-30 feet of water. The coral head rose from the sea bed to a height of 5 m. They say that the coral reefs grow about one mm a year. You can do the math. Old is what I came up with. Got some great diving pics.

After talking with Craig, we planned a two-day dive trip to Egypt, crossing at Taba. He had his dive boats moored there to avoid the lengthy customs process coming back into Israel. Just taking the bus was a two-hour process. I can imagine them stripping the dive boat looking for "contraband." Within his empire, there was a photoshop, and a staff diver would come along as a spare DM/Videographer. VHS back then on the PAL format, not the NTSC that, is the North American standard. The camera and case were as big as a boombox. Watch That '70s show for a refresher. They got to get that transferred over sometime. Add it to the list.

We did nine dives, including a move like a night dive. So many different species of fish and the corals' bright colours were illuminated by our high intensity underwater lights. Cuttlefish, Parrot fish, Moray eels, Yellow Barracuda schools, and the monster giant clam. Yes, sir, just like on Gilligan's Island that, Ginger and Mary Anne had as wash basins for the laundry. Just something that the Professor whipped up.

Back at the apartment, we are packing up for the now-dreaded trip uphill to the Golan Heights. Yes, it was a trek uphill. We went to the camp from sea level to over 1600 feet above. You could make it to Little T's pub in Tiberius for a burger if you're lucky. They had a monkey as the bar mascot, brought back from Africa by the owner years before, and he would tug on your pant leg to get some provided treats. He knew the drill. Get the new draft guys to feed me. After a few trips, the novelty had worn off, and he was seen as a pest just begging for scraps.

Now, on the last leg of a trip, one of the guys, Ed Butt, an electrician who also was my roommate, saw a scrappy little runt of a dog just before the turn into the gate. As soon as he opened the door, the dog took off into the field. I hope he knows where to run. Just outside the camp before the gates to the border crossing is an Anti Tank ditch 25 m wide and 5 m deep going to the Jordan and Syrian borders where the cliffs and valleys are not providing natural obstructions. In the middle of the road, you could see a maintenance hole cover. It's just an everyday thing that you would see anywhere else.

They had the same thing in Germany when I was with the Regiment. After WW II, the German people rebuilt everything for demolition in case of another attempt to be invaded again. The bridges, highways, and major intersections were prepped to blow. Under the manholes were regular concrete-lined shafts 4-5 m deep. Into these Measle shafts (?) I don't really know the proper name. We would place in these 50-pound wheels that looked like cheese, hence the term "Cheese wheels," that were high explosives to a certain mark in the shaft. The mark was a calculated charge load for a specific crater. Small, medium, large, or supersized. Just the road or the whole intersection.

So we were told on our first weekend orientation trip to the Sea of Galilee and the Jordan River that German Jews who fled to Palestine during and after WW II brought this idea with them. Hey, if it works, why break it? Sorry about that. Let's move on.

99

Lion fish off Moses rock in the Red Sea.

18 tanks. 3 each for 6 divers.

The advanced Open water course Akko 1998.

Chapter 15

Digger Dog

The next day, Ed Butt and I were going to Haifa to get some parts and, after getting our trip ticket, tools, and our AWOL bag, just in case. To this day, I still have stuff ready for my AWOL bag for an overnighter. Margret still didn't believe that when we went to Australia, all I had was my old NBCD suit bag, about the same size as a carry-on. Six socks, underwear, tee shirts, two long-sleeve tee shirts, two pairs of shorts, and a second pair of long pants. Sandals as second footwear. Shaving kit. Done. Buy anything else. We were staying at our daughter's place, so there was no hotel shock.

We did our pickups and a bit of the tourist thing before heading back to meet the 1600-hour return time. Just as I was coming through the S turn around the lava rock wall, Ed asked me to slow down. He was looking for the dog that we had seen last night. He finally saw him by the AUSBAT gate, so he got out, and I went to turn in the truck. He came back with this little dog. Hey, this guy's name is Digger, Digger Dog.

This was the start of his long and giving life. He became the Engineer mascot, with free rein over the camp. The section all chipped in for the vet to check Digger out. Shots and a de-flea bath, he was ours to care for. Dog food from a local store and carrots from the cooks, Digger had it made.

Now, why I brought this up is because when I went back in '98, Digger was still there, but the EME section now had him. He was in sad shape, and Ed quickly got him back after an argument came up with an old draft mechanic, "Who gives you the right to take our mascot. He has been an EME dog for three years, new draft fuck head."

Well, Ed was going to smoke him, but instead replied, "Well, new, new draft Fuck head, Greg and I found him back in '92. Come hear Digger boy, come on boy." Digger popped up his head and came to Ed. We looked at each other. Fuzzy cork soaker. (SNL). After a few weeks, he was back up to a slower but happier dog. On his collar was the number 16 for his tours. He would now come on the Friday 10 Km march up to Mt. Bental and back. He usually was in the truck, with the occasional lap or two around the groups before going back into the truck.

The driver was usually a guy named Terry Miller. He was an EGS tech. He worked on generators. Once he retired he went to work for CAT Generators. Quite successful, from what I have heard. Terry was also from Trenton at 86 ASU. We were 81 AEF at the time. He was also a Newfie and a hoot. Now, anyone who knew him knew that Terry had a special trick he would pull on the unknowing. "I bet you that I can drink my beer and put my foot on the ceiling at the same time."

Now, at this time, I will come clean and admit that I cannot remember which leg he was missing. You only got one chance at a guess. Sorry, Terry. So the bets were laid, and as he picked up his beer, he reached over with his other hand, popped off his leg, touched the ceiling, and then chugged his beer, or double rum and cokes, at the Club 125, St Hubert on our 10 day Middle East prep.

Needles, uniforms, UN IDs, training, and some time off. It was a great way to meet who you will work with for the next six months. Then the budget cuts came in, and that is with a broad stroke of the brush how the RTFs were conceived. The same thing was done to satisfy the voters with the disbanding of the Airborne Regiment. How many colours did they earn in all the conflicts that they represented our flag in, gone with a stroke of a pen. It is mightier than our swords.

Ed and I also did some diving together through the Med the Red and floated in the Dead. On one 60-hour leave, we went to Akko and did some diving with Remo and his friends. Great boat dives, and not so great for some. Baby Bubblers, as we called them, sometimes got seasick. Chumming up the Med on the way back to the club. The other great thing was learning about the local foods and culture was the need and nice to know. No shorts in holy places, don't talk to these ones, stay in this area. Also, it was for our protection. We were, for all intents and purposes, white, youngish foreigners with a bit of cash. Otherwise, why would we be here?

The nightlife was also a real eye-opener at some clubs. Hey, there are no Gentlemen's Clubs in Israel. I mean the design and music. Queen Sheba's on the waterfront had brilliant Egyptian decorations and design. We were in Akko one time and a Chuck Norris movie, "HellBound." was being shot. He was staying at the Carlton downtown. Some of the movie was filmed when Remo had his dive shop. I have pictures that match places in the movie. So we have just finished our diving and are famished from the trips, bringing the gear off the boat to the van, then to the hotel to rinse off the suits and lay everything out to dry off before it would be packed away later that night.

The search for a place to eat something began in the city once the parking was sorted. Since there were six of us an outdoor empty table was a hot ticket. One was situated across the street, and as some others were leaving, we snagged the table and got chairs for everyone. Drinks and food were ordered, person-watching began. After a few minutes, we all looked at each other and the same look was there. Something is different. A few more trucks are here, more IDF is coming in, Barriers, WTF is going on? Then there was a disturbance at the end of the cafe. It was Chuck Norris in the flesh. They were filming a scene here, thus all the extras that popped up.

We were given a choice: finish in 30 minutes and leave, or stay for the takes, maybe a few hours. So 1.) watch a live shoot with CN in a Middle Eastern country, or 2.) go and sweat your ass off walking around looking at trinkets. If you watch the movie and pause at the street scene, zoom way, way, way in, the second table from the right you can see us. I loved my fucken job.

We had patios set up in the Golan. Each section had a patio area for BBQ parties, and on the last Friday of the month, there were rotation patio parties where the different sections hosted the patio that night. They became a thing to look forward to, planning the food, signature beverage, and a theme game to do with the other visitors. A few jobs got the quick fix when that time approached.

Our fire protection for the base was a huge water reservoir powered by a BMW motor. It also was the unofficial pool. I even was a paid NPF employee as a life guard there. It seemed to be a plumber thing. So was the last plumber, RL. He was a good floor hockey goalie. Some great parties took place there. No swimming drunk was a rule that everyone enforced. The CO was strict, and if caught, the area would be off-limits for ALL.

We used to have Tuesday sports night that we would go to the little town of Metula, which is located very close to the borders of Lebanon, and Syria. A Canadian Jewish organization built a sportsplex with a hockey rink, pools, saunas, and workout areas. Around five or six went from CANBAT, and some from other contingents. FINBAT sometimes lets a few attend, and as Ed would say, Hear comes Jari Kurri on a breakaway. After the scrimmage, a hot tub and sauna to sweat out the dust that manages to get everywhere. We had found a local pizza joint that would make yours in the stone oven, charcoal dust included. After a few trips, the owner would have a place for us. We were also the delivery guys for the to-go orders. Sometimes, a dozen pizzas were in the passenger seat.

One Sunday, we got a camp-wide memo saying that due to the weekend shelling, Hockey Night in Metula was cancelled until further notice. As luck would have it, our pizza place got hit during the attack. Too bad they were good pizzas. We could not see the shelling take place because the mountain range blocked the view in that direction, but we could see the borders to the North and West. Monday morning, about 1100, and every morning for a week, Big Brother and Sister would fly over, usually a pair of F16s.

When they hit the border, the boom boom of the afterburners as they hit supersonic speeds. The sun reflects off the fuselage giving sharp flashes of the jets doing loops as they approached their targets. Sometimes, you could see the 500-pounders glint before two puffs on the hillside, then a few seconds later, a low rumble.

As mentioned before about the explosives in the road, I had seen this before in Germany, and on my EOD HA basic course. It was mid-October 1986, and because some of us had flown in from

105

Europe, the service flights were only once a week. We had some time off to see old friends. I made a few calls to a lifelong friend. Mike Stanford lived in Burnaby, and he was an RCMP officer. We did grade school, junior high, and senior high together.

We both went into the RCMP recruitment centre to sign up. Both in mid-grade 12, looking for something else. Wait for your school to be finished, then come back. The same at the Army recruiter: get your grade 12 diploma, then come back. So we did as we were told by two grown men with guns.

I got into the Army, and Mike into the RCMP, who retired with 35 years in. He is now a professional photographer with a studio in BC—the whole ball of wax. Mike is also the recipient of the Medal of Bravery. He was awarded for his courage in aiding a fellow officer through a house fire safely to the exit when the smoke overtook him.

Well done, buddy.

Well sage advice that turned out to be. That piece of paper is the first one in my binder of certificates. I had a conversation with someone a while back, and they never finished their grade 12 due to his circumstances and continued with his life. We discussed a GED, but it was just another piece of paper. Yes, it is, but the world runs on these pieces of paper.

Colour outside the lines if you wish. We are all entitled to our beliefs and convictions. Once I found that I actually loved to learn, then did the practical to prove the theory. I was a sponge. Courses were free in the military, and to go to college or distance learning, they would pay 50% of the fees. Some guys did sports trips, I did courses. This was probably the biggest decision in my life up to this time. Go back to school, or have a few at the Midtown tavern for the happy hour. We had a few at the tavern and, the next morning went back to JL Ilsley High for the last few months. Choices, choices. Some good, some bad. But you still have to choose.

Since the area around us was mined with both anti-personnel and anti-tank mines, staying on the hard stand was strictly followed. There were areas cleared that the farmers used, and roads around the camp were safe. What you see in the movies doesn't even hold a candle to the real-life experience. Smells, sound, heat, cold, where you are at that moment give you the total body surround sound and chair effects that the Source can't match.

"A mine is the perfect soldier."

A quote from Pol Pot, the leader of the Khmer Rouge during the Cambodian genocide in the late '70s, killing between 1.5 to 2 million citizens. Stuff you learn in the military history DL courses. It lies there just waiting, never asleep. After a while, the records, if any, were lost, and fields became overgrown. So what you can't see can't hurt you, they say, except for the forgotten mine. You could tell where an old field was when you would see dead animals lying around. They were called Poof cows. There they were, then Poof, flipping over in the air or seeing a chunk of flesh hit the ditch.

Anti-tank mines needed 250-350 pounds to set them off, whereas anti-pers mines only needed ounces to trigger. They usually just took off a hoof or the back end. To experience a few hours of mines going off around the camp was something else.

We were playing floor hockey on the parade square. It had a six-foot brick wall around the perimeter, keeping that orange ball in bounds. Someone called out that there was a fire in the field adjacent to the main gate. A Syrian was trying to get across the border, so the IDF was launching para flares like Natal Day on Citadel Hill, trying to get eyes on the line jumper, and that's when the fire started. 2nd period of intermission entertainment until the first explosion. Bang....anti pers..yup ....BANG anti-tank fucking YEAH.

The Eng O wanted Smokey to get the fire brigade to fight the fire. A Hard No. He is responsible for the Camp, but an orchard, let it burn. If you haven't noticed, it is a minefield in every respect of the words. BOOM. Bunker alarms going off. This is not a drill. We stayed in bunkers for about six hours, in whatever dress we had on at the time. You could change into your bunker kit, but lying on the cot in my sweats was good for me. Main Gate to CANLOG was changed to CANBAT just before my second tour.

Digger Dog.

Weekend service call.

UNDOF main gate, 1992.

Chapter 16

The orange card

The Orange card was one of the most cherished items you could have on tour here. This three-by-two-inch card enabled you to cross into Syria during opening hours without doing the three-day prior sign-up, and I hope the round trip memo makes it back from the UN HQ or the Pentagon located in Syria. We had a Canadian building with bunks, a coffee room, lounge area there. It was mainly for the few who had to do multiple days on a job over there, and the permanent CDN staff lived elsewhere. If you cannot make it back to the border and have an hour to spare, go through the first two check points, Alpha and Charlie gates. Charlie gate was in the middle and had MP's from the different contingents stationed there, as well as the K9 unit. A safe haven if needed. Then Bravo gate, the Israeli one. This had computers, a few offices, a driving well for inspections, and a 20-foot-high concrete wall around it, blocking the view of the camp except for the gates. On a bad day, they would even pop off the WV hubcaps to look for smuggled items. If the computers were down, no luck unless you had an Orange card. Every Engineer section had two cards each, so one guy didn't have to go alone. Other sections had the same arrangements if they were frequent flyers.

The Syrian LOs (Liaison Officers) were laid back and didn't care what was going on in Palestine. They do not recognize the '49 agreements. And just to piss off the IDF, they had a table and chairs set up on a hill with a thatched umbrella for shade. You had to have tea first, in full view of the IDF, just because they could. Are you going to shoot me for having tea? As you leave the LO position, you drive through the town of Quneitra. It was leveled in the seven-day war, and was never reconstructed. The population before was 80-90K, now just a few nomads. The area next on to the main road to position 28 which was an UN stop. The IDF stopped here instead of advancing forward to Damascus. It is only about 20 km from the city centre. Along this road, there were shacks made up from tin sheets, lava rock and jumper cables to the power lines for juice. Fraggle Rock is what we called it. The to the small shopping area. Popular because it was just across the line, and the parking was good. Silver Mike, The Penguin, The Cave outlet store, and the Gold Guy. Everyone's favorite spot. Margret has two, three, and four band rings, chains etc. If you had the time, Damascus had the Souk Market. Towels, bathrobes, shirts, suits, shoes, gold, silver, spices and anything else you wanted.

During my last tour, the NCT from Esquimalt BC along with 20 FDU - P divers, came to help with a 30-day re-wiring of the base job. Any longer in the country, all kinds of alarm bells go off at UNDOF HQ. Then special allowances come into effect. The same logic behind the 56 day roto's. Can't afford to pay you, so we will burn you out instead. The gold orders were coming in by the pad full. They were buying for friends back home, too.

Everyone wants a puzzle ring and gold dog tags with chains. We got paid in USD and then had to convert it to Syrian pounds. The base rate was around 50:1. But the barber shop on the Dark Side gave you a few points better. I think the most I exchanged at one time was $2500.00 USD @ 52:1= 130K pounds. So you stay, have tea, and watch it being counted out in 50 and 100's. Elastic bundles of 10K. Why only ten K? If lost, it is only about $190-$200, and it is easy to count quickly into the Adidas bag and off to get the gold. When you were coming back across, the guards could search the vehicle and any bags in it but could not search you. Sporting our Mr. T starter kits and rings to even make Birk's Jewelers look twice, off to the patio to give the owners they're slightly used gold. The price point on gold back then was about $290.00 per oz, and some single guys spent their UN pay on gold chains for an investment. Elias had a gold shop in Damascus with a shawarma wagon across the street.

Always fix up your hangover. A bottle of Fanta orange to wash it down while he opened up his shop and put on coffee. We were picking up rings for our wives. Elias showed us a chain he was making for an Austrian. It looked like a 5/16" anchor chain, 24 inches long. Each link was one ounce—his retirement investment plan. Didn't believe in Mutual funds, I guess.

They got way more pay than us, but all they got was uniforms, food, and a building to stay in. They made their own way home, ours were paid for. We had a theatre, Moral shows, subsided R & R. Not them. So, sometimes, it is not about the money. Three different messes. They had combined messes or just a room. Add a Duty-Free shop on the base, a pool, and lots of trucks, staff cars, and vans. At the back of the Ausbat compound was the Million dollar parking lot with about 50 assorted BMWs, AUDIs, and 911s of all styles and colours. Toss in a Corvette and a LandRover to be on the safe side. Then there was the wrecker pile—about 250K worth of Bad investments.

The NCT and the divers stayed in some apartments in a nearby town, Qatzrin. Our Israeli purchaser and interrupter, a retired IDF LCol, lived in the same town, so it worked out well. There was a small mall and a few bars/patios that were always full. Most times if someone was coming over for a visit on HLTA, they stayed there. The bus stop was there for different routes, east or west.

We had some fun section parties at his little Tiki bar camp on the Sea of Galilee. I remember being the DD one night, and on the drive home, we got lost in the fog and drove right up to the IDF base just down the road from us. Oops, wrong turn. At one point, you could hear the track vehicles in the tank tracks beside us that ran parallel to the road. The Merkava is a series of main battle tanks used by the IDF—the road tremors with the rumbling of a 50-ton tank cruising at 50 km 100 feet away. Again, thanks for the big white UN van with the blue and white plates. Our work van was being retired, plate 2424. Sgt Dale Gorman, a Carpenter, had brought that van up from the Sinai when the camp was stood up 20 years before on his first tour. The plate was mounted on a nice oak base with a brass plate and his dates. Fun and good memories. Some pictures I cannot look at because of lost friends who went way to soon. Remember a few chapters ago? Moving along.

During the tour, I got to travel to outposts from Mt Herman, which straddles the border between Syria and Lebanon, to Position 28, down on the Jordan and Israel border. Traveling from the camp to an altitude of 2810 m above sea level to Mt Herman during the summer tour could be done in a Pathfinder, but when the winter

112

came, three to four m of snow could block the road, and the camp could be isolated for several weeks at a time, so ensuring all the heating and cooking equipment was in good working order. It was usually a day trip there since it was a three-hour ride after you got thru the gates. The hassle was worth it. The cooks at the camp, Austrians owned their own Gasthaus back home, and this was paid practice for them. Some great meals came out of that kitchen.

Not the same at Position 60. Just across the Syrian border, Position 60 was a large Polish camp (POLBAT), with about 70 troops there. Their main job was border patrol and logistical support. Frank Piper and I had a job in the kitchen one day. The gas range and a steam kettle were down. The first thing we used to do was hit the side of the ovens with small wooden bats to get the mice and other things living in the dark spaces a chance to leave. The floors sometimes were covered with roaches and other creepy crawlers. Sometimes, it is a mouse that got into the control box and got fried in the process, or just months of filth built up. The cook here was Polish but big, with a wife beater shirt on, the stained apron just covering his gut, and clogs on his feet. The helper just brought out a pig body out of the walk in fridge. Supper, I guess.

The Jordan border is in the background.

the Dead Sea Salt Works. Dredges pumping out the water to dry

Diving site in Eilat.

Israel and Lebanon border.

Chapter 17

R&R

My first R&R was coming up after two months. You have to take one before the new draft arrives and the other near the end of your tour. We were going to Latakia, Syria, located in the northwestern region about 50 km from Turkey, with Cyprus 100 km west. The Mediterranean Sea ends just 125 km north in the Gulf of Iskenderun. Myself and a fellow Engineer, Mike Lalong, an electrician, were sharing a room at the Golden Beach Hotel. It was a long and dusty trip, sometimes waiting for the roto-till-drawn cart with eight people and a few kids to crest the top of the hill and pull over broke up the endless desert features and was the hourly excitement. I will never complain about an Irving gas station washroom again. Another lesson learned.

Having a ziplock bag with a roll of Charmin two-ply is a lifesaver on these road trips. Still have a roll in a bag stuck away somewhere, I'm sure. The restrooms here are called WC (water closet). It was in a closet, and there was water from a rusted spigot. Thus ended what was in the room, besides two foot prints and a hole. I will stop there. No further explanation is needed. The Syrian Army had check points at every other town, and the UN bus just stopped for a plate check and off on the bumpy road again.

On the side of the road were the contents of a beat-up Mercedes 200SE scattered like garbage in front of the car while the family watched in fear as the looting continued. We left them in a cloud of dust and diesel fumes. I had dozed off for a bit, and then the horns blaring woke me up as we reached the city limits. Right on the beach, our hotel is huge around 500+ rooms. This is going to be fun.

Now, here is another pearl of wisdom that the upper echelon thought would deter fraternizing amongst the troops on R & R. Since you shared a room for the whole tour, having a single room would have been nice for a few days, but nope. Even married couples had to be celibate. Our room was on the 6th or 7th floor, facing the town. The real expensive rooms faced the ocean—no big deal.

I didn't plan on spending much time here besides sleeping a few hours. There was a huge tub and a bidet in the floor-to-ceiling tiled bathroom. Two twin beds separated by a small night stand would fit the bill perfectly. We flipped a coin to see who got the beer and then grabbed some loungers, putting on a tee shirt to "reserve" it while the other got to have a bath first. A one-hour time was set, then switched while the other checked out the beach scene. I won the toss. See ya in an hour!

The tub was filled, beer on ice, and a Monte Cristo #4 cigar. About half the cigar and three beers in, there is a knock on the door, and then it swings open. In comes someone from housekeeping. She came right in with the extra towels and around the corner to drop them off without even noticing me in the tub. On her way back out, she came in to leave the hand towels, and got an eye full. Her biggest laugh wasn't me in the tub with my beer in hand, yes, a beer, but that the bidet was filled with ice and Carlsberg Gold beer, with the ashtray on the bowl lip.

Hey, I'm a plumber. Utilizing the resources available at the time and adapting it for your needs. And it was right next to the tub. No digging into a cooler or the trash can full of ice. Then later, all you had to do was get rid of the empties, and no water to deal with when you are hung over the next day. One of the things that the Pre Med briefing mentioned was to stay away from buffets and sauces. You didn't know how long the food was out and who had had their fingers in it, so if it is fried or BBQ'd, it should be safe. Only drinks from a can or bottle with a metal screw cap. Anything else, who knows what it is, especially water. Our clinic did some tests on the bottled water, and the water that we treated in the plant was better quality.

With Mike back, my turn for the beach. He gave me some quick pointers and the lay of the area. Chairs secured and I'll see you down there. The Beach was massive, with a huge yacht anchored only a few 100 m off shore. The Pharo is approximately 125 ft long with a beam of 30-35 ft. Their tender was a 35 ft Hurricane RIB with twin

250 hp inboards. Could that thing fly?

Now, just a bit off-topic for a second. Someone asked me why when explaining distances, I use meters and feet mixed. Stick to one or the other. Well, for long distances, I use the firing range and a football field for smaller items. On the Kingston 600 m range, we started the students at the 300 m line, had them load a mag, safe on, and advance to the 200 m line and adopt the prone position. Oh ya, they have 30 seconds to go 100 m with full webbing and gas mask carrier. We (the RSOs) would walk behind them, watching pieces of kit bounce off.

At the 200m, then ready the weapon and on the command, fire. Unload, load, weapons on safe and advance to the 100 m where the test starts. After 100's of range days, those distances are easy to guess at. A football field (NFL) is in yards. Sunday afternoon football keeps me occupied sometimes. Move the sticks 10 yards for the next down. And there are big lines on the grass for easy reference.

So, back to the boat. Later that day, we rented a paddle boat and went for a closer look. The crew was all in white, as well as the owner. A big gentleman, with a huge white handlebar mustache got behind the helm of the tender and put her on step as soon as he was untied from the yacht. The rest of the family was well dressed, even in riding gear, whip and all. Got a few good pictures. If I remember, I will dig up the old album—the day of the Kodak 110 pocket camera. No one had iPhones then.

We found a little cafe just outside the market, and the menu was all grilled items: kabobs, steak, fish, and veggies. A few of us gathered there for supper, and the food was really good. We got to know the owner, and one of his kids spoke English. After s few minutes talking with him, the Dad came over to us and brought the Turkish coffee over as a welcoming drink. That is one of the things that I used to love in Syria. When we were either working there or on leave, the locals wanted to make a friend first, then you could buy something. The trip usually was the whole day by the time all the coffee was gone and goods were loaded up. The market was a popup type, only for the weekend. All kinda of artisans practicing their trades, from pottery to trinkets of all fashion. Margret still has three small blue glass-blown pieces that I got that day. After all the moves and damages to our furniture, they are still intact. The man who made these for me took about seven to ten minutes to make them. Mike got a couple, also. All tolled, about three USD.

Wake-up calls were always ordered, so you didn't sleep the day away. That is what the beach lounge chairs were for. There is always someone selling something to you, just like in Cuba or the Bahamas, and no age restrictions. A young boy, about 10 or 12 was going around with a clear bag with different kinds of beer and pop. If you wanted something, he would go back to the stand and get your order. So it only makes sense to tip good and you get good, no great service. The Syrian pound (SP) was about 50:1, so 100 SP was two bucks. A beer was 75 SP, so two were 150 SP. We gave 200 SP, with a good tip left over for him. It didn't take him long to figure that the Canadians were good tippers and courteous, not rich, overbearing tourists.$200 USD = 10,000 SP. It was a good 60 hr R&R.

Chapter 18

Around the country

Although I have done some sailing in the past (the White Sail program back in the 1970s and a few Stink Pot and Rag races as rail meat), I am a power-boater at heart. We have a 34-foot Mainship Trawler, Tapped Out, which we have extensively travelled over the past seven years. With the revitalization of the race, which had not been run for several years, the Club was buzzed with activity in preparations for the BBQ and the Skipper's briefing. Several other power-boaters had been able to get on as crew, and in passing, I had been talking to Rick Tinga, who mentioned that he had just come in from Bluffer's Park on

Catlin's Nonsuch 33. I expressed some interest in the race and that maybe I could ride along as ballast.

Catlin is of Romanian background, having attended Naval Academy and served in the Merchant Marine for several years before immigrating to Canada, his piloting skills are definitely a notch or two above the Weekend sailor. He has been a member of the club for many years (known as the Weatherman) and has sailed around the County numerous times single-handed in the Red Witch with only minor incidents, as he described them. He was more than happy to have me as the fourth, which would help on the shifts. "We would leave at 0800 to get to the Murray Canal swing bridge at 0900. Grab your wet weather gear and spare socks, and see you then. I will convert you to a sailboater yet, my friend."

Now before I get further into the story, I will lay some background. I have never done the outside route, and also never motored/sailed through the night. The Race is approximately 120 NM, starting Presquile Bay at the fairway marker 1100 hrs sharp Saturday and ending at Myers Pier Mark Q52 at Belleville Sunday. Doing some quick math we would be under sail until around approximately 0600 hrs the next day. The weather is supposed to be not too bad, 15 - 20 knots from the SSW with a wind shift from the West and then from the North later that night. And just a small chance of rain. Seas about 1.5 to 2m. Sounds like a good day to go sailing, were his famous last words...

Reporting 30 minutes prior to launching for the safety brief and vessel familiarization, we slipped and proceeded to the canal. Just off B dock, Spank'n Mad was hard aground and with all hands heeling to free the keel. Now, for those who do not know, there is an unwritten law of the sea: if you come upon a vessel in distress, you are obliged to offer assistance. We received a tow line and with the 30 horses churning up the bottom, we got her free and out to the channel markers. We will just bank that good deed in Neptune's book for future use.

The trip to the canal was filled with anticipation and tactical discussions on when the wind shifts will aid the over 825 Sq feet of sail this Winnebago on the water boasts to carry. There was a piper on the lead sailboat piping the eight boats through the canal, with well-wishers on the banks waving and taking pre-race pictures. (it might come in handy for insurance purposes later.....). This seemed like the time to have the traditional good luck libation—Gin and Tonic to fight off scurvy and malaria. Catlin asked for the ratio, and I sang out 3:1.

Unfortunately, I neglected to say what to what. I think he forgot the tonic. Once out through Brighton Bay, we were on station 20 minutes prior and did some timed runs and a few jibes. With the sound of the start gun, all craft made it through with a clean start. Something that I had not previously experienced in the Wednesday night races at CFB TYC. With Nickelson Island in sight, there is only a slight breeze. Cruising at a blistering 1.3 knots we start to develop a beam slap with the boom violently jolting as it dipped into the water. The residual effect was that the second baton sleeve end came open, and the baton started to work out of the sail. It's not good, and we are less than one hour into this trip.

After some discussion (Rick and Catlin talking, I just smiled and nodded politely), we (me and Catlin) went up on deck, lowered the sail, removed the baton and decided to install it later.

With Scotch Bonnet abeam, the decision is to reinstall the baton, so we (me and Catalin) do the process again, and 15 minutes later, the sail is back up, trimmed and catching some wind. With the fleet in sight, the wind is picking up, and we are doing an enjoyable 5-6 knots, seas 1.5 m. Then, the baton sleeve end opens up yet again, and the baton gradually proceeds to work itself loose. Within five minutes, it gently slips out, and Catlin says to me, "Catch it if you can." I casually looked at the depth sounder.

181 feet. See ya.

Luckily, we got spares, so I am not diving today. The mid-afternoon meal of salmi sandwiches is served, and some dark clouds are visible astern, approaching rather quickly. Within a few minutes, the winds are increasing and we take turns dressing for the incumbent weather. I recall that there was a slight chance of showers. It is around 1600 hours and the rain is here with winds of 20-25 knots.

"This is good," Catalin says, "She needs wind."

Spoken like a seasoned sailor and within an hour, we have caught and passed three boats. One of the clubs entrants, LayLee, was doing some rather violent maneuvers and the last we saw of them, they were heading south towards New York. Several hails on the VHF got no joy so we hope for the best. I will let Eric tell his own tale. His rudder snapped off 18 inches below the waterline, so when the boat heeled, they lost steerage. I would not want to steal his thunder.

We are now approaching Mark K14 with Timber Island and the False Ducks in sight. The wind is shifting as predicted, and a sea state of 2.5 – 3 m is now the norm. Sustained winds of 25 knots on the wind meter with gusts of 30 + and the occasional rouge wave keep the crew on their toes. One of the crew that I have not mentioned up until now is Catalin's friend Shannon. A novice sailor, she was not feeling well, so Rick gave her some Gravel to help her out. She, as we politely put it, slept around the County... Things were looking good, on the course, Catalin on the helm, and I was facing the stern looking for the rouge waves, which were becoming more frequent.

At one point, Rick had her surfing at 11.6 knots, and Catalin was averaging 9-10 knots. Smoking. We are now at K11 and heading for the stacks at Bath, course 005°M, and the time is 1845 hours. Why am I so sure of the time and course, you ask, because we were just hit by a large wave, and another quickly followed, picking up the Nonsuch and turning her opposite to the boom. Not good.

"We just lost the boom," Catalin cried out as I looked up and saw the centre of the wishbone fold like a house of cards, and it sliced the sail a good 10 feet up, then the leeward part of the boom buckles like a cheap lawn chair and begins to thrash to the extents of the sheets. Catalin gives me the helm and orders us into the wind.

After a few anxious moments of cranking the engine, we are under power and plowing into the waves. Rick and Catalin secured the boom fragments and bundled the sail up as best as they could. I must admit with all the excitement and just trying to hang on there was concentrated effort by all, with no panic or uncertainty of the task at hand. Within 20 minutes, they were both back in the cockpit, and we tried to distill the past few moments. I stayed at the helm for the next hour as we discussed the whole event repeatedly, the adrenaline slowly wearing off.

Once we got to Cressey Point and into the reach, I took my turn to catch some sleep. With another 10 hours of motoring ahead, we would do shifts. After a few hours of shut-eye and a hot cup of tea, I am back in the cockpit as we approach Forester's Island.

At the skippers, briefing, we were told that there would be swimmers in the water, attempting to break a Guinness World record. They would be encountered by the Narrows and to heave to even though we would be under sail. They were kindly referred to as "pedestrians" and had the right of way. We actually caught up to them around 0100 hours as we were exiting the narrows approaching North Port and Big Bay. The rest of the trip was uneventful, and we spent it in discussion of the day's events and the trip to Toronto later that day. Details on documenting the damage once we were docked and how to secure the lake voyage consumed the rest of the trip. We arrived in Trenton at approximately 0530 hours. Once secured, I was off to the comfort of my vessel and a few hours of kip before the all-night trip to Bluffer's Park later that day.

That fall Catlin got his boom fixed, well replaced it with a new extruded wishbone and a new sail to boot. So now it's the next summer and we are going to do the Lake Ontario 300 race. Chris Sackiw, who also sailed with me from Shediac, NB, to Halifax when I brought Wind Gypsy 1 here, came along for the race. Catlin's son and Rick made up the rest of the crew: five crew, a big boat, and the lake. Preparations were made, and the entry forms were submitted for record. Each boat had a GPS transponder so the race committee could follow the tracks, and if an emergency arose, they knew where to go. The support staff was huge, with helicopters and high-speed chase boats. Canada 1 was skating around the fleet, getting pictures done for the around-the-world single-handed race later that year. Three spreaders on the mast. That boat could reach speeds over 20 knots.

I made up two large trays of food for the suppers: a hamburger, tomato, and elbow macaroni with cheese. Easy to heat in the propane oven at any hour. Beer and a single malt Scotch also were added to the stores' list. I was officially listed as the cook/rail meat.

Off to a good start; Catlin had to get his son, who was back in London, doing sailing school, so a turn-and-burn four-hour trip from Bluffers Park and back turned into a seven-hour trip due to an accident on the 401. Go figure. By the time they got back, he had been up for over 24 hours, so once we were underway to Port Credit, they both hit the rack for the 3-hour trip.

Good sailing weather gave us a chance to try out the new sail with all the reefs. Since the Nonsuch only had one big 800 square foot plus sail, it was an important lesson learned from the Around the County race. The welcoming committee assigned your slip; in our case, we rafted to another 35-foot sailboat on the wall. The swag bag had the regular stuff: a tee shirt, key chain floaters, drink covers, and the red Myer's Rum ball cap with LO 300 2014 embroidered on the back. This company supports some of the major races and to earn one, not as a freebee at the liquor store, is nice to have as a keepsake and conversation starter. Preparations had to be finished, which included a man overboard drill and demo on your vessel to satisfy the race committee. Serious stuff on the big lakes. Sunshine to shit in 30 minutes or less. I had my ass handed to me more than once by the lake, so a few pops along the way is ok, but for an estimated 45-60 hour race, depending on the weather Gods, the weekend party mode is stowed for the race end.

Off with the start gun for the different classes of boats. Slower first, then the fast ones, so hopefully, they will all meet at one point along the circuit, and the handicapped fleet will merge for a race to the finish line. In theory, anyway. We were in the middle of the pack, and it was awesome sailing amongst 60 + boats of all shapes and crews. Some were singlehanded, or a pair, then to your boat passenger rating. No pontoon party boats entered.

After sailing for seven or eight hours, the wind fell off, and we could see on the laptop the other sailboats tacks and tracks looking for some wind. Supper time and shift schedule for the night was made up. It was a clear night as we approached Scotch Bonnet, but there was very little wind for the SW turn to Niagara on Lake, NY, which was turn two.

Around midnight an alarm started to ring, and the battery panel lights were going red. Then the lights in the cabin lights went brown, then out—no wind, now no lights. Rick and I went down below, shut off all the breakers, and pulled the engine cover off. Well, we could hand crank the engine, and use it to recharge the batteries only. Guess what? No crank. Next, check out the wiring. All the switches were in the right positions, so look behind the panel. Grandmother's knitting after the cat got at it looked better than this mess. Since the previous owner lived on the boat full time, he had bypassed the battery switch, so all the batteries were on, not just the house bank.

Now, what to do?

You go old school. Since we had a compass and paper charts on board, so like a scene from a movie the salon table was cleared off, flashlights angled for the best lighting with the chart, parallel rules, and dividers puled from the nav station. "our last known position was…Break time."

The wishbone boom broke 22 feet from the mast.

Chapter 19

Fiona

We had a rough last few weeks all around here with Hurricane Fiona hitting us on 24 - 25 September. I will not go into details about the effect and damage to Fiona. It has been broadcast enough without another rendition of events. Our biggest thing around here was to get the docks and boats out of the water. If the wind doesn't get you, the storm surge will.

Wind Gypsy 1 was moored at AYC, storm-rigged the best that I could. On a ball is a lot safer for the boat. It can freely swing with the wind, whereas if tied to a dock, now you not only have the wind shifts causing unknown stress on the rig, but you have the surge and tides as well. She was on the ball for Dorian as well. Tough old gal she is. After it was safe to go into town, about five days later, when the grid was mostly back online, and the trees were cleared from the main roads, I went down to the club and got the tender to drop me off at the boat to see how she was.

As we came around the docks, I could see her just swinging slowly in the wind. Unlike that Thursday before when I was rigging the boat, the tender operator had to take a few attempts to get close to the boat and judge the actions of the boat. He tried to get close, but the wind caught the stern of the tender, pushing it forward into my Stainless Steel bow plate/anchor roller. Old wooden boat versus Stainless Steel. The bow went up as WG1 was coming down. The roller plate just shaved off a few inches of gunnel-like box cutter through well a box.

Shit happens, and that is why they never went to metal or fiberglass boats for tenders. They have to be able to bounce off and not hopefully sink after a small bump. It is better to fix the club's boat instead of the members. She was all good and only a few inches of water in the bilge. Not the same could be said for the cabin. It looked like a Sunday morning after a Dal homecoming party. All the sail bags, fenders, and cushions were on the cabin sole, so when all the sliding drawers opened with the wave action, dumping all their contents about the cabin, nothing was broken, just in a big pile. Now, there were lots of open slips since boats on the docks were more at risk from the wind, so about a third of the fleet was on the hard I could bring her in alongside. Tender service is going to stop soon, and haul out is at the end of the month.

In the last 25 years, the surge has claimed over 15 feet of shoreline, leaving the granite shelf exposed. The property is far enough (125 feet) and high enough (60 feet above the HHWM) not to get wet. The surge will just pound anything into ruins just from the sheer non-rhythmic actions. Heard of the rouge wave? There is a picture of a trashed fish store getting towed out to be burnt. This is off our front lawn.

We are located in what boaters affectionally call a hurricane hole. With the wind direction of NW, the granite mountain behind us and the one over Dutchman's Cove saved our village. A few trees down, and my next-door neighbour lost about 8 - 10 shingles. Our biggest problem, as was everyone else, was no power due to the massive amount of trees on the lines in the HRM area.

But living here in the "sticks" several have a long history here, so maybe the basic EM skills were not brought on because of an emergency, but out of growing up here. Generators, cisterns, septic fields, wood stoves, and propane for cooking. Securing procedures are passed down either from family or just observation. ATVs with plowing attachments instead of golf carts and a stocked pantry, not relying on Uber Eats for dinner.

Unfortunately, no matter how well you can prepare if it hits the fan, I hope the blowback is directed elsewhere. Our unit in Trenton 81 AEF was dispatched to St Herbert, Montreal 03 January 1998 and stayed there for 19 days for the Ice Storm. What you see on TV doesn't compare to real life. The same problem with the downed trees, but add 250-foot-high steel hydro distribution towers laying like trashed mechanical erector set creations. Miles and miles of crumpled towers. It's hard to use a chainsaw on them. Welding Torches and chop saws are now the tools of choice.

Meanwhile, the rest of the unit Crew Chiefs were given an AOR, do the RECCE, the COA, and recommendations for their specific skillset, and back in three hours for the Troop Commander to pass up to the Division heads for priority listing. After a few days, the HQ staff, who were in the HQ building, a good place for them, were still in the black, with minimum power, and wondered why the Engineers had lights, hot water, heat, and parking.

Well, that is what we do. So, the OC and the Chief came back from an O Gp with the news that we are moving so the HQ staff could be warm. Our Chief lost his shit, so we packed up everything, Everything. Generators were disconnected off the main grid, steam shut off, heat, all of our tables, chairs, well, our whole HQ, onto the trailers, and off we went to our new building. A few hours later,, we were reconnected, and I was brewing up a Timmie's in the coffeemaker.

Well, the OC and Chief went to the next O Gp, and well, they were pissed that the building was empty and the parking lot was full of sea cans. The CANEX was next door, so they were all hooked up. We need gas and snacks to do our jobs. So, now (and I am telling it like it was, less the PC /SHARP training), the Chief and the OC, who is French, are fuming at the A-hole French HQ, and our staging area was filled with Police cars there for a briefing. A call was made to the HQ to move the cars so we could get to work, but a wait-out was given. After two hours, the Chief ordered us to hook up the cop cars to the loaders and drag them away. We thought it was a joke, but he took us outside and directed what cars were going where. Just like a scene from a comedy flick, the cars were gently pushed out of the way using cargo straps and 2 x 4 planks for runners.

In a matter of half an hour, the lot was cleared enough for a 10-ton truck with a PLS (Pallet Loading System) to pick up a large generator due at a nursing home in the local area. Our days were busy, doing different jobs, and in a small town called St. Pie, around 10 km from St. Hubert, every hydro pole was snapped off or was tangled with tree limbs of some sort. Our section built portable showers in the community centre, and the Red Cross was doing wellness checks. The modifications allowed the centre to stay open 24 hours, now that showers were there for extended stays.

One of the most ingenious uses of a CNR train I have ever seen was about a week into the recovery efforts. Everyone was on duty for this one: carpenters, Plumbers, Electricians, Administration and support staff. A six or seven-story advanced care nursing home was demanding more power than the backup system could provide, leaving residents relying on battery power. Other units showed up to pitch in, working in -25 C temperatures. Frostnip still affects my fingers in the winter today. A 600 KVA transformer was delivered by Hydro Quebec, and their workers craned it into place.

Next was to build a 10-foot by 10-foot building to protect the transformer connections, and give a safer environment to work in. So here is where the CRN train comes in. It is just a big diesel generator with thousands of liters of fuel to idle for a week. The train's output was around 1.0 mW. Enough to light a small town of 750 homes. It got wired up and was still running when we left after 19 days.

Even McDonald Douglas had their turbines hooked into the grid, providing power to the city, and there were no real language difficulties between the staff and store employees when items had to be purchased. Even the local town mayor came and opened up the hardware store in the middle of the night so supplies could be acquired for a late-night repair. I found that in humanitarian missions, there is always a way to get your points across. Both parties want a positive result.

About a week into the ice storm relief, The Director General for Engineering Operations and Infrastructure, MGen Penny, showed up from NDHQ to see what the boots on the ground were doing. After the day of touring various sites around the greater Montreal area, a debriefing and observation from the General was held after supper, and coffees were brewed. When MGen Penny opened up the floor to questions and asked for suggestions, Ed Butt piped up and asked how much was in his (MGen Penny's) slush fund. A few dollars in his discretionary fund pot was available for what? Boots were the answer. "Working all day in -25 C weather with these combat boots is like wearing hockey pucks."

Two days later, the BATA Safety boot van pulled up beside our building, and a few at a time, we got new Gortex safety boots. Troops are happy, and as far as the bosses are concerned, money is well spent.

Storm damage. 03 October 2003

Chapter 20

CFB TYC

Canadian Forces Base Trenton Yacht Club (CFB TYC) was established in 1961, on Baker Island located in the Bay of Quinte, ON. We joined the club in 1998 after I bought a 1987 21.5-foot Bayliner Ceria cutty cabin power boat and trailer. We had made the deal, the water test was done, and the pick up would be that Friday after work.

The day finally came, and Margret was going to drop me and the girls off at the marina, and meet us at the yacht club in about half an hour. We got the keys and slipped off from the slip and I slowly got the feel for the boat. It was a stern drive so your steerage was in the forward propulsion. Simply put, the prop has to be turning to be able to steer. Famous last words....simply put.

Our first stop was the Trenton Marina for some fuel. It was supposed to be at least half full, 25 gallons. It has about a quarter tank if the gauge is working correctly. So my first docking attempt. Jenn on the bow, and Jackie on the stern lines. Line her up, slide in the stern, throw the line, good, stern line good, Bang, and the engine stops, and the bow is drifting away, WTF? Well, the bow line was thrown, but not tied, and dropped back into the river, and when I put her in reverse it sucked in the line around the prop killing the motor. With the aid of the staff, we got tied up and an inspection was done on what to do to remove the nuts and pins that held on the prop. The second problem, is no tools. No worries, I got a dive knife so I cut the line off so the outdrive could be raised up for better check. A small nick in the prop, and eight feet shorter on the bow line, not too bad.

So now that the engine starts and the drive is ok, I can get fueled up. $75 dollars and an hour of time lost, we got to get to the YC. "Where is my wallet" I ask the kids with the I don't know answer. Hell, just great. I must have left it in the car, and Margret has it. I offered one of the kids as collateral until I could get back, but just the boat registration number was needed. Thanks, and we are off back to the YC, now over an hour overdue. This could have been an end to my boating experience, but with reassurances from the marina staff that boating is really a lot of fun, we slipped the lines and headed to the yacht club. That was 17 years ago, and I now could not imagine a life without being on the water.

I have owned a 21.5 ft Bayliner, Buoy & Sea, a 27 ft Sun ray cabin cruiser, Aquahloics, our 34 ft Mainship trawler, Tapped Out, and our current vessel, a Mirage 30 ft sailboat, Wind Gypsy I. Why the change after so many years of owning powerboats one would ask, well after my release, we decided to make a long trip as a bucket list item before going back east. There are many different routes or well-documented trips within the Great Lakes, our choice was the Triangle route. The trip's first leg starts at Trenton, or somewhere on the lake, then off to Kingston, to Montreal, turn south at Sorel down the Richelieu River to Lake Champlain and the canal system, then turning east up the Hudson River, and then north up the Eire barge canal to Oswego NY, and across Lake Ontario back up the Bay of Quinte to Trenton. We were away and did not cross our wake until some 39-odd days and 760 nautical miles later. We were planning a move back to Halifax and the trawler was not your choice of boat where I now live. There is lots of open water and depth to go just about anywhere on the east coast, but sheltered harbours are sometimes miles and hours apart, rolling in a following sea in a shallow keelboat is unsettling and somewhat more dangerous than a sailboat with a mast and lead keel to somewhat ease the ride and with sails up, it is quite comfortable. The other things that I considered were long-distance trips, and what was more comfortable for the conditions that I would now be sailing in. Another consideration was in the event of an engine failure on a powerboat on the Atlantic, well you're screwed. You cannot anchor here like in a lake just dropping the hook over into the mud bottom with the flukes digging in quickly. The ocean seabed is mostly rock and rock formations well over 100 feet in depth. Just in front of my house, the cove entrance drops to 80 ft then to over 100 ft.

The great options are that you can have multiple sail plans for your boat, all weather-dependent, and an inboard diesel engine as a backup, not a primary source of propulsion. 50 consecutive days on a boat with 40 on the move, I would have never done the trip using Tapped Out. In some areas yes it would have been nice to have the horsepower on occasion, but there were many spots where the trawler would have been damaged or unable to get into a berth. This was a totally different trip than before, with no turning back.

2006, I was the 45th commodore of the yacht club, when I was 45. Easy to remember. I had taken over early from the present commodore, he was deployed on the DART team and was not going to be back until after his term was over. When it was all said and done, I was on the Yacht club flag and the CPS training Squadron for ten years. In the heyday of the late 2000s, the club had around 110 boats and a membership of 225. Lots of people were close to retirement as we were, and moved back to their own spots, then COVID-19 devastated clubs all over the country, and people's interests changed over the next two years so memberships suffered with a slow recovery all around. We left in 2016, and unfortunately since then many friends have either sold their boats and left, gotten sick and left, or have passed away. Margret recently came back from a surprise trip back to Trenton, and there was much sadness. We can never really go back to that great time, no matter how hard you try to make it so.

The Δ Loop, the Final Chapter

After a good night's sleep and some cleaning up, a rest day was in order. Saturday it was very windy 20+ and it rained all day. We just had a casual day reading and checking emails and getting caught up with friends and family. Sunday was clearing up a tad, but still a strong NW wind with gusts to 25. I had been informed by the crew, that in no uncertain terms, THEY would be going out in those conditions. Sounds like another day to relax. With a calmer day predicted for Monday, the plan to go to Picton for a day or two was dropped. We need a few days once we are back to get the boat ready for the lift out this Saturday. Besides, being this close to our home port, only 40 NM away, we felt that this was the best decision to make.

After the morning coffee, and listening to the weather on the VHF, the winds were going to calm down late in the morning, so preparations to get underway began. At 1030 things were looking good, so the lines slipped for the last time and we set off for CFB. It was a great relaxing trip, my wake was the biggest wave on the reach. Once at Deseronto, I put TO on autopilot and sat back while she took us home. Once back in Trenton, it was a quick trip to the pump out, and back to her home slip. It was a great feeling to "cross your wake" and be back from this adventure. I have completed a separate spreadsheet with all the places, distances, and fuel used. To summarize we did 760.1 NM over 39 days. We burned 148.2 US gallons for an average of 5.13 MPG. We stayed in 23 different locations and went through two provinces, two states, two countries, and 59 locks. This was the longest trip both by distance and duration that we have done in our boating thus far. It was a great learning experience, and not as scary as it seemed to be.

Breaking that envelope of the 1000 Islands and going into new waters can be somewhat intimidating but take your time, watch, and listen. Some of the best information you can get before and during the trip is from fellow boaters. Books, the internet, and guides are good assets to have, but to rely solely on them is a mistake. Conditions can change from publication time, or even within a few days of checking a website. We were lucky that we got through lock #13 the day before, or we would still be in the Eire Canal. I checked the NYCS site yesterday and it is still about a three-week repair time for the dam before traffic can move again.

Lessons learned along the way; Trust the boat. Do daily checks and she will do her thing. We had several intimate conversations along the way.

Once a week, do a comprehensive check. Tighten gear clamps, check through hulls, batterie levels, and anything that is screwed down. Most boaters do an average of 40-50 hrs a year, we did almost triple that in five weeks. Things will get loose. Don't get too concerned about the gel coat. You will get scratches, rubs, and a ding or two, especially in the locks, but you are using the boat. Chart plotters are a great tool, but paper charts are what I use daily. Several times in the canals, the course indicated on the chart plotter was down a highway or railway. (this is why you don't do this at night) Very few nav aids are lit in the canal and with the flooding in the spring, they are not as indicated on the charts.

We need bigger fenders. These ones are 8" dia by 26" and are 30 years old. In some locks they were literally crushed to about 3" in dia. The purchase of the 15" orange ball was one of the best things we bought. It kept the flared bow off the wall and was a good "spring fender" in getting out of some tight spots.

Fuel up when you have a chance, to avoid (1) a large bill, and (2) if you get some bad fuel it won't be a full tank. Take your time and enjoy the trip. We didn't really have a timetable as such, just be back here in six weeks. Unfortunately due to the end of the season, many places were closed, so maybe next year we will leave earlier in the summer.

If in question about the weather, and have the ability to hang for a day do so. We still, even after taking off lots of clothes, etc, still had way too much on board. Pare down to essentials and add one extra.

Have basic spares on board, oils, filters, impellers, belts but you are really never more than a few days from a town. We met some boaters with extra shafts, and props, and had a small machine shop with several hundred pounds of tools. That is a lot of weight to carry and space to fill. Plan stops to resupply, laundry, and maintenance day, if you can on Mondays. This avoids the weekend rush or the shortened hrs.

The trip was a lot of work, but fun work. Most of our boating up to now has been weekends or a two-week summer trip. Short trips, and party, party, party. After a day of traveling a drink or two and a bite to eat, bedtime was about nine o'clock. If we were going to stay for a day or two (weather days especially) we could stretch it to ten. All that fresh air, sun, and physical work i.e. locking and also walking around the small towns makes for a long day. We met some very interesting and knowledgeable people, and also some ignorant and clueless. Some big-money boaters were great to talk to, and some were dic*s (Richard's). But that also went for the average Joe boater as well.

136

We met a Canadian in Waterford going south who just gave one-word answers, and it was almost as if we were an annoyance. Who knows, maybe we were. He ticked off Bruce when they mentioned that OokPik was also going south, the eyes rolled, and a "whatever" expression came over his face. Bruce dropped that they had been to the Bahamas in their 42 Hughs sailboat, several times, and had done the GreatLoop the previous year, the ears perked up, and suddenly they were not lazy stink potters after all. You could tell (we never did get his name) that Buddy wanted to ask more, but Bruce announced that it was Attitude adjustment time, and off we went.

Would we do it again? Maybe not the same route, but definitely back down the Erie and southbound farther. We did not look at this trip as a 750+NM trip, but many day trips. Just plan a day or two in advance (only if there is a real need, i.e. Locks or bridge openings) and tackle the big water crossings when you come to them. Budget-wise, Canada is very expensive to go through. $211.00 for the locks and fuel was an average from $1.38 to $1.60 a liter. The NYCS was $75 with mooring for the season, and fuel around $1.07 to $1.30 a liter, some marinas were only a buck a foot, and there were also many free docks with power and water. Have a contingency budget for extras. (charts, replace broken items, binoculars $275.0).

We are now in the process of getting TO ready for the winter layup and then off to Annapolis for the Powerboat show next weekend. I hope these notes have been informative, and sometimes entertaining, and it was a great way for us to remember this trip. Another check off the bucket list as they say.

Greg, Margret and Zoey

Tapped Out

Chapter 21

41 AEF

41 Airfield Engineering Flight was located at CFB Cold Lake, AB. We were posted there in the late 80's between Chilliwack and Halifax postings. Every spring there is a NATO air exercise called Maple Flag, and as Airfield Engineers, we play a big role in the clearing, repair, and restoration of a combat-damaged airfield. More about that later.

For the last four years, I have been posted to 81 AEF, Trenton ON. Preparations were started and the old buildings next door to us were leveled with the utility junctions run. After 1 CAD did a reorganization then we were called the Airfield Construction Troop (ACT) the Wing lost 82 AEF in the mix, 50 people, and a building. I think it was an election year.

I was getting posted to 1 CEU, Moncton NB August 2001, so my last away with the flight was going to be that June to Cold Lake for the ex. Our Troop WO, Garry Moore had done a RECCE in April for our camp during Maple Flag. We would build a mini-camp for 30, including 4 Sgt's and our TC. Triple cat-wire fencing, in and out gates, MECC Ablution and Laundry units, a CP, Kitchen, mess hall /combined mess for after hours and classroom. The "Men" had their own modular tent sections, while the Sgt's and the TC shared a tent. Even though we are a strong team, there has to be a separation when living with each other for three weeks. That custom dates back to the Roman Times.

About a week before the trip, the TP WO got a gallbladder or some type of stone attack and was grounded. The TC gave me the nod to make up my team for the Advanced party, leaving in two days. Not bad, there was a good report, drawings, and locations for all the required setup, a store list, and contact numbers for the guys at 41. I could take seven guys, and me for a total of eight. We also had to rent two 15 pax vans at the Edmonton Airport for our three-week exercise. All packed up by 1500 the next day, flying out in the morning. What could go wrong, right?

Everyone showed up at the meeting point, a quick store, a kit check, and onto the bus to PIA. Great trip out, lots of fun. Eight Army guys on a road trip. We get to the Hertz rental to pick up our vans and load up for the three-hour trip north. Well, there seems to be a problem with the FIN code, the AMX number, etc will not enter. Ok, I have my CC for the deposit, then claim it after. Works like a charm that VISA card. A quick stop for some road burgers and on the way. Arriving on the outskirts of the Grand Centre fond memories of the places we frequented years before went by. There was a lot of new construction along the highway. It used to be a dreary, cold, long, and sometimes dangerous trip. Did that one more times than I wish to remember. Anyway, there was a newly opened Tim Hortons, with the drive-thru line out to the road, but when have you ever been in a short line? So off to 41 HQ to see the Chief for his briefing. Well, the Chief was golfing yesterday and popped his bad shoulder out of the socket, and was not in the best of spirits. Ok, seen worse cases. He asked for the RECCE report, quickly scanned it, and handed it back. Great report that WO Garry Moore did. The issue is, that the area has been changed a bit, and the frontend loader was in for a repair, so no moving the sea cans. "Get bedded down and give me a new layout for the morning." was his response. OK, been in worse situations.

Got rooms at the Yukon Lodge for the night, and for tomorrow we are under canvas. After a few beers at the mess, ideas and a game plan were drawn up. The rest of the flight arrives late tomorrow night, so our target time was three hours before. Coffee on, CP operational. We used to have competitions between sections on getting a MECC CP up, a 10 kw generator, and coffee on. Some sub-10-minute runs were done, so that was no worry, it was just the rest of it. The camp was done a few hours before the deadline, with no real panic. The rest of the Flight showed up, and we got prepared for some training days before the main exercise.

After breakfast, we formed up at the camp, and the rest of 41 AEF showed up. They were going to be running the classes on the different pieces of equipment that we were going to be using. Rapid

Runway Repair, Airfield lighting, Aircraft Arrester Gear, and so on. One of the first items was the MECC Ablution Unit, and MCpl James Morris was going to give the presentation. Now this is the overarching link to this chapter. The Tp WO had given us all nicknames in Kosovo, so when we were our Motorola radios, called the "Brick" for its shape weight, and usefulness, this gave us a little more freedom with the radio procedures. Short range only a few km, but great when working around the camp. Since we had our own frequency, a little latitude was given to the VP. Example: my call sign was E418D. A mouthful for sure. His nickname for James was Gerbil. He was a cheerful character with rosy plump cheeks and a bushy short blond stash. He was a history buff and created amazing scale models right down to the dirt splatters on the tank tracks. My other Ql3 was Cpl Jurzack. Jurassic was the Tp WO's name for him.. So remember this little tidbit for later. Maybe I will too.

My nickname was Plunger, the WFE techs were the Water Boys, the EGS Crew included MCPL Mark Browning, The Cardinal, his 2 IC Bishop, and their third was Deacon. The TP clerk/finance/admin/and all-around paper wizard, Radar. He even wore glasses. A few other guys names included Stormy, Izzy, Wolfman, Smitty, and Billy Vee. The WO was the Silver Fox. They reflected our job, or a nickname from years ago, and were also puns on the Military callsigns. Again with the examples. Well, I think it helps to see the parallel anyway. The Engineers were Holdfast, the Mechanics were Bluebell, The TC was Sunray, and the LT was Sunray minor. Military Police were Watchdogs. Moving on.

The rest of the unit showed up, and since we pretty well knew each other from somewhere along our careers, handshakes and a few quick stories from other times were shared over coffee in our mess tent. The next few days training schedule was presented and after break, we would start. So now back to the start of this story.

Their TC was a new Captain, new to the troop, a female, and an RMC ring tapper. Now before I go on I can feel the hair on the back of my neck go up. No intent to label or stereotype, just my observation. Now in comparison, our TC in Kosovo was Captain Van Oostrum who despite getting the dismissive looks when at O Gp's, (personal experience) stood up and got stuff done. She was later promoted to Maj and was the School OC at CFSME. We had a chance for a quick catch at a mess dinner when I was on my QL 6B. There were some bad days for everyone, and a few days away sometimes is what was needed. Since we were in full construction mode, in the winter, and going from camp to Platoon houses started to get to you. Today they call it a mental health day, back then it was a trip to Skopje, Macedonia where the HQ, stores, Admin, and major vehicle repairs were done. It used to be a bus terminal and repair station. You signed in, got a cot in the Modular tent, and then a ration card. Since this place was in the middle of the city, there was no need to wear full kit going outside the gate. Get into civvies, sign out at the CP, and off into town for a sit-down restaurant meal, with Two beers. Some guys were drinking Heineken, regular can size. We (three of us from up north) were drinking Stella Tallboys. "These taste better" one young base support person pointed to his green can. I was polite when I wrote that bit. Well one of the older guys brought up the point that the H is 355ml, and the S is 470ml, so almost three beers to your two. No rules were broken, just interrupted by the engineer's mind. Where was I going again?

The MECC Ablution lecture was next on the list for the demo. The TC asked Gerbil to get started, and he kind of smiled giving me a puzzled look, as if he was not sure what to do. The TC asked him if there was a problem, and quiet chuckles and smirks could be heard. "No Ma'am, " he said " no problem, but Sgt Tanner taught me and Jurassic all about these and how to repair oil burners." "You did not set up the unit ?". "No Ma'am. The guys from 81 did". Needless to say, we had a long coffee break that afternoon. No demo is required. With the fun aside, the three weeks were interesting, with a surprise Exercise mortar attack at 0000 hrs something before End Ex. Smoke, gunfire, yelling. Some of the great things about the Army, they are always on some sort of exercise, and Enemy forces are sometimes needed to add realism to the training. You knew the tactics, the training area, the planned routes, etc. While the troops were patrolling for hours, we waited with our traps set. Six weeks in Booby Trap school on our QL 5 gave you a whole new perspective on Guerrilla warfare. It causes lots of damage and messes people up mentally. A dead soldier is just that, dead. Maybe blown all to shit, and that will fuck you up, for a while, but someone yelling, screaming in pain, missing a foot or a hand from an unexpected action. Like opening a door, moving a log on a path, or unseen tripwires. Back to the last exercise. You know that it is just an ex, but still running to your stand to positions amongst the pyrotechnic display was heart pumping. The QRT loaded up, radios buzzing with orders. The whole thing lasted until the first light, then the Starburst flares for End Ex.

Now where this overarching link comes from. Gerbil later remustered to the Intelligence branch and was later posted to Trenton in the mid-2000s. We just happened to meet at a WgOps briefing and after had a few minutes to catch up on the past few years. Once we started to get involved in Afghanistan, a lot of confiscated items made it back to Canada for review and information sharing but on a tight leash. We got our foreign weapons for our classes from Afghanistan. There were lots of video clips of American convoys ambushed by Taliban IEDs, some near misses, and some not so. It's a totally different sensation watching the movie Platoon and watching vehicle cam footage of someone getting vaporized for real. As mentioned before I taught Mine Awareness Training (MAT) on the PSO course. The morning was the class, PPT, and inert mines to get your hands on. After lunch, we did prodding and basic minefield clearance to get yourself, or someone injured out of danger. Practicing the Liberace method flat on your stomach. This is in reference to the pianist Valentino Liberace and his nimble finger gliding across the keys. I remember that from Day one of our QL3 minefield training.

Some other captured videos were not for public viewing. Taliban beheading with shards of glass, old tin sheets, whatever was handy for an agonizing slow bleed out. Then they stood on their backs, grabbed a handful of hair, and jerked and twisted off the head, tearing the remaining flesh off from the back of the neck. The head, sometimes with the mouth and eyes still opening and closing almost like a fish lying on the wharf after he's off the hook, slapping the deck for that last few seconds. Just the nerves and muscle spasms, but it still freaks you out. The heads then rolled down in a small ditch slowly darkening in colour from the blood trails. It is the shock

143

factor that they want to hit you with first. The second reaction is WTF, third maybe closing your eyes for just that split second, fourth another look to let your brain analyze what your eyes are seeing, maybe disgust, or just nausea, and then when the clip is over everyone has their own comment and their feedback. Unfortunately, or fortunately, however, you look at it, the real world has to toughen you up a little bit.

Back in the 1980's there was no internet so all our info was from films, or pictures and later going to video. Our EOD films, were mostly from Northern Ireland, from the Royal Engineers doing car bombs and building clearing. The voice recorders in the Kevlar Blast helmet started automatically. This was one last thing to worry about. So needless to say some of the recordings ended rather abruptly. Sometimes remote cameras are set up in a danger-safe zone and their purpose is to capture external events that might affect the situation, and in the event that a high order happens, the footage can be used for reference for lessons learned. The other great resource of footage was the Montreal Mobster scene. Lots of guys with their legs blown off from car bombs, and accidental detonations. And you have to add in some Canadian bank robbers with dynamite vests on. Their trigger of choice was a wooden close pin, with a tack on each end, then a wire from the hot goes through the pin tacks. If closed, the circuit is made, and poof. A few good headshots when they were away from bystanders made a few dents in the nearby cars. One actually had half a face stuck on a car door window. Enough of that.

When I was doing my Emergency Management course at George Brown College one of the courses was on terrorism. Three months of research and a few rabbit holes were chased. Some really fucked up stuff out there. Our group had to create a terrorist group and write a paper establishing who we were, our ideals, cause, and intentions. It was fun, informative, and eye-opening to look through a different lens, as a civilian, not as an Army guy. One did the group intelligence, one did the radicalization propaganda, I laid out the attack and what resources were needed, and the last person did all the formatting, and editing and helped with the research. A long pause here. I was thinking of adding the paper here, but on further review, I think not. There was some weird, off-the-wall stuff that

144

some of the guys dug up. Being on the DWAN, my search engine entries were being logged, and one day my OC got a call from WTISS about some of the sites I was on or tried to access were questionable in their minds, and I should be cautioned on my interests and restrictions will be set up. A perfect example of being blackballed without just cause. The OC had proof read all of my assignments over the past year, so he knew what was going on. Besides the military was paying for this course because it was a requirement for my job. He straightened it out but it still took a few days to get my rights back for the DWAN, A-holes.

Chapter 22

DFTP

Every other year Canada and the USAF did inter-unit exchanges called the Deployment for Training Program (DFTP). One year we went down south, and the next year they came up. 81 AEF did trips to the 134th Air Refueling Wing McGhee Tyson Air National Guard Base TN, 325th Mission Support Group Tyndall AFB FL, 209th Civil Engineering Squadron Gulfport MS, and 107th Attack Wing Niagara Falls Air Reserve Station NY.

We were here for just over three weeks at the McGhee Tyson Air National Guard Base. There were several projects on the go, but some time off was also scheduled. It started out with a Parish holiday, so a three-day weekend unexpectedly came up at the start. The TC, Capt Healey got us SNCOs together and we sorted out what we could do in advance for the start, then weekend routine, but no road trips just yet. The Master Chief gave us the welcome speech, places where and where not to go as white folks. Knoxville still had some backstreets that were still living in the 1950's. As the final comments were given, arrangements to meet at the Club later were made. Then a brown paper bag appeared on the table. The CO passed it to our Capt and said " This is Moonshine that comes over the hills in jugs" The Tennessee Sour-mash was clear as water. Their rule was that everyone had a drink if they wanted to, but the Capt would have to finish the rest. To return a jar back with some left in after 25 guys drank was frowned upon. So just to make sure the Capt got his share, the last few guys added a bit of backwash for good measure. It was going to be a good trip. The core group of us were in our late 30's, mostly responsible adults, mostly, and had been together for a few years. There was a good rhythm between sections, trade ribbing always, but thats what guys do.

We had a three-day weekend while we were there, so Charlie Poisson, a Sgt Struct Tech that I had met on the Bosnia tour planned a trip. He was stationed at Coralici and was posted to 81 AEF after the tour. We had a good friendship outside the unit. Dinners out with the wives, events at the mess that sort of thing. We were going to Nashville for two days, and on the way back we stopped at Lynchburg to do the Jack Danials Distillery tour and do the tourist thing. With the hotel and rest stops planned, we just had to work for 14 days, then our break. Sunday routine was observed for the troops, and the SrNCO / Officer did our PER drafts and rewrites sometimes relying very heavily on the word picture guide book. Even away on an exchange trip, the paperwork back home still had to be done. jobs got figured out.

The first week went pretty well after some jobs had to be postponed due to the weather. A hanger retrofit was pushed back until the winds died down later that week. It was an active runway so the ever-present FOD (Foreign Object Damage) protocol had to be adhered to. Usually on each deployment, exchange, or course I have ever been on with the Engineers, a community improvement project is included in the scope of work so material can be prepositioned at the civilian address. This time it was grading out a field by the American Legion Post 13 in Blount County, the next Parish over from Alcoa. The little league ball-field was getting done with new dugouts and benches. The kitchen was open at 1000 for brunch, and the bar was open at 1201. While the Dirt boys played with the dozers, the rest of us worked on the structures. During our lunch break, the bartenders kept offering us Buds with our meal, but we all politely refused. We don't drink on the job, plus we had to drive back at the end of the day was the polite answer. No worries, he would bank our drinks for that Friday night. One of the renovations at the NCO's club was the stall and door replacement. They weren't in bad shape, but the new design had the sinks and toilets in a different layout. The ones at the legion were beat-up plywood frames with the many layers of cover-up paint chipping through. So while we waited for the contractor to tile the floor, we went to work at the Legion.

A truck full of guys showed up the next day, a Sunday in combats and unloaded our tools and the stalls. Sgt Steve Anderson, (deceased) the heavy IC got the dumps and graders warming up just as the Legion manager showed up with the keys. They normally are closed on Sunday until 4 pm, then open until midnight. That gave us the day, and lots of time. I guess no one told the manager about the inside renos, and when he heard the boys tearing the plywood frames in the washrooms he came running in with a bat in hand ready to swing if necessary. Judging from their condition it was not the first time he heard that sound. I don't know who was more scared, us or him. Everyone had a good laugh and a reminder that the bar was open later that night. With the job done by 1500, we packed up and headed back to the base for a shower, supper then back to the legion was the current plan.

McGhee Tyson AFB is the home to the Air Force NCO Academy. Four weeks of intense training. Real intense. Scenes from "An Officer and a Gentleman" Drill Sgt came to mind. The Trooper brim cap, number 0 haircut, the ability to chime off a rant extreme levels of volume, and the never-ending length of obscenities without breaking a smile. These guys were going to be these guys some day. Then they would be Staff at one of the schools in the American Air Force. We were in the mess one suppertime when a platoon from the NCO course came in for their dinner. Maybe the instructors have to watch certain movies as a requirement because this Top's voice gave you goosebumps when you heard it. "Full metal Jacket" comes to mind. Pte Pyle was slack and idle to the Drill Sgt (DS) who took out his rants and made it his project to see that Pte Pyle got into shape. The DS ends up getting shot by the Pte, then he blows off his head in the bathroom. Sorry to spoil the end if you haven't seen the movie. Anyway, it was a little freaky to see that it actually goes on in real life. Later we were having a smoke and the DS came over and was having a chat with us, just like we knew each other for years. He told us that they only ran a few courses a year, so they were aloud to have some fun. Might see you at the NCO's club later for a drink was the parting exchange and then off to get his course. You wouldn't have any voice left after a week, but it would be fun trying.

After supper, we had our meeting about what the jobs are going to be this week, who is going out tonight, sorting out duty drivers, and as long as you are back for breakfast roll call, all is good. Steve Anderson, Dale Gorman, and I sat at the bar people watching between NASCAR commercial breaks. The old girl that did the bar was anywhere between 60 and 90. A real Hillbilly and her husband died in Vietnam. One of the regulars showed up, gave her a nod of the head, and off she went to the kitchen. He never said a word. She was back and poured him two Jack and coke's in red solo cups. Out the door, he went, off to an old Chev van which looked a lot like Steve's back in Trenton. We gave her the "what's his story" look and she said that she'll be right back. To the kitchen, then out the side door over to his van with a brown bag. Interesting chain of events. I cannot remember her name, so she told us that he comes in every day, gets his two drinks, orders a burger and fries, and has it in the van. The van was his home for the past few years. Veteran and just never settled down. Did not get his whole story, just enough to answer the regular questions.

Around 2000 the bar started to fill up, and the crowd was very diversified to say it nicely. The banjo Deliverance scene was going on in a far corner, and some heavy pool table bets were being tossed around. The dollar beers were going down smoothly, but it was American beer, so trips to the restroom were more frequent. Once you break the seal....

Even though we left a dollar ever time the bartender brought us a round, a small pile of ones was building up in the corner. Some of the guys were in the backroom playing darts and an intense poker game was had a mix at the weathered six-sided table. There was a huge engraving under the rubbed varnished top of the Legion crest, the branch number, and the established date. Not unlike our legions, the walls were covered with pictures and medals from wars of the past. There are always in every group a few that are into serious poker games. I did that while on exercise in Germany. Had some good exercises, and a break-even or two, but Margret was wondering why my "field pay" was sometimes in cash. Needless to say, our first night out was interesting, and plans for the weekend were being made.

134th Air Refueling Wing used the KC 135 (E) as the refueling tanker. They were converted Boeing 707 passenger jets, with the seats removed, and extra fuel bladders onboard. There are six or eight big lazy-boy-type chairs at the back and where the refueling line operator sits. It looks like an airplane cockpit, windscreen facing down to the approaching aircraft. Pretty cool to see. We flew out over the Gulf and refueled some F-111 Aardvark bombers. Just like a scene from a Steven Seagal movie.

The airfield also serviced the FedEx transport fleet and was a major hub, so there was always something flying around. Since Knoxville was just down the road, it was fun to venture out and explore the local stores and the nightlife. Some of the single guys found a club called Cotten Eyed Joe's one night and we went into a country bar with huge TV screens around the whole place. Apparently, there were line dancing classes and you could watch the dance floor and the CMT station with the top 40 rotating every hour.

Once the waitress came over to get our order, four specials a jug of Bud, and a pound of wings. Then I think that it was less than ten bucks. A deal at any rate. After a bit of chatting with the waitress and some locals at the pool table, we soon were all old friends. Military in the states ranks up there pretty high with the population, and everywhere I ever went in the US, I always got treated well. Hotel chains with Veteran rates, and almost every restaurant gave you some type of discount. A blue plate, or window sign displayed gave you free parking at the meters. We went to the Season final NASCAR race at Homestead FL, when we were visiting our friends there, and I had my sign on the rental car rearview. After the driver's license inspection to make sure things matched up, we were directed to an area right up behind the track, next to all the driver's haulers. Back to the Nashville trip.

Our R & R long weekend was fast approaching, and Charlie and I made our final route and hotel bookings. Two days in Nashville, and a night around Lynchburg after the Jack Danials tour. Now before I get any further, the next part involved one of my subordinates, but as I mentioned in the beginning I won't slag or bring up any unnecessary background Bull that may not be relevant at this time. Cpl Bruce L. the night before got into an argument at a bar with one of the other sections guy and got a poke in the face for being a smart ass, and a whiner in a club. Bruce had been caught looking at the female restroom door a bit too much for the local boys, and when asked to move and drink up, the other section members also then had to go, which in turn pissed them off. Cover charge, two drinks minimum with only one in hand.

When Bruce got a little mouthy on the way out, MCpl Richard Amos gave him a backhand to the face with a "smarten the fuck up or the next one will really hurt" or words to that effect. I had to write up the charge report recommendations so interviews had to be done. Needless to say, they had to be separated for the R & R, so this is where we get back to our Nashville trip.

The Capt had us SNCOs in for the pre-trip standard briefing, don't go out on your own, don't leave anyone alone in a bar/club/etc, and stay out of the Out of Bounds areas for White people. No shit. Right from the Alcoa Sheriff, who looked like he just walked off the movie set for Brubaker. With the toolbox safety meeting done, the guys were dismissed and were changing into their civvies. The Capt had the leave passes, the rental van info, and the emergency contact sheet for just in case to give out in their packages. One other small bit of info to pass along. Since Bruce and Rick had their little dust up a discussion was held and by a majority decision, it was suggested that Bruce would not be going with the rest of the guys, which suited him fine. He didn't want to go anyway and was just going to stay in the shacks all weekend and watch Sat TV. Fill your boots buddy.

With leave passes, rental van keys, and phone numbers sorted out, we were off to our rooms to load up and go. A quick stop at the PX for some cigars, cheaper than downtown right? Knock Knock on the door, and the Capt popped his head in "Got a minute? Bruce is sitting in the TV lounge and he told me that he wasn't going with the other guys and was staying here on his own." I can see what is coming next…. and Charlie just looks at me rolling his eyes. We had a minivan with lots of room, so as we have been taught, leaders have to sometimes take one for the section. Bruce quickly packed up his Weekender bag (he wouldn't know a Go bag if he tripped over it) and slid into the back seat of the van.

Once on the road, the discussion turned to what we were planning to go, and some of the spots in Nashville that Charlie and I were hitting. Supper at a steakhouse was first on the list after checking in to our Holiday Inn a few blocks up from Main Street. As we unloaded and started to make our way in, Bruce started walking down the parking lot, and back onto Main Street. We both happened to look over and see him leaving and then both looked back at each other. Either way, we were going to be screwed. Leave him to wander off and get rolled, or have him with you for the next three days. I called Bruce back, and we explained that the Capt put him under our charge so you may as well check in here. "Charlie and I are going to get changed and then we are off to the Nashville Steakhouse. Meet you in the lobby in an hour."

A few cold beers and a hot shower after a five-hour drive felt great. We were looking at the Nashville Entertainment Guide for the directions to the Crazy Horse Saloon. It had been featured on The Nashville Network, TNN with some good bands playing. The Country/rock mix in the 90's was big then. The Grand Old Opera was a place that my parents visited a few years before, and although not country music fans, the whole town had lots to offer.

After an hour, we went to meet Bruce in the lobby and headed out to supper. Well, I am surprised to see Bruce there on time. "the restaurant is just a few blocks down the street, then to the CrazyHorse after. " I said. "Let go." Bruce wasn't moving and Charlie was walking by and he saw Bruce's kit bag on the floor next to his chair. "Why do you have your stuff with you?" he asked. "There are no rooms left, and I don't have a credit card to reserve anywhere else." Are you shitting me or what? I was thinking, and I could see what was coming next. Charlie just shook his head. Fucken idiot was all he said as I gave Bruce a room key. "Throw your shit in the room, and we will deal with this later." Not how I wanted to spend the next three days, babysitting a 45 year old 14 year old.

He was back down in a few minutes and Charlie and I had discussed a few different scenarios on how the night was going to turn out. Too bad was Charlie's stand. "We're here to relax and get away from work shit, not be babysitters and have to check our conversations. Bruce was also a little snake and at any opportunity would exploit any info he accidentally overheard. He already was written up for falsifying a leave pass and giving misleading statements. Fucken liar and he got caught trying to worm his way out of it. Consequently, the Capt had him on a short leash, even shorter after the smack-face incident a few days prior.

The Steakhouse was a few blocks away, and we still had about an hour before our reservation, so a stop at the closest bar was in order. Canadian Club and cokes for Charlie and me. If you ask for a Rye and Coke, you get strange looks. I think Bruce ordered a vodka and seven up, or something like that. We instantly had the same thought as the waitress arrived with our drinks, and was taking our orders, Bruce just got a salad. Trouble was the thought. He'll be loaded by 2000. " Is that all you're going to order?" Charlie asked him. Bruce gave him a snotty look and snapped back "What's it to you anyway?" He was about to say "Charlie", and thought better of it. There are rules for a reason. Now don't get me wrong, I'm all for first name basis on leave / R&R / dive trips, etc, with friends. But when this individual has been charged by the CO, and you marched him into the Charge Parade, had him placed on recorded warning, then C&P, and now babysitting after he cried to the Capt, first name basis is used to a minimum. This made conversations awkward because we would start talking about another deployment or something else but had to stop short because a funny event somewhere else with SNCOs now posted to 81 AEF, may not have been so funny back here, and big ears had to be shut down. As we finish supper we look for the nearest bar and check out the local music scene. Our first stop was the crazy horse saloon. We saw the dancers getting ready for the competition, the line dancing competition that is. We got to the bar and ordered a couple of drafts checking out the crowd as we looked for a seat away from the floor.

Unfortunately, it has been several months since I have worked on this project. Chapter 23 happened, and it basically consumed my time and life. I think that all my preparations have been done, and I'm just waiting for the final two pieces before I go forward with this. Stand by....

Chapter 23

CBC report

Veteran pushes for harsher penalties after service dog attacked by another dog | CBC News

Nicola Seguin CBC News Posted: Jul 03, 2023, 6:00 AM ADT | Last Updated: July 3

6–8 minutes

Nova Scotia

A veteran is calling for Halifax municipal officials to strengthen the bylaw that deals with dog attacks after his service dog was injured by another dog. He says the bylaw doesn't offer enough protection to service animals.

Greg Tanner and his yellow lab Barrett were bitten near their East Dover home

Greg Tanner uses Barrett to help him recover from PTSD and a broken back. (Robert Short/CBC)

Every time Greg Tanner takes his yellow lab, Barrett, for a walk these days, he puts on gloves, and extra layers of clothes and carries a big stick. The Canadian Forces veteran is nervous about what he might find down the road from his rural home in East Dover, near Halifax.

Two months ago, Barrett and Tanner were attacked by a neighborhood dog on the loose. Barrett is not just a companion, he's Tanner's lifeline, a trained service dog that helps him cope daily with his post-traumatic stress disorder.

"I lost it," Tanner said. "It was like I can't protect him, I have nothing."

Tanner is now urging Halifax municipal officials to strengthen animal bylaws. He's upset the owner of the aggressive dog was only fined and argues there should be harsher penalties for attacks, particularly ones on service dogs.

Tanner left the military after breaking his back in 2012. He was diagnosed with PTSD three years later. He said he had trouble walking and struggled with his day-to-day life. Then in 2021, he met Barrett.

"Before, I sat in my garage and drank," Tanner said. "I was throwing my life away. This is what brought my life back."

Tanner got his service dog, Barrett, from Kansas in 2021. (Robert Short/CBC)

The dog that attacked Barrett in April bit him on his hind leg, drawing blood and leaving puncture wounds. When Tanner tried to protect Barrett, he was also bitten. A neighbour had to fend the dog off with a golf club.

Barrett has recovered from his physical injuries but sometimes will refuse to walk near the spot where the attack happened.

Tanner said a Halifax Regional Municipality bylaw officer only fined the owner of the aggressive dog and no further action was taken.

"Dogs run around, fine ... but just the response, that's what's blowing my mind," he said.

Dog attacks fall under a Halifax bylaw labelled "respecting animals and responsible pet ownership," which puts the onus on owners to prevent their dog from attacking a person or another animal, damaging property, running loose , or making excessive noise.

"If a dog owner has violated the bylaw, either a municipal compliance officer or a police officer ... can issue a summary offense ticket or a bystander who witnessed the offense could report it to 311 for an investigation to be initiated," municipal spokesperson Laura Wright said in an email. N.S. woman was killed by her own dog while taking it for a walk, RCMP say

Wright said during the investigation, a compliance officer will gather evidence and consider the dog's history. If the owner is found to be in violation of the bylaw they could face a variety of penalties, such as fines and the requirement to muzzle the dog when it leaves the property.

The dog could also be declared dangerous and subject to various restrictions, such as the requirement that it be in an escape-proof enclosure if loose on its property, on a leash, and under the control of an adult when it leaves the property. It could also be seized by animal services.

Morse declined a recent interview request on the topic, saying the municipal staff report should come to the council in December, and "there is progress, it's just slow."

'Still nothing'

Tanner provided CBC with the information he sent to the compliance officer, including vet bills, an RCMP report, a witness statement, and statements from four neighbours concerned for the safety of their children.

Wright said she could not address the investigation into Barrett's attack because of privacy reasons. Tanner said he pushed for the dog to be declared dangerous, and to be reimbursed for vet bills, but so far neither has occurred.

"I asked the compliance officer to ask this person, 'What's your dog's vet status? Has it got rabies shots?'" Tanner said. "I don't know ... Nothing, still nothing."

Tanner said since the attack, he has noticed a psychological impact on Barrett. (Robert Short/CBC)

Paws Fur Thought, a non-profit organization that pairs veterans with service dogs, is supporting Tanner as he rehabilitates Barrett. They are also backing him in his fight to have attacks on service dogs treated more seriously than those on pet dogs.

"I consider ... the psychiatric service dog a medical tool," said Kim Gingell, the organization's intake co-ordinator. "They help the person with mental health issues get through the day, move forward, do things."

Gingell said a service dog being attacked can be "catastrophic" for both the dog and the handler.

"They have to trust their handler 100 percent," she said. "And if that trust isn't there, they can't work. So this could completely ... end things.

"It's like a diabetic losing their insulin."

Gingell said a service dog costs around $25,000 and undergoes significant training, so is difficult to replace. She said usually it takes her around 18 months to get someone a service dog.

Tanner said he is speaking up because he wants the dozens of veterans who rely on service dogs in Nova Scotia to not have to go through the same thing he is dealing with after Barrett's attack.

"I think I have to put my fears aside because that's what we were trained to do."

: Nicola Seguin is a TV, radio, and online journalist with CBC Nova Scotia, based in Halifax.

Needless to say, this event has had some lasting effect on both Barrett and myself. The dogs had been kenneled elsewhere until the owner came back from a trip. A few weeks later they were back in the village, and they're barking gave an uneasy feeling to the both of us. He sometimes refuses to go past the house where they live. When I see them my anxiety and anger build up. Because of the privacy laws and if I used a name, the individual would no likely push a law suit for slander or whatever else they choose.

WHY the tone? After a few friendly email exchanges, then nothing. No vet report from their vet, nada. My out-of-pocket costs were around $500.00 for vet bills and a new jacket. Not a whole lot of money involved, and just the fact that they live, well, rent a house here they might do the neighbourly think. Not fucken likely.

I am walking Barrett down by our park, part of my physical therapy, walking. I have progressed from a few hundred meters to an average of two km on a good walk. This particular day I got a call from an unknown number, and instead of hanging up, I decided to answer it.

The male voice on the other end asked if this was "Gregory Charles Tanner, home address is ......" This is the beginning of a bad afternoon. Only a priest, Grandmother, or mom when you were in the shit, called you by all three given names, and sometimes a bonus one is thrown in for good measure.

"Yes this is, to whom am I speaking with please?" was my authoritative comeback. "Constable M.W. from the Tantallon RCMP Detachment. What is your current location?"

After a quick exchange of information, he was on his way down and I was to meet him at my house. So now I am really curious, what did I do? Allegedly I just told a neighbour that I was coming over to her house right now to kill the dogs. Weapon unknown. The person was as the Constable said: "in hysterics and feared for herself and her pets." Interesting turn of events, no? Fucken bizarre.

On top of that, I got a call from her insurance company lawyer. They wanted an excessive amount of info and forms filed so they could review their client's liability for the dog attack. Really? Your insurance company lawyers? I was just wondering what her deductible was to go this route. Well, my reply was the CBC report.

Things seemed to quite down for a few months, with only and occasionally hearing or seeing of the dogs. Want to add another twist? Mid September a HRM Compliance officer showed up at my house with a subpoena for Provincial court. The person that was charged with taking care of the dogs that day was contesting the summary offense. Interesting, where is this going to go I wonder?

So October 26 arrives and we are going to court as a witness. Talked to the Lawyer briefly, and then the RCMP, HRM Compliance, and Daniel Burke showed up at the courthouse. (Daniel arrived on scene as the dog was on me, and using a golf club, was able to scare them enough for us to get away, seek shelter behind his

159

truck and call 911). I have been in a courthouse before, but getting sworn in and talking to the Judge was the second time I gave a witness statement in court. The first time was in Fredericton NB at a Coroner's inquest in 1982. Sapper Ross Carr, who was in our troop was going to Moncton for the weekend and was hit by a car later that night and was left for dead. I was called up because I was the last person from the Squadron to seem him before the accident. Ross needed a drive to the mall for an NBLC stop, and then he was hitch hiking to Moncton. Now back in the 80's everybody hitchhiked back and forth to Moncton, Sackville, and Halifax. I did it for a year before I could afford to by a $500.00 junker. Usually, I took the bus back Sunday afternoon so I knew I would be back at the base that night. After I got my car, Harriott, a light blue Honda Civic weekend trips were soon the regular. Dave Currie who lived in Truro was also on my TQ3 Field Engineer course in Chilliwack so we hung around with some other Maritimers. Gagetown was a posting of choice 22 Field Squadron and would go either to Truro, or Halifax every pay weekend. Sorry, a bit of scope/story creep going on. That's another chapter to work on. Back to it.

Back in court, I gave my statement and stayed to hear the rest of the testimony from the other witnesses. Everyone testifies and after about 1 hour the court is recessed. We are called back in and the Judge gives her decision. Mr D. and his partner were friends of the dog's owner's brother and agreed to do this dog and house sight unseen. During his statement, Jason produced pictures of the state of the house, dirty and mouse droppings about the place. Once they saw the dogs and the condition of the house, they didn't want to stay and were going to leave. After some discussion, and because the dog's owner was flying overseas later that day, other accommodations for the animals could not be sorted out until later, so they agreed to stay for the welfare of the dogs. The dogs were to be kept in a small fenced-in yard with a gate and a latch. This is where the Judge had a hard time coming up with a decision. She went into due diligence, the definition, and what the court looks like. They had only been at the house for about an hour when the let the dogs out into the yard, but Jason after describing how he locked the gate, the improper procedure was done and they got out. The judge based it on the fact that although he had thought he secured the gate, the proper way was not shown to him, thus letting the dogs run free. He admitted that they didn't know the dogs had escaped until they heard shouting on the road. During his statement, he apologized to me about the attack and had no idea that they had gotten out. The decision was that he had done all that he could with the information he had to lock the gate, so he was found not guilty of "owning an animal that attacks a person or other animals". Since she came back from her trip he has had no communication with the dog owner. She never got the ticket, so she shut them out and mentioned that it had been a stressful time, for him and his partner. After court was dismissed, Mr D and I had a brief discussion of the event and I could tell that they were upset over the whole thing.

So, a not-guilty verdict might seem to be a defeat, but far from it. Since the dog owner did not show Jason the proper locking procedure, should that make him at fault, no? I was going to get a process server to drop off a letter to her, but the cost was going to out weight the end result. Then her insurance company's legal person contacted me with a case number referencing the alleged dog attack. So that is my in to contact her. This will bring us back to the RCMP call about me coming to her house to kill the dogs.

So that brings us up to today. The package that I am working on for the insurance company will have the 90-page court transcript, a copy of the 911 call, victim statements, and what I will be asking for. What the insurance company wanted was proof that the attack actually happened. Well, this has been done for me, and the comments from the Judge will go far I think. Damages, what are the damages? This whole event has now taken off in a different direction. September 2022 I completed my Firearms Safety Course to own a long gun. Everything was processed, and in March a call from the RCMP to confirm some info, and off for the final check. It has now been over 20 months, and nothing as of yet. Some phone calls later, I found out that it did clear National, and was now to the NS Chief firearms Office waiting for final background checks. Interesting. I have had three background checks done in the last two years. One to go get Barrett Sep 2021, then one for HRM EMO as a volunteer in December 2022, and one for Team Rubicon in April

2023. All came back OK. Her call was in June. Talking to some retired RCMP friends in the Veterans group, they brought up the fact of the latest inquire of the mass shooting that was released, with the fact that she had used certain words I might have been flagged as a wait-and-see because there is an open case file on this attack.

In doing some internet searches about dog attacks, the laws vary not only by province but also by municipality. In Nova Scotia, there is no Provincial dog bite ruling. The dog bite victim may file a claim under the Occupier's Liability Act that can hold the owner responsible. Once I get all the information collected I will look for legal assistance to go forward. Punitive damages if the NRF safety course and permit have been delayed because of the false accusation. An email was sent to the Nova Scotia Chief Firearms Officer's office to do a follow-up on my FSC certificate a few weeks ago, and no answer yet but that is to be expected. I will wait another few then a further inquiry will be done.

Back at the writing again but now it is to keep my thoughts in some type of order. This event has by all intensive purposes been a consuming fire that it seems that just as it gets under control, another reminder or escalation of the situation (the RCMP call, the insurance company email, the CBC report and article, the court subpoena, the court testimony, the Judge's decision) have just been coming as waves with the occasional rouge one catching you off guard. Trying to suppress or concentrate on other things seems like an impossible task right now, and this is again one of those times that I have to either walk the walk or live with what has been going on for the past seven months and take a seat. Since sitting hurts my back I guess going forward I do need some type of closure. What I'm trying to do, no what I am going to do is have a claim ready to file in the new year. With a few quick calls to legal companies that advertise dog bite representation, not many are willing to even talk to you unless there has been serious injuries explaining that there is a lot of work involved in proving the case etc, etc, so that is their excuse. So this is why I am working to get everything that I can think of done, along with my executive summary cover letter. I understand that time is money and if I did learn anything from our SCAN workshops about resumé writing, no one has the time or wants to spend the time sifting through 100's pages or trying to as we were told, "pick the fly shit from the pepper" so to have most of the groundwork and a clear direction forward is a good start.

Hilary at TN and I talked about that day, and what can I do and are doing to deal or cope with this on every appointment since then so she suggested completing an assessment form to capture some clinical info that can be used in this claim. Another thing done that a lawyer doesn't have to get done. I think that if the FSC, the RCMP, and the subpoena weren't involved this might have faded away a little, but it has come to a point where I don't know what direction to go in. You cannot really cold call a law firm's office and getting in and being told "not interested" is what is my go/no go point right now.

My renewal notice for my cannabis prescription came in last week, so I made my appointment with Dr. Hernadas in mid-January and went to the website to complete the forms. That got me surfing and I came upon the Veterans 4 Healing site. It had been a while, well a few years since I had talked to Fabian and Juliane. We met on a Resurface North retreat that I had gone on before going to get Barrett. They have a place across from West Dover and their Main office is in Cape Breton. Maybe a fresh conversation will give me some ideas or some next logical steps forward. A phone appointment will do just because I could not do the day's drive to the Island. We went to MFT in 2017 to get my first script. A five-hour trip, a place to stay, then the trip back.

Had a good 1/2 hour chat with Fabian. I was expecting to have to talk to Juliane first and maybe set up something but he was available. That was one thing that I didn't have to do to go through the whole story/process again. Sometimes it is as simple as that. Well, I say simple but being able to actually press the send button on the email request, or call someone took an enormous amount. I don't know what you would really call it, frightening, heart in the throat, chest pounding sweating sick feeling with the ever-growing ringing in the ears to add some amusement to the mix. Time for a new chapter.

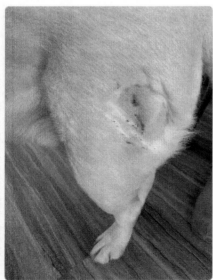
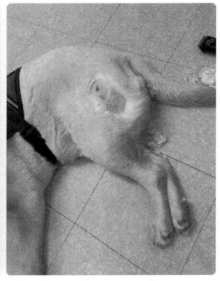

Photos entered into evidence by the Compliance Officer.

Chapter 24

4 CER

I posted to 4 CER (4 Combat Engineer Regiment) Lahr, West Germany from May 1983 to July 1987, and by far was the best posting we had. Ask anyone who was in the CAF and was posted to Germany during the 1980s and I'll bet they will say the same. It was a culture and a right of passage of sorts. The Special Service Medal (SSM) with the Nato bar represents a tour in Germany.

I started out posted to Two Troop, one section. It was an APC Dozer with an eight-man section. But getting over to Germany was a bit of an extended trip. I was going over early because the Regiment was getting ready for a field exercise the first week of June for three weeks, then back for the regular posting rotation. Margret at the time was five months pregnant with Jennifer, and we had just found out when applying for our passports Margret wasn't a Canadian Citizen. WTF was my first comment to the passport officer? Her parents were Canadians, he was a Sergeant MSE Op (Trucker) posted to Germany from 1959 -62. Margret was born in a German hospital on a British Base and we had all the papers, SIN #, and tax returns. **Well** somewhere along the way something wasn't recorded and she was a German, not a Canadian. After several months of calls back and forth, the citizenship came through. Her last month to fly was mid-August because she would be too far along in the pregnancy for flying so the push was on, otherwise, it would be November before they could fly over. I think that it was the last week of August when I got the PMQ, and almost lost the PMQ that same weekend. It was a fun weekend just getting back from Fall EX Part 1. In garrison for three weeks, then back out to Hohenfels training area for six weeks. It is a big American Armed Forces Base home to the 7th Army Training Command. The training area is 163 km2 and 319 km of off-road and trails. *This is from the official Hohenfels website. It is about 1 hour from Nuremberg. A city within a city. There was a huge stone wall all around the inner city where all the clubs and bars were. We got to go there for a mid-exercise R&R. The different sections usually gathered at one of the big Gasthaus for a good meal and some beers, and shots, and off to some bars. The last bus was at 0200, or a several hundred Mark (DM) taxi trip back.

So, my flight was on the May 24 weekend. Just the way the flights were. I left Shearwater at 0700 Sunday to fly to Trenton, then to Ottawa, then over to Shannon Ireland, then Lahr FRG. A long long day that just got longer. Having made it to Ottawa, we deplaned and waited in the AMU holding area. There was a CANEX snack bar, a pinball, a video game area as well as a small gift shop. Off to one end was the Sgt's and WO's area, the Officer /VIP lounge. It was Ottawa after all in the '80s. Anyway, there was an announcement looking for about 10-15 persons to come up to the info desk with our travel claims. A different priority was assigned to your claim. A priority 5 is for leave or nonmilitary related, then on course, posting, etc. You could also get bumped if a higher priority came up and needed a seat. I was on a posting so I was safe, but some others had to get the next flight. The Prime Minister at the time was Pierre Elliott Trudeau, and his plane had some sort of mechanical issue, so they were going to commender our flight. The problem being that it is going to take the night to re-configure the aircraft for the VIP package. The people from Ottawa just went home along with the ones that got bumped from the flight. That left about 100 or so of us Cpl /Pte's who were unless giving proof via a claim that you are entitled to a hotel for the night were not permitted outside the AMU for security reasons. You know, as soon as a Corporal or Private got loose from the Regiment we would tear up the town, end up in cells, (jail) and miss our flight. Funny how they applied those lessons learned to us, but as they say RHIP. Once the Boeing 707 was unloaded all the luggage was re-xrayed and secured in the hanger with the MP's on the door. The SR NCOs and Officers had their mess to go to and stretch out, have a drink and a bite. Meanwhile, the rest of us searched out spaces to get comfortable for the night. Some small groups who were traveling together returning from a course were playing cards in the smoking area. Since you had to wear your S3 dress uniform, the old green bus driver style itchy scratchy tunic when you traveled on a service flight, and shoes that were a killer. Normally in the Army, your footwear was the combat boot or your dress parade boots. The problem is that after week ten at CFB Cornwallis (am I permitted to use his name since the statue was taken down?) you were able to get double soles and clickers put on your boots. This gave that distinctive cadence when marching on parade giving that authoritative sound that makes a head turn. Unfortunately, the Air Force saw the metal clickers as a sparking hazard, and they were forbidden on the hanger or the tarmac approach to the aircraft so you either had them pulled off for the flight at which the loadmaster produced a smile and pliers, took them off, taped them up, which would also destroy the glossy hard earned spit shine or wear shoes and pack very carefully in your barrack box for the flight. My size 12 boots took up a lot of space. That used to suck coming back from a course in Chilliwack and the warm December to CFB Gagetown's winter four-foot snow banks. By the time you got off the plane, walked through the snow to get the base taxi back to Base accommodations, and made your way home from there, your feet were soaked, and raw leather spots and scrapes appeared on the once highly shone to a deep reflective gloss toe cap.

The next morning the CANEX coffee shop opened up and the line went the whole distance of the area out into the AMU. Back in line as your name was called, seat assigned and we were airborne before 1100. It was a long flight with a stopover we got into Lahr early the next morning. I got my kit bag and rucksack and made my way to customs. That was a long process and after being up for over 36 hours in the same uniform with a two-day growth. Feeling like 10 pounds of shit in a 5-pound bag was the general feeling. The RSM was waiting at the main door with one of the regiments orderly room Cpl's. As our name was called, from the attention was called "Sir" out. Once the dozen or so of us were collected up, the first blast of shit from a crusty old Chief Warrant Officer Regimental Sergeant Major commenced. CWO Mushrow was about five foot five, tuff as nails, and didn't care who you were, or where you were if he wanted your attention he got it. If he had his pace stick in hand that would be brought into the conversation with pointing, swinging gestures, and the occasional light poke at a button on a pocket or some other out-of-place accruement. There has been more than one chin tapped on parade for not having "shaved for that day".

Welcome to Germany. The first stop was to the regiment Orderly Room to clear in, get your ration card, and room in the shacks, followed by the quick rules for the next few days. We were not able to leave the base until we got our Canadian Forces Europe ID cards, so the guys in the shacks all got introduced, finding out who was who and where the places were on the base. There were lots to do with the Centennial Club, the Junior Ranks and event hall, a bowling alley, a movie theatre, five or six different places to eat, and many clubs and hobby shops to keep you busy. When I was in 22 Field, I did the 2-week Combat Diver preliminary, but because I was a V3 vision, being nearsighted it was a medical fail. I needed my glasses to drive so even though your sight is about 25% better underwater if you had to RECCE a bridge or fording area at night I could not see enough unless I had my glasses. Not to be put off by that news I did my NAUI basic open water diver at the base pool before I flew over and later joined the Lahr Sub Aqua Club to complete my open water check-out dives. I still got together with some of the combat diver-qualified guys and we dove all over Germany, France, Spain, and Austria's Lake Konstance. Completing several more civilian diving courses and eventually became the Vice President of the LSAC. If the Regimental dive team was going off for an exercise, they would come over to the club and fill some tanks there. The club had just got a new big compressor and a six-bottle cascade system capable of filling about 25 80 cubic foot scuba tanks in an afternoon so with their compressor and the clubs going cut down on the after-hours work. The filling room was nice and cool especially when it was scorching out. There was a two-foot by six-foot metal tank used to keep the tanks cool during filling. Also kept the beer cool.

Waiting for my PMQ (Private Married Quarters) to be available, I moved into the shacks for the next few months while the Regiment finishes the exercise cycle and when leave comes up in July I will get the keys to the PMQ and move in August before Fall Ex, which was six weeks or so long. I almost lost the PQM the first weekend I had it. The welcome-in party got a bit out of hand, and they drew the line at going between balconies. We were on the fourth floor, so not too smart playing daredevil after several rounds of Jaermeister mini bottles. A case of 24 was 24 Deutsche Mark (DM) so a four-way split was only 6 DM. Durning playing Euchre, the loss of points required a shot. Tap the mini bottle shake, twist to break the seal, off with the twist top, between the teeth, and tilt back your head to chug it back. You then chase that with a Heineken (a green grenade) and play another game. Wash, rinse, repeat.

Margret showed up in mid-August, eight months pregnant. Our PMQ was on the top floor, so eight levels of stairs to get to our apartment. Our address for the next four years was Area 30, building 5, apartment 15. A 30-5-15. Easy enough to remember for taxi drivers to know where you want to go, as well as the German address on a laminated card, 22 Swartzwald strasa, #15. Most of the Taxi drivers were pretty good at getting you back. One card that you got from the troop clerk was a "Don't be AWOL " card. It was a laminated card with a list of phone numbers ranging from the Unit Orderly room to the Padre. If you were away from the area or couldn't get in during a snowball you could call in. A snowball was when the 4 Canadian Mechanized Brigade Group (CMBG) was going to emergency deploy to the field. The whole Battlegroup had time to meet for around three hours to have the Units all packed up and we would either just roll out the back gate and park in a staging area to wait for further orders. Sometimes we sat for a day and then rolled back to the base. Sometimes we loaded up on a train and deployed out somewhere along the German border set up a harbour area checked out a bridge or two then loaded back up.

Back out for Fall Ex part two in the field again. A few weeks later, with a check-in phone call planned to get updates from Margret and what the Doctor was saying. We didn't have a phone in our place, so you had to coordinate with someone in the block who had a phone. It was expensive to call from the phone booth at the American PX. There was a sitting/smoking area with a few dozen booths. With a few 1000 soldiers posted there on long exercises, that or the HAM radio were the only ways to talk. No internet then, iPhones, or Facebook, just handwritten letters.

After about three weeks of exercise, I called her and she told me that it was false labor pains, but the Dr said any day so that I should make my way back to Lahr on the next daily run. The calls and memos were done, and the following day I had my AWOL bag packed for the trip back in a 5-ton cargo as a co-driver with the rest of my kit secured in the QM Paul Bunion. The Exercise was over in another week, so if I couldn't make it back, it would come back in the secure stores to the hangar. Jennifer was born two days later 26 September 1983, after the afternoon coffee break. Went to check on Margret at the Base hospital, and during a contraction she grabbed onto my hand, and wouldn't let go. One of the staff had to call the ROR to let them know where I was. As the RSM said, "You were involved in the laying of the keel, no need to be there for the launch"

Later that fall I was selected to go on the EOD Basic course (HA) in Chilliwack in November-December. Since Jennifer was just two months old at that time, going back to Canada for two months while Margret stayed behind seemed ok to me. Well, I was told that I thought wrong. She was not going to stay in a foreign country, with a new baby, with no friends while I am in Chilliwack, with my friends, in a familiar place, no baby, and going out on the weekends with the boys. Or words to that effect. Hence the calls to and from the Orderly room and after a stack of paperwork was stamped in triplicate, Margret and Jennifer were booked on a priority 5 seat to Ottawa. The civilian airport was just on the other side of the airfield a 10-minute taxi ride. As we were reloading the aircraft for the next stop on the trans-Canada milk run, Margret and Jennifer were safely in the taxi off for their flight to Halifax. They were going to split the time between my parent's place here in Halifax, and her family in Oromocto NB.

In January 1984 I moved to Ammo and was the driver of 28 A. My section vehicle was an M548 cargo carrier track vehicle. In the Field Troop, you usually spent on average seven months away on exercises for the year with the year's training schedule all laid out so you could plan your year. The many Troop BBQs and Pig roasts for rotation/promotion parties were always fun. Everyone in the troop paid 5 DM every payday so over the course of four to five months there is a healthy balance. This resulted in a nice bank account balance that paid for these. Our first experience with this was the

170

Two Troop Tramps Oath. All the new guys that were posted in lined up at the head table with the Troop Commander (TC) and Troop WO. One by one we were handed a scroll to read and a full liter of beer. "Repeat after me, " said the TC and we did. After each paragraph, we drank a beer. First standing, then kneeling, and the third was the Pukka Sapper. You were held upside down by a few guys and you drank the beer upside-down. A bit of a challenge keeping it out of your nose. Not hazing as such, because you had a choice of beverage besides beer. A passage of rite. The whole unit bonding thing. Great memories.

My first exercise winter exercise was REFORGER '84. It was a big NATO exercise with the American Military mobilizing their Battle Group from the States to Germany. The main emphasis was the actual deployment of several 1000 troops from other participating NATO countries. The Regiment was part of 4 CMBG. During the weekdays the military was able to travel on the main roads, up to and including the Autobahn, but from Saturday 0000 hours to Sunday 2359 hours track vehicles i.e. Leopard tanks, Mobile Artillery, APC must park for the 48 hours in a Harbour or Bivouac area. Since 4 CER was all track or heavy equipment we set up for the weekend and were looking forward to the Sunday routine. Once the vehicles were parked, the halt inspection was done the kitchen truck was set up the section Sgt went off for the nightly O group. Since it was mid-February in Northern Germany the Fasching celebrations were being held in the small towns in the training area. These parades and dancing shows were specific to the town's main attraction. There would be 30-40 people all dressed up in the same costumes which looked really interesting. You could also buy plaster of Paris figurines or masks from each of the different groups. That Saturday night we were all going out as a troop to the arena and watch the 1 1/2 hour show and then have dinner at the local Gasthaus. There were 30 of us all dressed in green combats sitting in four or five rows. And we fit right so well dressed all the same. After dinner, the transport Troop had 5/4 pickup trucks to bring us back to the harbour area. Each pickup could hold six to eight guys. We take our turns waiting for the next ride, finishing up our beers. About 30 minutes later the other three trucks arrive. As

Jimmy Willmore and I undid the straps to roll up the tarp on our truck the RSM CWO Spruce got out of the driver's side and came to the rear of the truck giving a hand if needed getting into the truck bed. Some of us had a few beers with supper. As long as the eight-hour rule wasn't broken, and you didn't get too loaded all was good. The truck started off and we were all really preoccupied with talking about the night's show just rocking with the swerves and turns when the truck stopped and stayed still for a minute. All of a sudden the truck was backing up to turn around and we felt, then heard a crunch and the sound of metal on metal. Jimmy flipped up the tarp and we saw a dark Volvo fender crunched by the bumper. He had just backed into the car turning around. The driver's door flies open, and you just hear the RSM cursing as he comes to the back. Then he turned and saw the eight of us in the back just looking at him. "Nothing happened here, understand" or words to that effect said the RSM. Holly fuck. This is the real army. Almost just like something out of a war movie.

Back in our CP with the Penthouse setup. It was a set of rails that came down the sides of the APC then a tarp over it. This gave the section a more protected living/cooking area. Sunday routine was next so a few games of cards broke out and conversations went back to earlier about that night and soon the term "Volvo Killer" was being whispered. The 5/4 in question was not involved in an accident, and there will be no more of the Volvo Killer or any other reference to this was laid out pretty clearly in the next O group. As a side note, RSM Spruce was later posted to Cold Lake in charge of the Primrose Training area. There was a section of Combat Engineers posted there to maintain the range and do any EOD that might have to be done. The CF18 target range was located there, with a sort of Rod and Gun, (cast and blast) club. Besides it was a good place to fish for Pickerel.

We had a section supper at the local village Gasthaus. They are usually small in size with the customary stone above the door with the date of the opening. 1874 and earlier were some of the places run by the same family. They made the beer, and cherry snaps, and had the hogs and chickens from the farm. Inside were a few long tables and 10 or so smaller. There always was a table off in a corner

172

with a big ashtray and a Stadmish sign. This was for the locals. When they built the Gasthaus the local population was the main village and the surrounding farms, not for 25 guys dropping in for supper, so calls were made, and each of the Field troops had places to dine out. Since this exercise has been going on for years, they are prepared and really roll out the welcome mat. There was an expression over there," The farther away from the base, the bigger the schnitzel". These were huge mounds of spaetzle noodles with a Hunter (mushroom) gravy and pom frites. I was also introduced to a drinking game that was a first for me. There was a one-liter beer mug filled with beer and five shots of cognac (the cheap type). The top was a wooden circle with five hoses around the outside and a larger one in the centre. The five on the outer hoses sucked to create a small vacuum, and the sixth person blows in pressurizing the mug, and in a split second, the mug is dry. Rack them up. Well for five more times anyway. You have to pay to play. It is something along the lines of shotgunning a beer. Google reference if unsure.

Mexican Overdrive. That is what you called an out-of-control track vehicle going downhill. You steer with tiller bars instead of the traditional steering wheel. When pulled back on a tiller bar it will cause that track to slow down making the vehicle turn in that direction, but they also are the brakes. We were on a Fall Ex '84 and the afternoon ammo run to a section was ordered in. After the route/map check, we loaded up and made our way through the mountains to the sections obstacle they were completing. Unloaded and back to the harbour area. Also in the Cargo carrier were Mike Fowler, and Sylvester.

As a side note, 28A had been in for an inspection /work order a few weeks before the exercise, and some bolts were replaced as per the hour meter maintenance book.

We are about 15 km from 2 Troop's area, starting down the other side of this mountain with the grade a little more going down. As I applied the right tiller bar a huge bang and something exploded underneath the floor boards. They started bouncing and lifting up and down. The track started to drift left across the double lines as I tried to regain some sort of control. With a weight of 12 tonnes, and a few more as cargo (" this ain't no feather duster you know"). With

173

the carrier's overall dimensions of 20 feet long, and 9 feet wide now, she was now free running down a steepening grade with only trees on the big hill to the left stopping the long trip down to the rushing river below. Sylvester had put his feet on the dash to keep from getting hit by parts or fluids coming up from the engine. I couldn't make the turn, so I was carefully pulling on the opposite bar to scrub off some speed. Not that we were going over 30-40 kph, but that is a big rolling hunk of metal so aim for a soft pile of Fir trees off onto the left hillside and squeeze those arse cheeks tight. In retrospect, those few seconds it was just the survival instinct, seemed to be all in slow motion. We got stopped, but it wasn't pretty. Most of the trees were 4-6 inches in diameter so as the M-548's slopped front end rode up over them, they actually acted as a sort of catch fencing, slowing us down. Finally stopped a few 100 feet in and I hit the engine kill switch. Everyone does the quick running of your fingers over your face and quickly downward to the rest. No one was injured, a few bumps but otherwise all ok. Now, what the fuck just happened.

Once outside and walked around the crash site for a further look, a nervous smoke followed. Since there were no iPhones or wifi just the tray-mounted low-range RF radio, which did or did not work in the hills and wooded areas we gave it a shot before the batteries died. A part of the propeller shaft ripped a hole in the rad, thus the hot fluids to spray up. Got a hold of the CP, but no one is around for recovery. The Battle Group was on the move and we just had to hang tight. We had 72 hours of rations and lots of water, but nothing else. Within a few hours, a vehicle from another Troop came by and got Sylvester, he had to get back to his section. Mikey and I had to secure the vehicle/weapons and just wait it out for a few days until they rolled back this way. Needed a bigger tow truck to get her out of the rhubarb.

As our first night closed in, the green Coleman cook stove was broken out, and water was on the boil for supper and some hot coffees. US Meals Ready to Eat (MRE) were what the field troops in 4 CMBG consumed when not on hot rations. These came in a carton of 12, with 4 each for breakfast, lunch, and supper. Since it was just the two of us the pick of the pack was up for options.

Breakfast for supper, why not, and some John Wayne cookies for dessert.

With the carrier sorted as best as we could, sleeping bags laid out, and a last look around before going to ground. We decided that since the track was so far off the roadway, no one would be snooping around so a full night of sleep was welcomed.

The next morning after coffee and a quick wash, I was going into the village to find a store for some real food and some cokes. Most towns have a sports complex where you can, for a few marks, get a shower. Some of the troop harbours / Bivouac areas were next to soccer fields, so this was a common practice. Mikey was going to do the afternoon walk after my recce and would stay by the road in case a Regimental vehicle came by.

In my broken German, I managed to get my message across to the store owner, an elderly gentleman. He came out from the counter and motioned me to follow him. Ok, I thought, great he will give me directions. Instead, he again gestured with his hand to get into his car. Even better, now I don't have to walk in bad directions. Getting my *rechts and links* straight might have been a challenge. As we were driving, I noticed that the town was in the opposite direction. The driver didn't speak much except *"ein paar minuten."* In a minute was my translation. We pulled up to a small typical German farmhouse, and he went in returning with a male in his mid 20's over to the car. Now totally confused the only thing I could come up with was " I'm Cpl Tanner with 4 CER and I think that there is a misunderstanding." After my explanation of the situation, he replied back in English that he was on leave from the German Army, and was a Tanker. With that sorted out they were offering to bring us back for supper, a shower, and our laundry. War movie stuff for sure. With the logistics worked out, the shift was made up and we took turns for supper. With a clean set of clothes and some homemade bread, I made it back just before last light and Mikey still had not heard anything. Oh well, at least we had a good night with that family.

Just after our morning coffee a REME truck came by to check out the recovery job and a ride back to Hoenfelts training area. It was the end part of that phase of the exercise, so back to camp and got ready for the train to move back to Lahr.

Nicknames. It is unenviable that somewhere along your life's journey you will acquire a nickname. Coco Adams, Chicken Arms, Johny Mac. Other nicknames around the regiment were Tex, Bubbles, Woody, Droppings, Pig Pen, Ducky, Roscoe, Exadore, Chisel Chin, The Silver Fox, and The Easter Pig. My second fall ex with The Two Troop Tramps as 28A's driver I picked up the nickname. Comatose, AKA Coma.

Coma. Now at first reading this reference you might not know what to think. I've had a few that I can recall. Some are not so PG-rated. I digress.

We were off doing an Ammo run during the afternoon time so road snacks are thrown into a combat coat pocket for the road trip. Once we got out of the harbour Mikey was asking me what I wanted to eat, and "What do you get" was the standard answer. The choice was fudge brownies and chocolate cookies. A brownie sounded good as I eased onto the checkered route and out for our first drop-off. Driving with my legs holding the tiller bars I started on a cookie, not bad, and the brownie next. It was small so the whole thing was chewed up and chased with some water. Almost instantly my ears became ringing and I could feel my face and tongue swelling up. Shit, that's not good. The MREs only listed a generic name on the wrapper and preparation instructions, and no other ingredients. I was deathly allergic to Walnuts, cashews, and pecans, so I am mindful of what I eat. Anyway, as full-blown anaphylaxis kicks in, I manage to pull the track over and almost pass out. All I can hear is Mikey yelling over the radio that I am having some sort of reaction to something. A No Duff was called in. During an exercise, if a real-life incident happened, accident, etc, a No Duff call clears the radio frequencies until the situation is under control.

A 5/4 was sent out as the call went out for the Field Ambulance to RV at our bivouac at the CP 29A. I do remember some bits and pieces of being on a litter in the back of the box amb and then going down to the post-WW1 hospital with its bleached high tiled walls. Four of the guys from 2 Troop were on the corners of the green

WW2 era litter humping down to another room for a few checks by the ER doctors. It now feels like a scene from any war movie. Everything is just like you can imagine but with smells, noise, and other voices that you cannot understand. In the elevator and up and out somewhere else. The hospital staff then took over and the guys were sent out.

IVs in each arm, my combats just cut off, boot laces and all to get me stripped down. A lot of talking and at one point I remember puking. Once in the half-moon pan, and the next was, not so nice. Well, they had to force it out of my system as it was later explained to me.

I have the release report from my 2-day hospital stay. The original and the translated versions. Interesting reading for sure. It was on very nice letterhead with crests etc on it. When I was discharged there were only a few days left before the train moved back and on excused duty for another 2 days I went back to Lahr and reported to the Rear party and get ready for the train unloading and store cleaning. Everything was cleaned, tagged if broken, and given the once over before the Regiment was dismissed for a three-day weekend.

The moral of the story, watch your nuts!

My next posting was in the 48 Squadron, as the Regimental Ammo NCO and it was a job with a bit more responsibility. I was driving a 5-ton with a trailer, with the other three section ammo reps working with me sorting and delivering the different troops' daily requests. You could be doing the demo range for the morning, then the cases of link rounds for the machine gun range. When the week was over the non-used ammo and explosives had to be counted, verified, and stored back in the Ammo compound. It was quite the deal getting in and out of the compound. Armed patrols, German Shepard guard dogs, double gates, one bunker open at a time. Your paperwork was good from the night before, your order is ready to load up. If not, some delays can really mess up your whole day, so there was an agreement of sorts between the different regiments. I have something that I know that we are no longer going to use, i.e., para flares, and someone needs some for a night shoot, and they have something you could use some more of, i.e., Bangalore torpedoes. The end result was that you didn't want to take any extra ammo back to base except for the regular required load. I'm pretty sure nowadays that would be a chargeable offense under some munitions act somewhere. No Names, No Pack drill. Got to do what you got to do, within reason that it is.

For my last year in Germany, I was posted to the Three Troop Vagabonds HQ section as the Dispatch Driver. I had my CSC MC instructor course, so after teaching a few DR courses ripping around the German wood line sounds like fun. Back then the "Stars and Bars" daily was mass-produced for the US forces stationed overseas and covered the big joint exercises in the paper. I happened to find a clipping from a 4 CER Field Engineer Camp in April 1987. The article was written by LT Keith Moody and covers "the wonderful three weeks we just spent in the US Army controlled Wildflecken Training Area (WTA) …somewhere northeast of here about 20 km away from the East German border…with the rain also came the dreaded wind; through the night the sound of madly flapping tents kept one in a justifiable state of fear as to whether the tent would stay up or not … Guess what? On one particular night, our nightmares were realized. During the deepest darkest hours the wind gusted fiercely and tore several tents from their moorings. Our field orderly room was one of the casualties causing correspondence to become airborne and fly into the nearby woods… Finally, after two and a half weeks of exercising, End Ex was called and we started the long process of cleaning, reorganizing, and refueling ourselves and our vehicles for the long trip back home. 4 CER is well prepared to support the brigade in any future endeavors. Chimo!"

And that was only one exercise. Well written, Sir.

We called that exercise Mud-Flicken. Mud and wind and mud. It was everywhere and on everything. Soon most of us had some sort of hack or cough starting and chills so someone, I don't know which SNCO came up with it but it seemed to work as I recall. Their version of a hot toddy. Two sugar packets, two aspirin from the FA kit, two oz of Bacardi's rum, and a few oz of hot water. Stir until it all dissolves then drink it up. Into the fart sack and lights out.

That May we started the process of getting all the paperwork in line for our posting back to Canada. I was going back to Chilliwack for my QL 3 Plumber Gas Fitter. After I had been accepted for my remuster course the CM posted the option of a four-year extension, then the close out of CFB Lahr. We had a few long discussions about going either way, but ultimately to take my remuster and return back was the decision. If you sit around with a few beers/scotches and play the "could have, should have, and would have game", then that starts to bring into question other decisions. I did go down that rabbit hole more than once and it is highly Not recommended.

I would be remiss if I didn't mention the 4 CER *Dirty Thursday* Ruck marches around the Lahr Airfield. When in garrison, for PT a few times a month the Regiment did a forced march with weapons and webbing around the 10 km permitter road. Someone posted a video from '86 of us running to the music of the Scorpions. A good laugh from the past.

3 Troop Vagabonds 1986.

CFB Lahr Who was there and when   ...

Picked this up from one of the towns during a fasching parade. '78'-'82'. Fun times.

1w   Like   Reply   4

Mask from a parade

Cab of the M548

Rafting across the Rhine on a Fall Ex

Chapter 25

EM WO

EM WO 8 Wing CFB Trenton was my official billet description at RTF with the occasional FSM duties to attend to. This position has morphed from when Captain Bill Ramsey, the Base Emergency Response plan guy and also the bi-annual Wing OSCER (On Scene Commander) airfield training exercise planner. The OSCER students were ATC officers and Sr. NCOs who were tower assistants. The ex was the last day of course. Bill had on his last posting been the SME on this subject giving courses and guidelines on procedures to other Squadron OC's and senior staff over the years.

January 2006 I moved into the newly created Standards cell. Since we were giving the same course material as the PSTC in Kingston to the Camp Mirage roto, the reviews and quizzes had to be administered and checked. Captain Ramsey asked me if I was interested in Emergency Management and learning how the Air Force works in panic mode. Incidentally, Bill was a Warrant Officer MP in the Army before going to the dark side. Catching a theme here? Why not. Your position number is attached to the unit's nominal roll, but where you work is at the OC's discretion so all is good.

My first OSCER exercise started at 1000 that Thursday morning with the crash bells ringing followed by " Exercise, exercise, exercise. Inbound aircraft has declared an inflight emergency. Master hydraulic failure warning indication. Exercise, exercise, exercise" Ok let's rock and roll. Inject number one was sent and the show unfolded. The script is moved along at the Exercise Director's orders, ensuring checklist items were followed, and if for some reason there is a problem, quickly follow the flow chart arrows for the Go/No-Go answers.

Off on one of the taxiways, there was a CF18 Hornet airframe with patches and marks all over it. There was a mannequin in a flight suit sitting in the cockpit and a smoke pot was letting white smoke simulate a crash. With lights and sirens blaring the Crash Rescue trucks are rolling from the firehall and approaching the crash site. Meanwhile, the students are either participating or taking notes for the hot wash (air force for debriefing) later that afternoon. Pretty sweet that getting access to places that the average person doesn't adds a bit of coolness to the job. Moving from Tactical, the boots on the ground stuff to Operations. Next-level shit. My old Secret clearance had to be verified and soon my clearance and Air Field ID card with lots of letters on it representing areas of access.

The Wing Ops CP was located deep within the building where the Wing Commander and his senior staff could manage an event in the "cone of silence". A Get Smart reference for the older crowd. Before gaining entrance into the Vault your cell phone and other electronic devices had to be secured in a bus station-type locker. Put your stuff in, and take the key with you. Then swipe to get into the inner offices, and then another swipe to get into the CP itself. The term cone of silence was coined because you were basically isolated from the world. The Motorola's that everyone used at the crash sites could not be transmitted into the CP, so updates were delayed and sometimes not complete. At the time the Wing was using the *Crackberry* as the main tool of communications and because of the cheap barebones plan, they were falling far short of what was needed. Buying bulk sometimes has its disadvantages.

I remember when our OC Maj Brendon Abram was deployed during the Haiti earthquake emergency. He was sent to Jamaica as one of the administration staff for the arriving goods and materials to be sent further on when required. You know send boxes 1-25 first to set up, 26-50 next then finally 51-75. Simple concepts aren't always so simple. The first flight was rerouted to Tyndall AFB Florida, the second's load was mixed, and the third was "commandeered" by some other agency for their shipment, so load three was shuffled back in the cue, and so on, and so on… Brendon ended up being there for about six weeks instead of three. Meanwhile, the MSS is trying to build a camp with critical components missing. Back to the Wing Ops CP story.

Since then, I have already mentioned Maj Brendon Abram was

my OC, during his term I do remember one or two other times that I made a few trips to Ops was for the charge parade. Since the Maj was the OC, and I was the FSM, he could lay the charge after I wrote it up and gave the member notice of the proceedings. The CO was a LCol and the RSM was a CWO, (enough acronyms for you?) they were the authority for delivering the punishment after the charge(s) had been laid, and a summary trial or court martial had been held, evidence presented, defense, and the decision. I have over my military have been the Accused, the Escort, and marched the member into the CO's office.

Everyone on our ALQ had fun rehearsing Charge Parade procedures and taking the opportunity to role-play each part, but on course and in the CO's Conference room for real is a different story.

It was about 0315 hrs and the phone was ringing. Probably a telemarketer's auto dialings from another time zone, but I grab the landline. It was the Maj on the other end. "Call Sgt Chalmers and the both of you get here soonest. One of our guys was in a fight downtown, and he was in the hospital getting treatment. At the request of the attending ER doctor the Quinte West Police were there and then brought him back to their station. " Ok, what, ok, call Dave.

When we met the OC, instructions were to gather said individual, bring him here so he could be cautioned, etc, and return him home to sleep. It was a weapons training day and he definitely could not teach drill or drive.

We pull into the QW detachment parking lot at 0410 and go inside to talk to the watch commander about what is going on. "He just left in a taxi a few minutes ago. Probably just missed it." Really, I thought that he was here and we were coming to get him was my understanding" Still a bit confused I continued "If he was impaired and injured, why did you let him go?" That was my next question.

"The hospital said he was ok, and there are no charges against him, so when he asked to leave, we had to let him go. That's the law"

Ok, thanks. A quick call to the Maj and back into the office where the next moves are discussed. No one was answering the number listed so wait out until 0730 and see if he shows up. Stranger things have happened.

It is now approaching 0500, so a Tims run and back for the OC's next instructions. Dave went down to sort out the training roster, and I got to work on my morning emails, doing the Monday morning delete routine and any other small fires that needed to be looked into.

At 0745 the phone rings, and the OC has a plan he wants to discuss. In short, Dave, MCpl Shelden Clarke, RCD, our CBRN instructor, have all done a few tours to go by his home and see what is what.

The individual was home, a little bruised, and had some facial cuts, but he was home. A few hours of discussions between all of us that stayed there in that living room. It was now time for a shit, shower, and a shave, dressed in uniform and face the music. Back in the OC's office after lunch where the charge report was read and acknowledged. We were dismissed I drove him back home in the Blue crew cab. A mature conversation between us discussing what was going to happen, and there was total acceptance on his part.

Back at work, rumors are starting to circulate that it was not fair that the member was also being charged. Give him a break already. This is where leadership, and the command team, as we are called now, OC and FSM, are the midlevel decision makers with the Col's and RSM's as our reporting supervisors. Tough decisions and discipline are not as easy as it looks sometimes. The old stereotyped British Indian War era RSM's high voice yelling the cadence at 120 beats per minute waving a drill cane. The 1978 Richard Burton and Roger Moore mercenaries movie "The Wild Geese" comes to mind. 30 days without a doubt, RSM march the guilty bastard out.

The summary trial was slated for 1300 hours at WOPS, so the procedure was reviewed and then we made our way over to the CP. I don't know who was more nervous, him or me walking. The commands and orders were going over and over in my head. Call the Halt on the left step, right turn to the CO's deck. Not too close as to kick the desk with your boots, and don't get tongue-tied.

Section 129 (1) of the NDA charge. "Any act, conduct or neglect to the prejudice of good order and discipline" constitutes a service offense. The others were dropped, with a $500.00 fine as the CO'c punishment.

As far as everyone was concerned, the subject was dealt with, and let's move on. Back to business.

That was the only time I had to do a charge parade. One of those things that some may never get to do. It all sounds very neat and tidy, but tons of paperwork goes between the base legal officer reference wording, charge selection, possible scale of punishment, etc. Lots of reading and deciphering terms. Worse than the PER word picture guides.

The exercise cell had been stood up for 18 months when Captain Ramsey decided he was retiring and going back to the big rock. With this, a message was sent out and a new Captain was arriving that March- April. Capt Jana Kozicki and her husband had been living on their sailboat at their last posting, a good start, and also a qualified ships diver. Another check mark in the good side. I was on the CCC course when she popped in during their HHT, so just a quick intro until posting season.

The OC was big on education and creditability for the RTF since training was our bread and butter. You needed something to back up the PPT besides " this is what 1 CAD sent to us" Otherwise the eyes just start to glaze over. It is sometimes unfortunate but at the operations level of things, courses and secondary schooling are required when addressing COs and civilian town council members. The NATO standard answer of" I'm not sure about that, but when I get some information I will contact you" During tabletop and full-scale exercises just don't cut the mustard. Since all I had in my portfolio was Grade 12 JL Ilsley Spryfield NS 1979 certificate an upgrade was in order.

For the next four years, the EM exercise cell members that I worked with were Capt's Jana Kozicki, Jim Boland, and Konrad Ostner. The Maj was the Exercise Director and jumped in when needed signing the memos for training funding. We all attended several conferences with other Emergency Management groups, (a subject at my DWD. Something about Konrad and pre-drinking in

186

the hotel room...) Police and Fire Chief, and cross-border training with the US Military Hurricane and Disaster response teams.

At a World Emergency Management conference in Toronto one year we had signed up for the JIBC intro to the EOC. The courses and seminars from design to small population cities. Exercise design was our main focus and there is always a better mouse trap out there. In short, I signed up with Jim to do the first few courses, and later on I went and completed my EM Ex Design program. This was now getting into the ICS system and the command structure, which is the emergency management guide structure. Scaleable and can be used with or without certain components. My next move was getting the full EM certification. Good memo coaching gets good results. "Research schools and get back to me by next week. You have funding for a multi-year course." Sweet.

A two-year exercise program was then developed from a symposium to a three-day full-scale multiagency agency exercise. This was a great learning experience with the information and best practices shared between the OPP, RCMP, and local fire and police forces was the best of both worlds.

I have throughout this discussion paper referenced my time at the RTF so as to not get caught in that loop I will move on the final chapter, the sum up.

The Captain's office after leave. We needed a bigger section, so on paper we do now...

Chapter 26

Sum up

Once I decided to go for it and after reading several online writing guides and visiting more websites than I can remember, there were two common threads that all stressed:

First, you need words on a page to edit. Not necessarily all the right words, and not in the right order, but just your words.

Second, if you want to publish your manuscript, you have to end it sometime, otherwise, it is an ongoing journal. If for some reason, your muse has arrived and auto-writing has kicked in, do as Clive Cussler, James Paterson, and Tom Clancy do. They add a sneak preview with the first few pages from their next book in the series. Might just do that.

Looking at the word count it is obvious that verbal diarrhea has taken hold so.. Sum up your ineffective SLUG. (Student Learning Under Guidance). That is what was taped to the back of Sgt Smith's clipboard and yes that was his real name. You had 40 minutes for your lecture, 39~41 were the limits so if you were getting close, you got the sign. He was our section commander/ course instructor on my Combat Leaders Course I completed while posted to 4 CER. Sorry about that …squirrel…..

After reviewing what has been written down over the past two years or so, hopefully, I did learn something under his guidance and it's time to wind this down.

So, on the first page the title was, So, how did I get here?

This is the Coles notes version or something that resembles it. I had mentioned that I had written a cookbook when we rented a place in Florida to Linda Mosher, a lady who we see at church in passing one Sunday morning at coffee wanted to read it. Linda recently self-published a book, "Surrounded by Death And Bureaucrats" stories from the Nova Scotia Medical Examiner's Office and commented on the book and wondered who set it up. It was just me, a vacation project to share with friends who know my second passion is cooking. Her comments were surprisingly very positive and put the bug in my ear to maybe self-publish. Linda gave me a few sites to check out in my spare time.

Over the course of a few weeks of detailed research phone calls and emails, I came to the conclusion that to promote, discuss and blog about cooking wasn't my thing at all. It is a fun pastime, but MasterChef or Chopped Canada competitions are fine on TV thank you very much. That is the main reason why I gave up teaching Scuba Diving after 15 years. It was no longer fun chasing after students and the long hours filling tanks for the next morning's check-out dives. That was my main concern about doing a cookbook. Promotion of the product. But, I do have a 55k-word manuscript about myself and my struggles with PTSD. Now that I could promote. Awareness about Service dogs and a possible funding stream for Paws Fur Thought. Thoughts become things. Giving back or paying it forward wherever you want to call it, with this book being published it is my overwhelming gratitude for the gift of my Service dog Barrett.

I am sometimes asked what Barrett does for me, and how they get their dog certified. Since I am all for public awareness and education on these wonderful animals I address the training question by explaining what CARES stands for. Canine Assistance and Rehabilitation Education Services where I spent a week training at the Concordia Kansas facility. If I have my cane, the first and not too far from the truth assumption is that he helps with my mobility issues. I'll have the blue plate special ;0.

The walks keep the joints and muscles moving, but our morning walks are the ones where we take a break sitting on the top of the hill, overlooking Whistlers Cove and out as far as the eye can see. The ocean is just an ocean. Flat or boiling with storm surges, it's a place where your mind can just drift with the swells, sometimes having a deep and sometimes emotional conversation with Barrett. He is always listening never interrupting. Almost as if he understands me. But he does. He keeps me grounded when I am thinking those not-so-pleasant thoughts, seeing something familiar when I suddenly jolt back into this world at 0130 most nights. My Protector is always seated in front of me looking at the door when we are having a meal out. The servers are always surprised when Barrett does not move when they walk by. Eyes on at all times though. Very positive comments always towards Barrett and sometimes a thank you for your service thrown in to boot. And I see the looks when they read the PTSD Not all wounds are visible and the Paws Fur Thought patches. Time for the hook and my 30-second PSA about the program. That is what a Real Service dog does.

Practice what you preach.

Since that day we were attacked by the dog at large, the following 7-8 months consumed my life reliving that day, with a different outcome before jolting me awake almost every night. Not that there was really anything new about waking up several times a night. It is either pain-related or just a Bang.. you are wide awake for no reason. The thing is that I always hear the click of Barrett's nails on the floor just as he is coming over to my side of the bed. "Hey buds, how are you? "I'm fully awake now and he rubs up on my arm, his wet nose pushes up for that contact, the grounding, yup, I got your six. A few pats on the head he does his circles and then I walk him back to the couch. Early days with Barrett I had tried to stay in bed, but he needed to see my feet on the floor and get out of bed. Over to the couch, up he goes and is snoring before I get back into mine. I kind of figured it out later that because of the Major Depressive Disorder diagnose symptoms his training and alertness was to get you up, even if just for a bit. When I caught COVID 19 there were a few days that bedrest was an essential part of the recovery, Barrett found it hard to understand why I was in bed mid-afternoon. Not in his schedule so it was several attempts later before he finally jumped up on the bed and curled up next to me facing the door. On duty always.

Hey, I thought that this was the Coles notes version. Look Car….

I won't rehash chapter 23 anymore, but directing that amount of energy from some sort of legal quagmire not to mention wasting money on what is really to be gained by a PTSD-enraged motive. Not the way to go. A few days into the new year, Margret asked me what was going on. She had "lost me " for a few days. Disassociation and drifting away had been a problem in the past. Not good, where are you? We talked about that day, and as she put it, "You have never been the same since that happened no trust, exploding over stuff for what. Talk to me".

What I had been writing over the past two years and where it was going was my next thing. I have to get this under control, so this book is my way of doing that.

The point is that you went where others would not. I have civilian friends, that openly said to me that they could never be away for those extended periods of time, let alone the where or why I was deployed.

My injury was job and work-related, but nothing very flashy or even headline-worthy. 30+ years doing my job. The forced marches for the BFT and deployment training, the Dirty Thursdays march around the 10 km CFB Lahr airfield full webbing and weapon plus just the hard physical work that our trades did. Injuries are a part of this way of life. They just add up after a while. As I mentioned prior, I had gotten an Exempt on my last express test that March for the year's end PER.

A few weeks later, we were at the CFB Kingston 600 m ranges running a crew through the level one weapon qualification. There had been a freezing rain/snowstorm the night before, but a lot more ice here. Depending on where along Lake Ontario you're located, the temperature difference can be quite different over the 100 km trip from Trenton.

We arrive to clear into Range Control around 0730, and then off to open up the range and get the morning started. The first thing is the inspection of the range firing positions and the butts. Sometimes the RMC Cadets leave things thrown in, not patched so that is where we started.

With things opened up and the guys assembling the ammo loading area, Dave and I walk the firing line being cautious of the iced-up areas. If the ice interfered with the shooter's spots the range practice would have been delayed or postponed.

Now as RSOs on site, we are directed in the CF Range Safety Manual, that you may, can, shall, or must cease training if conditions are determined unsafe, or words to that effect. The funny thing is that was did that before, and we caught a bit of flack from the current OC. Because it was sunny back there, and some of the Air Crew were hot on their Blackberrys already bitching that some NCMs had stopped the training without consulting them, etc and it wasn't really that bad...now. As not to get into a pissing contest that I would not win, especially when talking on a shity DND cellphone cruising down the 401 West by the Odessa exit, "Yes Sir when we get back into your office. Yes sir"

Big fucken deal, shit happens. The rest of the trip back was taunting and jokes. One of the aircrew had even suggested that to save time on the bus trip to the ranges they could load the ammo into the mags instead of outside when they got there. Nice suggestion, but a few faults in that scenario:

1. the 30-round magazines are prohibited because of their overcapacity and must be transported secured especially a few 100. We also have the bolts so the C7s they have on the bus cannot fire any rounds.

2. the loads are different and must be marked 5,10,15, and 20 then secured. My instructors are not doing that.

3. what happens when the bus hits a bump just as Lt Jones has opened up a 20-round box on the seat and the clips and loose rounds go scattering on the bus floor?

4. was that 19 or 20? and,

5. what happens when the bus stops for your Tims and a place with a warm washroom (instead of the range Porto potty at - 20c), and some loose 5.56 mm rounds roll off into the parking lot snow? Risk management and the Criminal Code of Canada... sir.

Back to that day. A Simple stupid accident that happens all the time, you slip and fall on your ass. This time it was just a little

193

different landing and the lights literally went out. Knocked the wind totally out as I lay on my right side. Dave was busting a gut, then helped me to the crew cab to catch my breath before the bus showed up. If you went in every time a small thing happened, your medical records would be in volumes and be termed a " MIR Commando" We have all fallen a few times over the years. The Cpl that I mentioned earlier about joining Bruce Nuclear had the year before, on the range acting as an ARSO did the exact same thing I had, but landed on his arm. He shook it off and sat it out in the truck for a bit. When we got back to Trenton, his arm was bruising so he went to the Wing Hospital to get checked out. His tendon was damaged and required surgery. See what I mean? Stupid. Squirrel.

We finished the day, and back in the classrooms, the students cleaned the weapons and magazines before going home. In my office still nursing the throbbing pain I finish the day's paperwork and lock up.

Back at the house, Tylenol and a heating pad on the puck-sized bruising that was getting ugly looking. Had worse playing in a weekend hockey tournament at Cold Lake.

As the weeks go on, things are getting slightly better and I have changed my gym routine a bit to give my back a break. Free weights are exchanged for elliptical or treadmill workouts.

The pain was not really backing down, but not really unbearable at this point. Tingling in my toes and leg had started, but not too bad. The five of us were still going to the gym 4-5 days a week, but I had been trimming back my routine to 30 min instead of 45, and an extra 10 in the sauna. One day in June as we were getting dressed back up, I bent to get something and the jolt of pain and tingling went right to my toes. Konrad was the locker beside me and I told him that I was going to see the doctor because something wasn't quite right.

Naproxen 500 mg 2 x daily and light duty for 14 days, then recheck was the suggested course of action and an MRI was the next move. The good news is that only six weeks to wait instead of six months. A new hospital in Coburg had just opened up so the times were down. Summer leave was in a few weeks, then back at it.

194

All throughout my leave, and back at work sitting and any bending caused more than some discomfort. Jennifer and Peter were visiting with us for a few weeks and were staying with us. I got the call for my MRI, on the following Wednesday night. By now the pain was nonstop and I could not even drive, so I had to be driven for the appointment.

It was a Saturday morning. Margret and I were having coffee on the back deck. I was standing/leaning with my cup on the flat wooden rail topper, Peter and Jennifer fixing their java and were coming out to join us. I just remember turning to my left and lights out. Dropped like a sack of potatoes. Margret said I was unresponsive for about 15-20 seconds. I just remember Peter and Margret calling my name, being tapped on the shoulder, and PAIN. Paralyzing, poker hot burning down my leg. They got me to the bedroom, but I could not move on my own. No matter how I moved the daggers kept coming.

Arriving at the QWH and just by chance my Dr. was on-call that shift. He wanted to know what happened. Wednesday I was walking, not today. He had not even gotten the chance to read the MRI CD that arrived yesterday. Admit and observe for now. Consults were being arranged.

On 26 October 2012, I had my back surgery done at the Kingston General Hospital. Procedures: right side discectomy and laminectomy.

I dug out the QHC discharge letter for reference before the rest of the files were pulled out and sifted through. Before I got too deep into the past, with the surgical notes out only, the rest can wait for another time, maybe. Unfortunately, I cannot destroy these banker boxes of documents.

1. Legal reasons, you are supposed to hold onto seven years of taxes, disability pension and other deemed important or irreplaceable documents, and

2. the day after the big fire pit, VAC or some other agency will request that last bundle of files that went blazing up with some fire additives that sparkle. Never need it until tomorrow, right?

"The fascia was opened and the muscles stripped from the posterior elements on the right L5 and S1.....The ligamentum flavum was excised piecemeal using a Cloward punch....There was significant lateral stenosis affecting the right S1 nerve root due to the focal disk herniation as well as facet and capsular hypertrophy...The annulus was intact and when incised, disk material oozed out. A single loose bone fragment was removed. The remaining loose disk fragments were cleared from the disk space using a series of pituitaries."

I'm glad that I was put out for that. "muscles stripped from...excised using a punch... when incised, disk material oozed out" Oozed out was the only medical term that I did not have to look up.

Education, what do the $10 words really mean to me, and to understand the long-term forecast. In other words, how far am I away from a wheelchair? We built our house and designed the property for that exact reason. Maybe when I am 80, or when I am 65, but now looking at the far right of the project management plan with a somewhat less critical view and assessment of what is really important. So back to the previous paragraph and my dumbed down from my Dr. so I can understand it.

BTW, these sentences were underlined so they must have been explained. The piece of bone that was removed was the one he suspected fractured and was part of the issue, and the stenosis can affect my bowel and bladder incontinence (my having to piss problems) and tingling sensations as well as the pain. Nerve damage is an educated guess. You can run a sharp up and down the underside of my foot and not a twitch. Bang on my ankle with the rubber hammer, nada no movement. I had to learn to overcome and adapt as they say in the Army.

I am asked what Barrett actually does for me. At first glance, besides lying down with his head resting on my foot and checking out the room? To the average Joe, that's about it, and that is what they should see. Someone sitting in an open public place and not having some sort of mental meltdown because of an unknown triggering action that to anyone else would not pass a second thought.

Barrett's sense of smell is about 10 thousand times better than a human, and when an anxiety attack is starting or if some disorientation happens (getting lost in Walmart) he picks up on the chemical and temperature changes going with me and reacts to bring me back. He lays down looking at the exit, I have my back facing the wall. Depending on the event it can be as simple as a wet nose glance on my hand to whining and a paw or two to keep me in check to the let's go for a walk tail wag and have a break at the lookout look.

So, that's how I got here.

Greg

The End.

The Menu

Your sampler today will be four recipes from my next release,
Tea biscuits for breakfast.

The famous Primanti Bros sandwich for lunch.

Supper is a French Canadian tradition, Tourtiere Pie.

The dessert presentation is Flaming Bananas Foster.

Please enjoy.

Some of my
favourite Recipes
with a few
Stories
How food and friends
complete a meal

Raisin Tea Biscuits

This is a great side to a full breakfast, or served with a coffee or tea on a cold winter's morning. When we anchor out at Sandy cove I have been known to bake a batch of these and go around in the dinghy delivering them to fellow yacht club members also on the hook. You can make these with or without the raisins, or substitute them with dried cranberries or try pieces of ham and shredded cheddar.

If you have some bacon grease leftover, split the biscuits and quick fry them for about two minutes in the skillet, and then set them on some paper towel for a minute to absorb any extra grease. They taste really good with a slight crunch and the raisins heated up. This also eliminates the problem of where to dump the bacon fat.

Raisin tea biscuits

2 cups flour
4 tsp baking powder
1 tsp salt
1/4 cup cold butter
1 cup milk
1/2 cup dried fruit of your choice or ham and cheddar cheese

Preheat the oven at 450 degrees F. Mix the dry ingredients in a large bowl, and then cut in the butter until small crumbs form. (make sure the butter is cold and use a grater to cut it in). The cold butter reacts with the heat of the oven to make the biscuits fluffy. Slowly add the milk and stir about 10 times until a ball can be formed. On a pastry sheet, sprinkle some flour and roll out the dough to a thickness of a 1/2 inch. Hint: I have two 1/2 inch square pieces of wood, some old trim that was kicking around, and with the dough between them, the rolling pin makes a quick square and even form. I book the dough into thirds, then roll it out. Book it again and roll it out.

I then use a 3 inch round cookie cutter to make the biscuits. If you want you can give a small sprinkle of sugar on each before going inn oven. I lay them out on parchment paper and bake for 10-12 minutes. You can also go with square biscuits if you want to be different! Easier to cut freehand than a circle. The booking process creates layers and the biscuit is fluffier and comes apart easier

Square Tea Biscuits with Monteray Jack Cheese
at Eric and Lois's in Homestead FL

The famous Primanti Bros sandwich

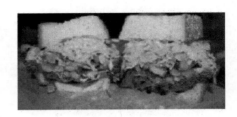

Now if you ever get a chance to go to Pittsburg stop at the Primanti Bros restaurant. We were in the area for a conference a few yeas ago, and the taxi driver gave us directions to the place as a _Must Go spot_. The sandwich combinations are crazy but taste exceptional. I made these on occasion and they are a real crowd pleaser. Serve wrapped in a sheet of paper to catch the droppings.

The Sandwich Ingredients:

2 slices of thick-cut Italian bread. You can butter it and grill the bread if you wish.. This adds another layer of texture
sliced pastrami (or your favourite type of meat)
2 slices of provolone or swiss cheese
a handful of crispy french fries (KFC fries work in a pinch)
a handful of oil and vinegar coleslaw
2 slices of tomato

Coleslaw

1 head green cabbage, thinly sliced or shredded

3 tbsp white vinegar

1 1/2 tbsp vegetable oil

pinch of granulated sugar

salt and freshly ground black pepper, to taste

Toss the sliced/shredded cabbage with the vinegar and oil, tossing to coat evenly. Add the sugar, salt and pepper and toss again to evenly distribute. Refrigerate until ready to serve.

Tourtiere (French Meat pie)

This has been a family tradition to have
Tourtiere at Christmas. This recipe I got
from Mom and over the years have added and
removed some ingredients to taste but here is the mainstay recipe
containing pork and beef. Some recipes call for two meats, pork and
ground beef if you prefer. Pictured below are the mini pies I made for
Christmas eve appetizers one year.

Ingredients
1 pound / 500 grams each ground pork and beef
2 onions chopped
1 1/2 stalks of celery
2 large baked potatoes
1/4 tsp allspice (a must)
1/2 tsp crushed garlic
1/2 cup water

In a large saucepan mix the meat together with your hands and then add the spices. Have the potato mashed up and add to the mixture. Then stir in the onions, celery and garlic. Add the water and heat to a simmer, for about one hour. Taste and season if required.

Have two pie plates prepared with either the ready made crusts, (I find that it is a hit and miss with these) or make your own crust. (Recipe later in the bread and rolls section). Spoon in the mixture and cover with pastry. Cut in steam vents and brush with a beaten egg. Bake for about 50 minutes at 350 degrees F.

Serve with ketchup and a homemade green tomato chow chow (chutney).

Bananas Foster

My attempt at this famous desert. I had a butane burner set up in the
dinning room, and once the rum ignited, we turned down the lights.
(remember to stay far away from the drapes...and don't drink too much
Rum)

Bananas Foster

Serves 4

1/4 cup (1/2 stick) butter
1 cup brown sugar
1/2 tsp cinnamon
1/4 cup banana liqueur
1/4 cup dark rum (Smuggler's Cove from down east works well)
4 scoops vanilla ice cream
4 bananas, cut in half, lengthwise, then halved

Combine the butter, sugar and cinnamon in a flambé pan or skillet. Place the pan over low heat on an alcohol burner or on top of the stove, and cook, stirring until the sugar dissolves. Stir in the banana liqueur, then place the bananas in the pan.

When the banana sections soften and begin to brown, carefully add the rum. Continue to cook the sauce until the rum is hot, then tip the pan slightly to ignite the rum. When the flames subside, lift the bananas out of the pan and place four pieces over each portion of ice cream. Generously spoon warm sauce over the top of the ice cream and serve immediately.

From Brennan's Restaurant photos

158

IOS inspections

Local bus stop.

Swinging ISO's into place.

Getting ready for a convoy south to Kljuc.

Pay your debts.

22Field Squadron, 1 Section prepping basic charges for RV 81.

Wind Gypsy I sailing into Learys Cove.

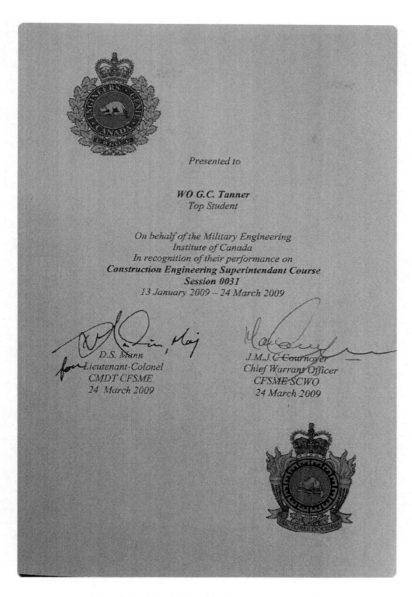

Presented to

WO G.C. Tanner
Top Student

On behalf of the Military Engineering
Institute of Canada
In recognition of their performance on
Construction Engineering Superintendant Course
Session 0031
13 January 2009 – 24 March 2009

D.S. Mann
Lieutenant-Colonel
CMDT CFSME
24 March 2009

J.M.J.C Cournoyer
Chief Warrant Officer
CFSME SCWO
24 March 2009

My 6 B Qualification course scroll.

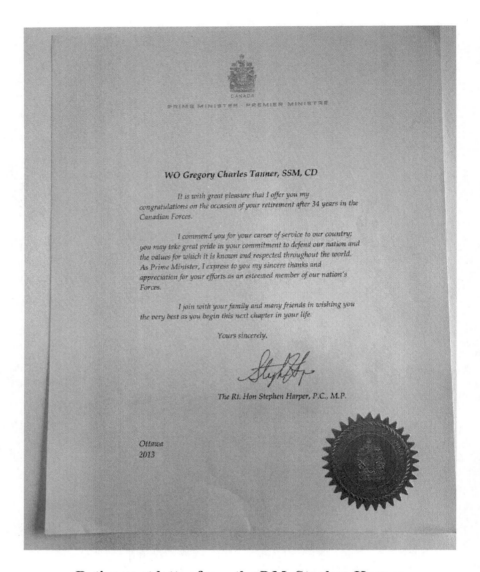

WO Gregory Charles Tanner, SSM, CD

It is with great pleasure that I offer you my congratulations on the occasion of your retirement after 34 years in the Canadian Forces.

I commend you for your career of service to our country; you may take great pride in your commitment to defend our nation and the values for which it is known and respected throughout the world. As Prime Minister, I express to you my sincere thanks and appreciation for your efforts as an esteemed member of our nation's Forces.

I join with your family and many friends in wishing you the very best as you begin this next chapter in your life.

Yours sincerely,

The Rt. Hon Stephen Harper, P.C., M.P.

Ottawa
2013

Retirement letter from the P.M. Stephen Harper

215

Glossary and Terms of reference

Canadian Military Rank Structure

CHIEF WARRANT OFFICER
(CWO)

MASTER WARRANT OFFICER
(MWO)

WARRANT OFFICER
(WO)

SERGEANT
(SGT)

MASTER CORPORAL
(MCPL)

CORPORAL
(CPL)

PRIVATE (TRAINED)
(PTE T)

PRIVATE (BASIC)
(PTE B)

Acronyms:

A3 RTF- Readiness Training Flight

APC D-Armoured Personnel Carrier Dozer

Fallex 82, 4 CER, M113 dozer in Germany, 20 Sep 1982. (Library and Archives Canada Photo, MIKAN No. 4940591)

BCD- Buoyancy Compensator Device

Bars- On some medals there were different identifiers called Bars, i.e. the SSM can have a NATO bar, like mine (4 CER Lahr FRG 52 months) but it depends where you served. Navy was for the Nato trips 180 days plus. These are just two examples.

CD-Canadian Forces Decoration (12 years service)

CD1-A clasp for an additional 10 years of service

CD1-Second clasp for another 10 years service

Numbers- 2, 3 etc tours at the same location is signified by that number. My UNDOF ribbon has a number 2 on it.

CFSME-Canadian Forces School of Military Engineering

CFPM-Canadian Forces Peacekeeping Medal

EOD- Explosive Ordnance Disposal

FNC1- Service rifle

FDU (P) - Fleet Diving Unit Pacific.

FDU (A) - Fleet Diving Atlantic

FSM- Flight Sergeant Major

HA- EOD basic course

HHT- House Hunting Trip

IDF- Israeli Defense Force

IFOR- Implementation Force

JIBC- Justice Institute British Columbia

KFOR- Kosovo Forces

M548-A Tracked Vehicle that has a flat deck for carrying six mine racks, or ammo and explosives. My call sign was 28A. (2)Two troop, (8)Supply section, (A) Ammo Carrier

MLVW, HLVW, HL PLS- Military vehicles

MSDT- Master Scuba Diver Trainer

NAUI- National Association of Underwater Instructors. (no longer exists)

PADI- Professional Association of Diving Instructors

PSTC- Peace Support Training Center

PLS- Pallet Loading System

PPCLI- Princess Patricia's Canadian Light Infantry

QDJM- Queen Elizabeth II Diamond Jubilee Medal

RCR- Royal Canadian Regiment

RECCE- Recon

SME-Subject Matter Expert

SSM- Special Service Medal

UNDOF- United Nations Disengagement Observation Force

Ql 3, Ql 5, Ql 6A, Ql 6B.- CFSME career courses

CLC, ILQ, ALQ - Leadership courses

1 CER - Combat Engineering Regiment. First located at CFB Chilliwack BC, then moved to CFB Edmonton AB after the base was closed in the late 1990's.

2 CER - is located at CFB Petawawa ON.

4 CER - Was located at CFB Lahr Germany until the base closed in the mid 1990's, then moved to CFB Gagetown NB. The unit, merged with 22 (FU) Field Sqn and was renamed to 4 ESR, 4 Engineer Support Regiment.

5 RGC- Regiment Genie du Combo - is located at CFB Valcartier QC

From the Red Book

"bars of God Save the Queen are played. Then, raising their glasses, they say "The Queen" or "La Reine," and immediately drink to her health. No other words are said after the Loyal Toast (i.e. it is inappropriate to say "God Bless Her" or words to that effect).

0720. Toast to the CME. At a CME mess dinner, the PMC then invites the Colonel Commandant or, in their absence, the senior CME member present to make a toast to the CME. The person making the toast rises and may briefly address the diners after which all present are invited to rise and join in the toast. If a band is present, all guests rise for the opening bars of Wings during which time the glasses will remain on the table. At the conclusion of the short piece of music all diners raise their glasses, exclaim "Chimo!" and drink to the CME.

0721. Toast to Fallen Comrades. It has become customary in most messes to toast fallen comrades and many messes set a separate table place setting in honour of the fallen. For the CME this toast may take the form of a simple toast "To Fallen Comrades" or a brief but more meaningful toast delivered by the PMC or one of the members present. Alternatively, and perhaps more suited for training mess dinners, an explanatory description of the place setting may be presented as described at Annex C.

0722. Marches. After the toasts, the authorized Regimental Mess Dinner toasts.

0719. The Loyal Toast. The Loyal Toast is always the first toast. At mess dinners of units in which the Sovereign holds an honorary appointment, the address to the VPMC may include that appointment. At a CME mess dinner the toast may be, "The Queen, our Colonel in Chief." or "La Reine notre Colonel en Chef." When a representative of a country that is a member of the Commonwealth of Nations is present, the loyal toast shall be made to "The Queen, Head of the Commonwealth." or "La Reine, Chef du Commonwealth." Diners should then stand at attention, with their glasses on the table, while the first six Marches of the diners' regiments or branches are played. The order of playing regimental marches is laid out in The Honours,Flags and Heritage Structure of the Canadian Forces (A-AD-200-000/AG-000). When all members are Engineers, Wings is played in its entirety during the toast to the CME instead of only the opening bars and no other marches are played. All CME members will stand when Wings is played."

References and interesting reading

pawsfurthought.ca

veteransunnato.org

https://woundedwarriors.ca/our-programs/ptsd-service-dogs/

Resurfacenorth.com

V4healing.com

caresks.com   cema-agmc.ca

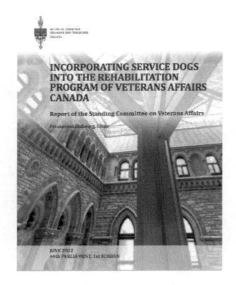

publications.gc.ca/collections/collection_2022/parl/xc78-1/XC78-

1-1-441-6-eng.pdf

CBC |

 Nicola Seguin · CBC News · Posted: Jul 03, 2023 6:00 AM ADT | Last Updated: July 3, 2023

https://www.cbc.ca/news/canada/nova-scotia/veteran-pushes-

penalties-service-dog-attacked-1.6892429

vtncanada.org

Thoughts become things... choose the good ones! ®

To reprint today's note, please give attribution to ©www.tut.com

Note that 100% of the book royalties and donations will go to funding these much-needed service dogs.

I would like to Thank you for taking the time to give my story a read and if by chance you were given or borrowed this book from someone else considering visiting the pawsfurthought.ca website and read about the people who are dedicated to this life changing service.

We were in Nassau for our 25th anniversary and took a small boat trip across the harbour to get to Atlantis Paradise Island one afternoon coming from the Straw Market. The gentleman helping you on and off the boat after a short five minute cruse with a big toothy smile called out in a thick Bahamian accent......

"You know what the greatest nation is? It's A Donation folks, pass the hat"

Manufactured by Amazon.ca
Bolton, ON

40313460R00136